BRITTANY ROBERTS

When The Flame Goes Out

First published by WTFGO Publishing 2025

First edition

Proofreading by Elisabeth Roberts
Proofreading by Emily Murdock
Proofreading by Ashley Murdock
Proofreading by Matthew Roberts

This book was professionally typeset on Reedsy.
Find out more at reedsy.com

To my husband, Matthew, my daughter, Lyra, and my friends and family. Thank you for your love and support. I love you all.

Insanity is doing the same thing over and over
and expecting different results.

Contents

Preface

Trigger warnings: This book contains moments and mentions of the following. Reader discretion is advised.

- Symptoms of mental illness and mania
- Hospitalization in a behavioral health unit
- Mental health stigma and self-stigma
- Profanity/strong language
- Suicidal ideation/self-harm
- Childhood trauma
- Drug use
- Disordered eating
- Hallucinations related to bipolar psychosis
- Mentions of pregnancy loss

Acknowledgments

This book would not have been possible without the support of the people in my life. A heartfelt thank you to my husband, Matthew, my mother-in-law, Elisabeth, and my husband's aunts, Emily and Ashley, for being the first readers of this story and for their tireless help in proofreading and giving detailed feedback on every page.

Lastly, to my own mind and body, for getting me through my own difficult days. This story was inspired by my time in a behavioral health unit. It is my hope that in sharing Brina's story, others may feel a little less alone.

1

There Are Six of Them

Six. I have six diagnoses. Some of them were obvious, but others? They felt redundant. I know the majority of what's wrong with my brain. ADHD? Yeah, already diagnosed, but they took me off my meds for it. Bipolar 1? I thought it was Bipolar 2, but what do I know? I'm not a medical professional. Anxiety? Yeah, no-brainer. Drug use? Dude, it's just weed. Nothing hard. I'd never done anything other than weed or alcohol. Boring, I know. Suicidal ideation and trauma in childhood? I felt more judged by those two diagnoses than the others. More vulnerable and called out. Not a fan of either of those feelings. Not really a fan of feelings in general.

The behavioral health unit. Somewhere, I thought I'd never be a patient of. I prided myself on my self-control and my intelligence. I guessed those don't really matter much when you have a "serious mood disorder", as the first psychiatrist called it, in that too bright, too sterile-smelling consultation room in the emergency department. A kind-eyed, middle-aged man. He kept telling me things weren't my fault. That bipolar disorder can be difficult to manage even with medication, something I had been without for a long time, thanks to a rare side effect of an antipsychotic I was on for nearly 10 months. He told me all of this after his assessment, but before he said he was going to admit me.

There I was. Embarrassed and ashamed of the actions I had taken that landed me in the hospital. I was voluntary, lucky me, but I still couldn't just leave when I wanted to. I went in expecting plain white walls and structured routines to help people get through the day. I was wrong. The walls were light blue, almost a powder blue, but still slightly too dark for that. And structure? The only thing we had to mark time passing was set group therapy times twice a day. Meals and snacks had a window of time when they were ready, but nothing concrete. Other than those, we had no structure.

I walked in with the intake nurse, or was she a tech? I didn't remember. She took my vitals, told me my heart rate was high, and asked if I was anxious. "A little," I replied.

No fucking shit, I thought internally. I didn't wanna be rude to her, but did she really think I wouldn't be anxious? I was just there after waiting in the Emergency Room for several hours, where they assigned me a sitter, despite my husband being in the room with me, with the door open. I wasn't dangerous... anymore. I wasn't going to hurt anybody. This truly felt punitive and performative, as the sitter often had to help another keep somebody else in their room. Somebody who needed more help than me. Or, at least I thought so. Eventually, after my intake, a nurse came in to talk with me about why I was there. Getting preliminary information. I liked him.

"Oh, you know, screwy brain chemicals," I joked, trying to bring levity to what I knew was a serious situation. My husband, Alex, shot me a look. I was underplaying what happened, and he was calling me out on it. Luckily, the nurse laughed, but asked me to elaborate. I took a breath, steadying myself before recounting the events that led up to my seeking help.

"I swear, it's not as bad as it sounds," I started, trying to control the direction of the conversation, not wanting anyone to feel scared of me or feel sorry for me.

"Well, I still need to know what exactly happened. Can you walk me through things from the beginning of this episode?" The nurse questioned, clearly experienced with people trying to divert from talking about their situations.

"Hun, I need you to be honest with the nurse and yourself. It was that bad. Stop screwing around," Alex said pointedly at me, not to me. No room for misinterpretation or any of my bullshit. "You said it yourself. Things aren't okay. It's bad enough that you're seeing and hearing shit."

I sighed and started talking about my four-week-long manic episode. I went into the details of it; how it didn't really feel like much of a difference at first, just that I was a bit more energetic. How I had so many good ideas that my friends and Alex's family recognized. I felt validated at first, so I didn't think anything of it when I stopped eating. It felt like I had no appetite, so I focused on world-building for Dungeons and Dragons, and, eventually, food no longer appealed to me. I was still sleeping, which I thought was important to note, but when asked how much, which was between two and five hours a night, all broken up, I was met with a frown by the nurse as he noted it in my chart.

"Okay, I can see how the mania was building up, but that still doesn't tell me why you're here. And what is your husband talking about when he says you're hearing and seeing things? Are you currently?" The nurse asked patiently but firmly wanting me to get to the climax of this little tale.

"No, nothing currently. When I say things are bad, it means I start to see shadows running around the bottom of things. Sometimes it's more faint, like a trick of the light, and others it's like there's a person in the distance. I can never see their face. It's always in darkness. As for hearing things, I often heard people shouting, arguing with each other, either in the hallway of my apartment building, or outside my windows, but when I go to check by my front or back doorways, there's nobody there," I explained.

The nurse added that to my chart and asked me more about what led me there on that day. "What about this episode was different enough to warrant getting a mental health evaluation?"

"So, I was in my bathroom, playing with a blowtorch," I started, as the nurse nodded along, asking why I had a blowtorch.

"Do you know what dabs are? Not the weird dance move," I inquired for clarification.

"Enlighten me, if you would," he replied, looking a bit bewildered behind the professional facade I could see right through.

"Well, dabs are concentrated cannabis or hemp products. You need a blowtorch to heat them up. That's why I had one. At first, anyway," I trailed off, not wanting to elaborate further.

"I see. Continue, please. I know it's probably not easy to talk about all this, but I need the full story," he pushed me along. *Damn it.* I really thought that would be enough. *Now I've gotta share the weird stuff.*

"Okay, like I said, it's not as bad as it sounds," I started, followed by another look from Alex. "Fine, it might've been a bit much," I added, still not thinking it was that big a deal.

I sighed, trying once more to settle myself before telling the next part. Were they going to put me on a hold? Would they keep me there against my will? Questions that ran through my head. I didn't wanna miss out by being there over the weekend. It would really be shitty if I missed my daughter's birthday party over all this.

"So, after I was done doing a dab, I was feeling on top of the world, really. I felt excellent. I kept raving about it, over and over again, thinking nobody could've even come close to understanding, let alone feeling, how good I felt. That's when I started laughing and waving the blowtorch around, clicking it on and off in the middle of swinging it around," I managed to get out, not making eye contact with either the nurse or Alex. "That's when I started talking to, raving at, really, people I imagined were in the bathroom with me." I was dishonest about the shadow people I did see then. I didn't want to make myself sound crazier than I already felt.

"Is that all that happened? Were you actually seeing these people or just imagining them?" The nurse pried further. I didn't blame him; it was his job, but I really didn't want to say it. Saying it out loud made it too real. I already told Alex what happened. I really didn't want to recount it once again.

I looked up at him. He was staring at me intently, willing me to share the rest of the story of why I was there. The nurse shared a similar look, but not to the same depth as my husband. Alex nearly told the nurse, but I cut him off, wanting to reclaim control of the situation that I never actually had.

"No, I was just imagining them," I lied. Alex didn't even know I was seeing the shadow people when that happened, and I didn't want him to. "And there's more. As I was swinging it around, I pretended I was in a group of people. Realistically, I knew there was nobody there, but I pretended I was scaring them with the blowtorch. I was saying things like 'What, are you afraid of me?' 'You scared I'm gonna burn you?' 'Don't be a wuss,' laughing at their imaginary, terrified reactions. I thought I was hilarious then. I don't think so now. I realize what happened next could've ended very badly, but I want to point out that it didn't," I tried to rationalize. I felt bad for omitting the detail about the visual hallucinations, but I couldn't even admit to myself how real they felt. That would've been too much, and Alex would've been pissed about me not telling him. I decided to keep that detail to myself.

I saw the nurse's face change a bit, more concern present that wasn't there before. I really didn't want to say what happened next, but he insisted I continue. I looked to Alex, seeing if he would explain for me. He started to open his mouth, but the nurse insisted it must come from me in my own words. *Damn it. Stupid hospital rules.*

"Look, I wouldn't do this now. I'm fine now. But at one point, the blowtorch wound up right next to my temple, less than an inch away. I pretended to press the button, all while smiling, laughing, and ranting about how scared other people were of me because they couldn't understand how amazing I felt. The safety wasn't on, but I wasn't trying to hurt myself. I'm not suicidal. I want to live, and I've got goals I'm working towards. I know what could have happened. I don't need the lecture," I stated as fast as I could, desperate for a shred of control over the situation. I knew from the look on the nurse's face that I was going to be admitted.

"Well, thank you for sharing. I'm sure that wasn't easy. The psychiatrist on rotation will be here as soon as possible for an evaluation, and we will go from there," he finished quickly. I thought I freaked him out. That was the last thing I wanted. I just felt deeply ashamed and embarrassed for sharing an incredibly vulnerable moment that I truly just wanted to forget. Not just that moment, but that whole four weeks. The impulse purchases, the reckless behavior, the random arguments I picked with Alex and other family members. All of it. I bunched my hands up I my shorts, wringing them up as I was filled with nerves and restless energy.

An hour or so went by before the psychiatrist was able to see me, and I ended up having to completely retell what happened. *What's the point of telling the nurse everything if I need to repeat myself?* I wondered. Eventually, the shrink said he was admitting me for observation, more or less to prevent a bipolar low, a depressive episode. I'd dealt with them before. I knew how to get through. I wanted to protest, to say I was fine. But logically, I knew I wasn't fine. I needed help. I needed to get back on meds.

I asked him directly how long he intended for me to stay in the behavioral health unit. He told me it should just be for the weekend, and we'd reassess on Monday. It was Thursday. So, I was definitely going to miss my daughter's birthday party. *Fuck. Fuckidy fuck fuck.* I swore internally. I was livid with myself, not the doctor. Why couldn't I just have a normal brain, like other people? Why did I have to be the bipolar bitch in my family? It didn't affect any of my sisters on either side of the family, two on my mom's side, one on my dad's. Not like I could confirm on my dad's side, though, as he and I weren't on good terms, or even in contact.

Alex's phone alarm went off. It was time to pick up our daughter, Luna, from school. He gave me a sad look, knowing he had to leave me there. I gave him my own reassuring look and squeezed his hand. I swore I saw a tear start to form in his eye, but he looked away before I could tell. I knew that all of the hospital stuff was getting to him, and the fact that he was about to leave me there. He thought going in that they'd just wanna get me started on new antipsychotics for my bipolar disorder. I knew better. After a final glance, he kissed me goodbye and promised to visit me the next day.

After a few hours, they were able to transport me to the unit I was supposed to be in until my release. I was met by either another nurse or a tech. I wasn't sure which. They brought me a wheelchair. *It's my brain that isn't working right, not my legs,* I thought sardonically. The tech was nice enough, but after transporting me through a series of twisting and turning hallways and two different elevator rides, I was taken to the consultation room before the unit, where the medical professional questioned me once again before giving me the medium-sized, powder blue scrubs, which fit surprisingly well. I also got a pair of large yellow hospital grippy socks. I guessed people called the behavioral health unit 'grippy sock jail' for a reason. The socks were much larger than my feet, but I didn't ask for a change, too embarrassed to do so.

Once I was dressed, my black crop top and khaki shorts taken from me and put into my belongings bag, the same professional walked me down the hall to the unit. The door had to be buzzed open by the professional's ID badge, and we then walked in. My head hung low. My dark, inky hair hid my reddened face, cheeks aflame with nerves. My right arm cupped my left, like a child who had just been scolded. I really didn't want to be there. Inside the ward, there were a handful of other patients, all wearing identical powder blue scrubs. One woman strolled right up to me, eyes wider than her smile. Her hair was a bright pink with no roots to be found. It was waist-length and tied back. Must've been dyed recently.

"Hi there!" She exclaimed. "First time?"

I nodded, confused by the brightness that was this woman, a figurative lighthouse. A beacon, really.

"Yeah. Yours too?" I mumbled, suddenly shy in her loud presence.

"Oh yeah, here anyway, but I'm also a mental health professional. Got my master's and all. But none of these assholes seem to understand that. Anyways, what are you in for?" she inquired, the mania on her face abundantly clear to me after the first sentence she spoke.

I was taken aback by how direct she was and how quickly she insulted the people charged with our care.

Before I could say anything, I was interrupted by the nurse in charge of the ward for the night. She was a tiny woman with greying hair. I thought she looked as though she might snap in half if someone breathed on her the wrong way. "Sabrina? Hi, I'm Tabitha. I'm the nurse in charge of your case tonight. Did you get a chance to eat dinner downstairs?" She asked, genuine concern on her smiling face.

"Umm, no?" I replied, as I looked over at the sole analog clock posted in the nurses' station, I could see on the left side of the ward.

"Of course, they didn't feed you," she said with exasperation. "Well, I'm gonna make sure you get a snack after I take you to your room, which is..." She paused to look at the notes in my chart. "Room twelve, down at the end of the hall. If you'll follow me, I'll explain some of the basics here."

I looked back at the pink-haired woman and shrugged. She smiled back at me. Her face looked seconds from splitting apart. She launched into a conversation with a young woman nearby. Maybe 20 or 21? I wondered briefly if that's what it looked like to others when I was manic. The young woman looked terrified.

"If you need to brush your hair, teeth, or get things for a shower, you can ask a nurse or a technician to unlock your hygiene basket for you. If you need a change of clothes, please don't hesitate to ask. When you go to change clothes after a shower or whenever you feel the need, there's a shared laundry basket you can dump the old clothes in down the hall near where we entered. If you wanna watch something on the TV, again, tell a nurse. They'll unlock a mouse and keyboard, and they'll type in whatever it is you request, within reason. It just has to be rated PG-13 or below," she rambled off, clearly used to giving this speech. I wondered to myself how many times she had said that same thing to other patients who came there before me.

"Questions?" She asked me as we arrived at my room. "Your bed is the one closest to the door."

"I'm not sure what to ask. Are we allowed hair ties or anything like that? I know my hair is gonna eventually get to me, and I'll either wanna put it up or cut it off. What about visiting hours? It's just for adults over eighteen, right?" I asked, wanting to make sure my daughter wouldn't be brought to see me like that.

She smiled at me. "You can ask for a hair tie up front. You're also allowed to have any visitors over eighteen you want, but no more than two at a time. When you're ready, please come see me up at the nurses' station. I'll make sure you get at least something to eat. Lights out is at 10 PM. You've got a few hours until then. Why not try and get to know some of the other patients?" She suggested.

She walked away after affording me yet another small smile. I looked around what would be my new room for the next few days. It was spacious enough. Just two beds, and I didn't see anyone in the bed next to mine. To my immediate left was the wardrobe, which was locked, keeping my toiletries from me. To my right was a bathroom. It had a door that only closed thanks to a magnetic strip. I opened it and looked inside. The shower was weird. No stall. Just a showerhead near the toilet and a drain in the center of the room.

Efficient. At least there was an actual door.

I left the bathroom and looked further into my new room. It was spacious enough. There were two beds, both made up in plain white sheets, blankets folded neatly at the feet of them. I decided that then was as good a time as any to make my bed. I grabbed and unfolded it, waving it up and down to shake out the folds. It wasn't the softest thing in the world, but it wasn't as rough as I was expecting. I put the longer end of the blanket along the length of the bed, tucking in the edges lightly as I looked over my handiwork, proud of myself. I hadn't made my bed in months. I tried to fluff the single pillow on the bed and found it to be lacking. It was the thinnest pillow I'd ever seen. More air than stuffing. That was going to be annoying and uncomfortable.

I took a minute to seriously take in my surroundings and consider why they surrounded me. I thought if I had felt like my normal self, I might've cried in this situation. Might've been devastated. But I hadn't cried in months at that point. I shook my head, took a breath, and turned around, ready to leave my room. I took a look at the switches next to the wardrobe and saw they were labeled 'Door' and 'Window'. They each had three buttons. One for normal light, one for reading, and one for turning them off. I played with my side's light for a moment, watching it brighten and dim. I saw a camera in the corner of my bedroom's ceiling. *No privacy except the bathroom. Got it.* I took a final breath, turned off the lights once more, and left the room, ready to get something in my stomach.

Once I was in the hallway, I took a better look around. There were maybe seven of us total that I could see. The pink-haired woman saw me and waved me over. I held up a single finger that signaled I'd be there momentarily. I'd been there since just before noon, and all I had was a light lunch that was given to me two hours later than normal, according to the sitters downstairs. Tabitha, the nurse from earlier, greeted me with a smile and asked me what kind of snack and drink I wanted. I asked for a banana and a Sprite, something I saw a few of the other patients had.

Once I had been given my snack from behind a locked door, I walked over to the pink-haired woman once again, taking a bite of my banana, prepared to talk with her then and more confident about my assessment that she was manic. She approached me quickly, her pupils huge and her words coming out rapidly, with a lot of added emphasis.

"Oh my god, hi! It's Sabrina, right? I overheard the nurse. I'm Veronica," she said as calmly as she could muster.

"Just Brina. Sabrina for paperwork, Brina for the streets," I replied, not liking the sound of my first name. Too many comparisons to the teenage witch I wasn't a fan of.

Veronica guffawed at that. I wasn't expecting such a full belly laugh from such a lame joke.

"You're hilarious!" She exclaimed for everyone to hear. I turned bright scarlet and muttered a thank you.

"Seriously, you're fucking funny, Brina! Here, let me introduce you to some of the guys. You're gonna need friends here, because even if you're voluntary, like me, they don't just let you out whenever you want. They keep you trapped here. Like rats in a maze. But I'm due to get released tomorrow, so there's that. Oh yeah, also, don't forget they count your sleep here, but only after 9 PM. So, if you want to go to bed by 8, they don't count that as an hour you slept. I don't understand why. Sleep is sleep. We're all here to recover from something. The assholes running this place seriously need to get that through their damn skulls," she remarked rather quickly. Luckily, I was able to keep up with her. *Weird about monitoring our sleep,* I thought.

She was practically leaping around, hurriedly introducing me to some of the other patients. "That's Killian. Like a pirate!" She pointed to a guy with a bleached blonde mop of hair, dark roots just starting to show. I couldn't make out his face, his shaggy, bleached hair covering it. I wondered what his deal was.

"Over there is Olivia. Olive but with an A," Veronica blurted out. It was the shy girl from earlier. The one who looked like she was in her early 20s or even late teens when I got a better look at her. She had very long, mousy brown hair.

Veronica pointed to two middle-aged women playing a card game with another guy, also middle-aged looking. Looked like Uno. "Okay, the one with the short hair is Alice. The one with her hair in a bun is Renee. And the guy over there is Lucien. No, for real. That's his name. Badass, right?" She exclaimed once more.

"So, are there more people around here? I figured that with how long it took them to find me a bed up here, most of the beds were full."

Veronica calmed for a moment and explained that sometimes people didn't come out of their rooms, but everyone was out in the common area at the time, so she didn't understand why it took the hospital so long to get me a bed.

After introducing me to everyone who was in the common area, I really took a look around. Taking in the common area for the first time. The floor was an ugly carpeted neutral grey with stains scattered about. The couch and chairs were all a weird type of cushioned plastic. Not very comfortable, but they'd do. All the furniture was either light grey and sage green or just sage green, if it was something like the fully plastic rocking chairs that were scattered about. There was a flatscreen TV above a built-in lower cabinet, where I assumed all the cables and such were hidden. I could make out a mouse and keyboard stored underneath. Maybe we could look up videos online later.

The dining area had four tables total, with four chairs at each table. It looked like two of the tables had been pushed together, and a bunch of art supplies, like crayons and markers, were placed in a few containers along with both blank pages and pre-printed coloring pages, lying on the table, waiting for whoever wanted to draw or color. *Maybe I'll try that later,* I thought to myself.

I also noticed a smaller gathering area off to the side, separated by a partial wall and a smaller nurses' station that was unoccupied. I saw the sign next to this area. 'Quiet Social Area'. That's what the plaque on the wall called it. I noted that and moved on. There were twelve bedrooms on each side of the hallway, one side for women, the other for men, I assumed. There were windows in each room aside from the main living area and dining room, but with how open the floor-plan was, I could see how natural light would make its way in.

"Earth to Brina! I asked you if you wanted to play Uno next time they start a round." Veronica was inches from my face, a huge grin plastered across hers.

"Umm, sure. Let me just make sure I don't need to take any meds or anything first," I stated, giving myself a reprieve. I remembered that the time for meds was never mentioned. I walked up to the larger of the two nurse stations and asked Tabitha what meds I had and when I was supposed to take them. She looked at me for a moment and asked me to give her a little bit, and she'd get back to me. After what seemed like five or more minutes, she gave me a reply.

"Okay, we don't have anything specifically ordered for you yet. Have you spoken with a psychiatrist since getting upstairs?" She asked. I shook my head. She gave me a small frown, displeased not with me, but with my answer. "Well, what I can do is give you something that'll help you with sleep. Do you want that tonight? We normally do meds between 8 and 9," she offered kindly.

I had an aversion to sleeping in front of other people, let alone when I was being actively monitored. I accepted the meds, and she went to get them for me. As I was waiting, Lucien, the middle-aged man who was playing Uno earlier, called my name, saying they were waiting for me to start. I guessed Veronica got to them fast. I held up my index finger and pointed to the door the nurse went into, indicating I was about to take meds. He waved me off, but seemed to accept my nonverbal answer. I looked over at the clock. It was just past 8 PM. I wondered if time was just passing more slowly than normal.

Eventually, Tabitha returned with a small cup and a pill package, which she opened in front of me, where I saw a medium-sized, round white pill.

"This is trazodone. It'll help you sleep," she calmly explained. "Most people here take it. No worries."

I looked back at the Uno table and saw the other two patients from before, Olivia and Killian, had gone to play as well. It looked like this was a community favorite. Maybe I could learn to like it there. As long as I needed to be there, that was. I figured that would be a good chance to try and get to know people. With me there, that made seven people all wanting to play Uno. I figured that this would be as good a chance as any to try and get to know people. I waved to the nurse and went over to join the Uno game, eager to get to know the people I was going to be around for the next several days.

2

Wet

Uno was definitely interesting. And surprisingly noncompetitive. Completely different from what I was expecting. Veronica was leading the group's conversation in a million different directions as we were playing, with her in the lead, only three cards away from Uno.

"So, with that all being said, I think we can all agree Devil's food cake is way better than Angel food cake. Or are you all crazier than me?" She burst out laughing at her own joke.

There were a series of nods and a brief silence from what I assumed were three of the more religious members of the group, Alice, Olivia, and Renee. I noticed Renee clutching a book about walking in Christ's footsteps. Don't get me wrong, I respected other people's religions, I just hoped these women weren't the type to preach. I was not in the mood for it, but I would be polite and listen if I needed to.

"So Brina, you never did answer what you're here for," Veronica stated loud enough for the entire group to hear, causing them to look between me and her. I swear you could hear a pin drop with how quiet things got. I could feel my face flush red, and I started to mutter why I was there so quietly that nobody heard me.

"Jesus, Ver, can't you tell when people don't wanna talk about things? Were you born without a filter?" Lucien popped off, coming to my rescue.

Veronica shrugged at him. "I mean, yeah, pretty much." She looked back at me and apologized for prying. "I know you were trying to say something earlier. You don't need to explain all that to me. We're all here for a reason. Mine is mania. But I swear this place makes it worse." A collective groan escaped the group. Seemed like she'd said that quite a few times already before my arrival.

"I know, V. We all know. It's making it worse for you. Why don't you go walk laps again or something? The rest of us just wanna play a game," Lucien retorted, clearly annoyed by Veronica's statement. Or rather, the implied repetition of it. Veronica scoffed at him and practically launched herself from her seat to walk around the large living space that was currently empty. All while ranting to herself about how he doesn't understand.

Now that I was up closer to everyone, I could kinda start making out their facial features. Lucien had more hollowed-out cheeks than I'd seen on most people. I wondered what his story was. Drugs? Starvation? Eating disorder? Olivia had a very round baby face with the biggest blue eyes I'd ever seen. She looked like a doll. Both Alice and Renee were in their late 40s or early 50s, but Alice's short hair was completely grey, unlike Renee's bun, which was still speckled with greys here and there amongst her dark brown. Under Killian's mop of blonde, I could make out a very impressive beard as well. I guessed he had to be around my age. Early 30s or so.

As I refocused on the game, I realized something. Everyone in there had a reason to be there. They weren't going to judge me for needing help. They all needed it. I played a yellow three on top of a green three, successfully switching the colors. A few people groaned at me. I clearly ruined their plans of card game domination.

"I'm also here because of mania. I nearly took a blowtorch flame to the face," I stated as the next player, Killian, I think, placed his card down on top of mine, a yellow four. Everyone looked at me with varying faces of horror and sympathy. Veronica was close enough to hear my reply to her earlier question and perked back up, going over to the group once more as she bombarded me with questions.

"Was it on? Why did you have a blowtorch? I wanna know whatever you're willing to share," she burst out, barely coherent through the rapid-fire speech.

14

"Umm, it wasn't clicked on, but it nearly was. Right next to my temple. I didn't have the safety on. But I swear, I wasn't trying to kill or hurt myself. I was just playing with it, and things just got out of hand," I replied, wanting the conversation to be over, but also feeling a strong urge to elaborate, noticing some people looked intrigued. It all just happened the previous night. So much had changed since then. I wasn't at home. I watched my husband fight back tears as he left me there. The smell of the butane torch mixed with the wax I smoked was still fresh in my mind from the night I previously thought was hilarious. The elation I felt was still palpable.

I shook my head. Thinking about it wasn't going to change the fact that I was there. In a mental facility. With a bunch of people that I felt I was going to get to know very quickly. Nobody but Killian offered up their story in return. He was quiet, clearly not wanting to share fully. "Drank a bunch. Said some stuff that I don't remember. Now I'm here until I get cleared. Looks like that'll be Monday," he said nearly silently. I gave him a nod, acknowledging what he said without prying further.

After the round dragged on with Killian pulling a sharp lead, two cards from Uno, I could feel the edges of my vision start to blur. I looked around. Others in the group started looking tired as well. I figured it was nearly time for bed. I looked back at the nurses' station at the only clock we had in there. It was just past 9:15. I was normally a night owl. Up most of the night, if not all of it. That night was different. Probably had something to do with the trazodone. I still had five cards, but I felt like I had maybe another twenty minutes of consciousness left, so I moved to excuse myself, stating, truthfully, that I was tired.

I shuffled off to my room that was nestled at the end of the far left hallway, not fully picking up my feet as I moved. My limbs felt heavy. I shut the bedroom door and moved to go and use the restroom. I could feel through my socks that the floor was wet, but I didn't fully register it until I sat on the toilet. It was wet, too. Covered in water. I opened my nearly closed eyes further and looked over at the weird showerhead. Droplets of water were sneaking out of it. *Guess I have a roommate now.* She must've showered while I was playing Uno with everybody else.

I finished using the bathroom and washing my hands, and exited into my temporary bedroom and found the bed across from me occupied, covered with what I assumed was dark hair, though it could've just been dark with water. I could hear from her soft snores that she was already out cold. *How was she able to sneak past everyone?* I wondered. I didn't hear her enter at all. Was that was normal?

I settled myself into my bed, the weight of everything that transpired in the last twenty-four hours not helping with the feeling of being sucked down into a black depth that was sleep. I remember thinking that I hoped my roommate was okay, and then nothing.

The dreams were pretty vibrant flashes, however. Seeing my reflection from when I was a teenager, my hair cropped short, a stick of a girl. So small and nearly like what you'd expect a stereotypical person suffering from anorexia to look like. The problem wasn't that I had anorexia. I just couldn't seem to gain any weight no matter how much I tried.

I saw further flashes. Me arguing with my mother, arguing with my younger middle sister, Abigail. I threw my phone at her and missed by inches. Screaming outright at my youngest sister, Zoe. Picking arguments with Alex back when we were teenagers, before we started dating. I kicked a hole in my bedroom wall, furious with my mother over something trivial. Angry. So angry. Why did all of my dreams have to be so angry? Not dreams, exactly. Memory fragments. Things I hadn't thought about in years. *Why now?*

I woke up to a bright light suddenly coming on in my bedroom, and I shot out of bed, a cold sweat on the back of my neck and face, my breath coming out in hurried gasps, and my eyes still blurry from the medication, even more so now than previously. I blinked several times to try and clear them and gave myself a moment to steady my breathing. I slowly removed my blanket and wandered into the hall, still with a staggered gait, wondering what time it was and why the lights were on. Was this just how we were supposed to expect to be woken up?

I found myself at the nurses' station and saw it was still only 4:30 in the morning. Way too early to be up. The staff from last night were still the ones on duty. No way we were expected to be up by now. I asked what was going on.

The nurse looked up at me, having just noticed me there and other patients gathering outside of their rooms, all wondering what was going on. "Power outage. Emergency lights come on when we lose power. Sorry, not much I can do about the lights in your room. They'll go off automatically when normal power is restored." She went back to her notes on the laptop in front of her.

As if she'd willed it into existence, the lights in the rooms all went off, and things returned to normal, or at least as normal as things could get in a psych ward. I shuffled back to my room, still half-asleep, where my roommate had resumed her snoring. I didn't even know if the lights affected her at all. She seemed completely out. Just as I was settled in under my blanket again, my head resting on the world's thinnest pillow, the lights popped back on. *What the hell?* I wondered, my eyes snapping shut, brows tightly furrowed, trying to hide under the blanket from the abrupt return of an abrasive presence.

"Seriously?!" I heard from down the hall. A woman's voice. Sounded like Veronica's. "I'm trying to fucking sleep here!" She did not sound happy. I couldn't blame her. Who wants to be woken up like that at 4:30 in the morning?

As I laid in my bed, I wondered why the power went off in the first place. There was no storm outside, as far as I could tell from the looks of my window. No strong winds. What happened to cause it? I might not have ever known.

I lied awake, my thoughts running cyclically. I wondered when the lights would go off, then strayed to the circumstances of my being there and not at home, in bed, with Alex. I missed him. I missed Luna, our little girl. I missed my phone. I wished I could reach out and text him, asking if they were affected by the power outage as well. I wished that I could just get up and write on my laptop, but that would have never been allowed in. Even if I explained how my thoughts got out easier when I could type than how I physically write; my handwriting looked like a five-year-old's. I wasn't even allowed a pencil or a pen in that place without direct supervision. I was stuck working with crayons and markers.

Eventually, I gave up waiting for the lights to go off once again and headed back out to the main hall, where everyone from the night before already was, feeling far more awake than I felt an hour ago. I didn't see any new faces, but the day was still incredibly young. It seemed like they had all gathered in front of the TV, watching one of the Jurassic World movies. I decided to join them, not knowing what the day had in store.

Instead of simply walking around the couch, I kinda made it to the edge and jumped on, as I'd seen both Killian and Veronica do previously last night. I was met with a series of nods from a few in greeting, while the rest were all actively engrossed in the movie on the screen.

I leaned over to Veronica on my immediate left and asked her how she slept last night, quietly, not wanting to disrupt the movie.

"Fine until the lights kicked on. Same for you, I guess. It happened not just twice, but three times. I wonder how we all slept through the first time. I mean, I get it, we're in a hospital. I betcha anything that they've got people on ventilators or whatever other machines needed to keep them alive, right? They need those generators, but somebody overseeing the hospital grid needs to know about this. We're all here to heal and get better, and what do we need to do?" She paused dramatically, waiting for my answer.

"Rest?" I guessed.

"Bingo! This chick gets it," she replied, pointing at me to anyone who would listen.

I continued my conversation with Veronica, and it naturally migrated into the quiet social room, so we didn't disturb the other patients who were enjoying the movie. The topic had shifted to us talking about our daughters.

"Oh yeah, my daughter is a real asshole at times. I get that she's only seven, well, about to be seven, but I wish I could tell her 'kid, if I have to listen to Let It Go one more time, I'm gonna lose it.'" I say, laughing.

Veronica held out her arms to her sides, gesturing to our environment, the behavioral health unit.

"If there was anywhere to lose it, this would be the place. Let it... out," she teased, seeing the mom-look on my face. The one every person knows by instinct.

"But yeah, wait until she's a teenager. Mine is fourteen. She thinks she knows everything and can't wait to grow up. She doesn't get all the responsibilities of being an adult. Hell, I'm still figuring it out and I'm nearly forty! So much bureaucracy and paperwork. Going to the doctor, going to the DMV, maintaining your house... It's all work. Kids really just don't get how much freedom they have. You know?"

"I know. I can look back and see how I was so clearly back then. But my circumstances were different. I was very much a product of my environment. Every teacher loved me, I was a joy to have in class, but I was also bullied a fuck-ton in middle and high school. Teachers kept reiterating their bullshit policies of 'zero tolerance', but still only ever gave kids slaps on the wrist when they saw it. Detentions, at worst. I was also a nightmare for my mom. Constantly lying to her, picking fights, stealing her makeup. Teenage shit," I replied.

Rounding the corner was a staff member in grey scrubs. A tech, Veronica told me. She explained that techs wore grey and nurses wore red.

"Excuse me, ladies, but it's time for vitals." She wheeled out a mobile device for checking blood pressure and temperatures. "Sorry to interrupt. Sounds like you were really into your conversation. Who's first?"

I held out my arm, offering to go first. She smiled at me and skillfully wrapped the large cuff over my arm, tightening it perfectly to my size. She then put a thermometer under my tongue and waited. I noticed the cuff was wrapped a little tighter than I had seen before as an adult in my 30s. Had I lost that much weight in just a few weeks?

"Okay, the temperature is normal. Blood pressure and heart rate are a little high. Are you in any pain or feeling anxious?" The tech asked me.

"I mean, I'm here. I have a small headache, probably from the lights turning on earlier, and I guess I am anxious, but it feels normal to me," I replied, not sarcastically at all. Completely serious. The tech frowned at my answer, but nodded.

"Do you need anything? Tylenol? Want me to ask about meds for you for anxiety?" She offered kindly.

I nodded and thanked her. She moved to take Veronica's vitals, and I could hear that they're normal. *Do most people not have anxiety about being here?* I wondered to myself. I decided to ask Veronica about her emotional state after the tech was done with her.

"Okay. Normal temp, heart rate, and blood pressure. Anything you need, hun?" The tech asked.

"Nope. Just to get out of here as soon as possible. ASAP. You know? I don't do well in captivity. Nobody does. That's why most zoos are unethical." She started into another tirade from her seemingly vast depth of knowledge on a broad range of topics. Her brain seemed to work a lot like mine did. Just without the filter I've spent 3 decades building.

The tech nodded and looked for an out to return to taking the vitals of the other patients there. She took advantage of Veronica's need to breathe and said she needed to get back to work and wished us well. I wondered how Veronica was going to be released if she were still like that. Or was that her baseline? Chick had way too much energy.

"So anyway, you said something about being bullied in school. Tell me more about that. I'm a mental health professional by trade, and I won't bullshit you with some fluffy therapy nonsense. I'll tell it like it is. Hit me. Do the trauma dump thing," she stated, smacking her hands to her legs, showing her enthusiasm.

I blinked at her. Most people wanted me not to do that upon meeting me. I had a bad habit of over sharing that I'd worked hard to reel in. I was surprised by someone other than a close friend wanting me to open up like that. I decided not to question it and went into a deep dive into my middle and high school trauma.

"So, it's complicated and long. Let me start by asking you a question. Have you ever just known something you should have no way of knowing? I did. And I told people about it. At first, I thought they were genuinely interested because they kept asking me questions. Asking if it was ESP or something. I figured out years later that I just have really good pattern recognition and was good at reading people. But anyway, the next day in seventh grade, people were laughing at me. Calling me 'Ghost Girl,' thinking I was talking about hearing ghosts and demons and shit. That wasn't the case and never was. I just understood things I couldn't explain well. Why do kids have to be such assholes?" I lamented, remembering how awful those years felt. I was glad for the one person in my life who saw what I was going through and didn't question my entire being. Alex.

"So, because you're built differently, you got made fun of. Sounds about right. Kids are pricks. That's why I didn't originally want any. But when my daughter came into my life, I knew I was meant to adopt her. What kinds of things did you know that freaked out the other kids? That's interesting, by the way," she replied, reminding me of the fact that we were both parents.

"When I was younger, I kept telling my mother I wasn't supposed to be the oldest child. That I was supposed to have an older brother, and his name was supposed to start with a C. She just kept telling me 'Well, that's what you are. I can't change it.' Guess what? I was right. On all three counts. My mom had a miscarriage at twenty weeks with a little boy she was going to name Cameron before she had me. I didn't know that until after I graduated from high school. She asked me when I was an adult if I ever read her notes she kept in our important documents folder. I never did. I didn't even know she wrote him notes," I answered with full honesty. I took in the shocked expression on Veronica's face, the first time I'd seen her truly speechless since my admission.

"Wow. Just... wow. How did you know that? Maybe it is ESP," she mumbled that last statement.

"Well, even if it is, I'm not sure I believe in ESP. I know there are just things in life we can't explain, and my knowing things is just part of that."

"You should write about all this when you get out. I bet you have one hell of a story to tell."

I felt my cheeks redden and grow hot. I used to write a lot when I was a teenager. It was my one escape. Reading was great and transported me to other realms, but I've always preferred building my own. I wrote anonymously, posting fanfiction stories online that led to quite a following before I stopped. Before adult responsibilities took over.

"Maybe," I stated, with no real intention of actually writing. Who would want to read my story if they knew it was about me? That felt very self-centered, in my opinion, and that was the last thing I wanted; to be self-centered. I truly believed I was here, on this earth, not the ward, to help

21

others. To learn as much as I can and help to do whatever is possible to use that knowledge to make a difference. A positive impact. Lately, I felt like I'd been entirely too selfish and self-serving. Probably due to the mania.

A nurse eventually popped up around the corner, carrying a small tray with four small cups on it. Two with water, two with meds, and mine and Veronica's initials written by each.

"I've got your meds, ladies. Sabrina, you said you had a headache earlier, so I got you Tylenol for that. The other med, I have the info sheet for back at the front desk if you have any questions. You've got Abilify, which is an antipsychotic, hydroxyzine and buspirone for anxiety, and lamotrigine, which is technically an anticonvulsive, but is used to treat depression with bipolar disorder. Any questions for me?"

I thought to myself. There was nothing for ADHD there. I was on meds for ADHD before I came in.

"What about my ADHD meds? I was on them before I came in. Started with a v. Vyvanse, I think?" I asked, curious as to why I wasn't given any.

She frowned slightly at this.

"I can ask the psychiatrist about that when he gets here, but that won't be for several hours. I'm sorry for the inconvenience. My best guess, however, is that Vyvanse is a stimulant. Stimulants can make mania worse. So, he probably took you off of it for that reason." She shrugged shyly and turned her attention to Veronica. She also had a small handful of pills she needed to take, some looked to be the same as mine. She swallowed them after arguing briefly that she didn't want to take them, but the nurse reminded her of her upcoming departure from the unit later today. That seemed to motivate her enough to take her meds.

I glanced back at the faraway nurses' station towards the analog clock. I couldn't make out the little hand's position at this angle, but I could tell the hour was about to turn. Maybe 7 o'clock? I heard the entry door buzz, and immediately after, the sounds of footsteps walking. It sounded like two women, or lighter men. There was also something that sounded heavy, like it was made of metal on wheels. *An occupied gurney?* I wondered. One of them sounded like they were in a bad mood or at least needed coffee. Their footsteps sounded heavy, however, too light to belong to somebody heavy. More like someone smaller and just out of energy, and like they were dragging, but not angry. I've been able to identify people by the sounds of their footsteps since I was twelve or thirteen. It used to freak people out when I could tell where they were and how they were feeling by the way their feet sounded. Only because I told them. So, I stopped telling people.

A sudden whine and a voice brought me back to our immediate surroundings. "It's 7 o'clock. Breakfast is served in the dining room for the behavioral health unit." It started before cutting out. I shook my head slightly, trying to get back to where I was meant to be. Which was the literal psych ward. For a moment, I considered trying to shake my head the opposite way and see if I could just go back to that. But my stomach was basically empty, and I was not going to say no to food. I practically leaped from the sofa, if you could call a bunch of plastic or rubber concrete a sofa. Veronica was way ahead of me, despite being the same height as me. I guess you don't miss meal times here. That gave me hope for the quality of the food.

3

Breakfast is the Most Important... Never Mind

I followed the lead of Olivia, Veronica, and Killian and took a seat at a table with the three of them. It looked like the staff delivered your meal to you. I didn't like that. I was a doer; I did things for others. It wasn't supposed to be the other way around. I felt my hands start to tremble slightly, but I quickly balled them into fists under the table, unseen by anyone. I forced myself to breathe as quietly as I could, hoping nobody was focused on me right then. Despite struggling to identify my own feelings, I had been told they were always clear on my face if you paid attention. Hopefully, the promise of food would be enough of a distraction to those around me.

My suspicion about the food being a distraction was proven true when Veronica's neck nearly snapped at how quickly she turned as her name was called for the next tray of food. Or, I thought she would get a tray. There was a gray tray, a white striped tray liner, and then her covered breakfast in plain white styrofoam with milk and orange juice on the side. The person serving her expertly pulled the liner and food off the tray without disturbing either or spilling a thing. A feat I never truly mastered in my limited years in a customer service role. Or rather, service roles. Plural. I had worked so many jobs. It was kind of ridiculous.

"Sabrina?" A woman's voice called out. I turned and saw a woman wearing gray scrubs very similar to the techs, but with a red and white line going around the collar of the neckline and sleeves. She was holding a gray tray with covered food for me as well. I only saw a milk carton, and it was vanilla. No juice for me. I frowned slightly for a fraction of a second before fixing my face and waving the woman over politely.

She deposited my food on the table with a smile. A genuine, warm smile. I didn't get how she could smile like that if she was constantly serving others. *Whatever floats your boat, I guess.* I understood the irony. But while I enjoyed making my loved ones feel seen, loved, and cared for, I didn't like constantly being the one doing the serving. I hated going out of my way to do things they never would have thought of doing for me, simply because the way I thought was different from theirs. Not through any fault of their own or mine.

"Thank you. And it's just Brina." I offered with a small smile of my own.

"You're welcome, Brina. Enjoy your breakfast. The default is pancakes and sugar-free syrup," she told me with a bright grin on her face. No sugar. That was practically a war crime.

Wait a minute, no sugar. That probably meant no caffeine. No caffeine meant I was shit out of luck. I was going to be extremely irritable in a few hours, and that probably explained why I woke up with a headache, other than the lights abruptly turning on. *Crap, crap, crap!* This was bad. I was going to have a perpetual headache while I was there! I thought to myself, allowing my hand to instinctively reach up to my head. Killian saw the look on my face and realized immediately what was up.

"No caffeine, right? You'd better let a nurse know so they can get you Tylenol when you need it. They do have coffee, but it's decaf," he stated, very helpful, but also very matter-of-fact. Almost snarky. He was probably bitter about the lack of caffeine, too. "You can also ask for a Sprite. It doesn't have caffeine, but it's something."

I lifted the lid of my meal, the styrofoam squeaking open from the friction of the connected lids touching and scraping against each other. I strongly disliked this sound, but I dealt with it. It made me shudder slightly, but when I used to speak up about it as a small child, I got told that everyone hates it, but you just need to deal with it. It's not that bad. So, I pretended it wasn't. I didn't want people to be annoyed with me for expressing what I felt, so I had to find a way to deal with it. And for me, that was just shutting it out as best I could.

Inside were two medium-sized pancakes, a sealed packet of syrup, a plastic spoon and fork, some scrambled eggs, which immediately made my stomach turn, and an actual cup of orange juice. I offered up my eggs, and they were quickly absorbed by Olivia, who had been so quiet as Veronica spoke aloud between bites of eggs to nobody in particular. Something about the bureaucracy in mental health facilities failing its patients. I could see some of her points, but they were very extreme.

In return for my eggs, Olivia offered me her extra orange juice. She had seen my face when I saw Veronica's orange juice and thought I didn't have any of my own. I really was being watched here. I needed to keep an eye on Olivia. She may have seemed quiet and meek, but she saw everything. Even if her intentions were good, I didn't like people being able to read me so clearly. I saw how this was also ironic since when I met people, I tended to be very friendly, warm, and open. It threw some of them through a loop, and I could always tell they had been through something they probably shouldn't have.

"Thanks for trading with me. I can't stand eggs unless they're hard-boiled or deviled. Something about them smells like sulfur to me. But I really do love orange juice," I thanked Olivia genuinely.

"It's no trouble. I love eggs. Good protein. And the orange juice was just an extra I had ordered. Didn't you get a chance to look at the menu last night?" She asked.

"No, I guess I made it in too late for that," I replied.

"Well, you should definitely make sure you get a menu today and make your selections for tomorrow. I have no idea what default meals tend to be like."

"I gotcha. Thanks for the advice. I'll make sure to do that," I said as I used the plastic spoon to cut my first bite of pancake. No knives, I guessed. It made sense, but didn't make the task any easier.

I looked back at the other two at the table, having an animated, or rather, one-sided, debate. Killian looked barely interested but kept replying to Veronica's rapid-fire insights and questions for some unknown reason.

"Okay, but have you ever thought about it like this before? Like seriously, how cool would it be if people could regrow limbs like a lizard can regrow its tail? I know it'd probably put a lot of doctors out of business, but it would be so great for humanity, you know? Not that humanity is all that great. Sure, some people are fantastic and want to go out of their way to help others, but that number is seriously outweighed by the people who go out of their way to be selfish and hurt others for their own personal benefit. That's why billionaires and their very existence should not be allowed to exist. They should be taxed to the point where they are only capable of reaching 999 million dollars, and then nothing else should be able to be allowed to enter their accounts. Don't you all agree?" She shot out, jumping from one topic to the next.

"Totally, dude. Billionaires suck," Killian agreed with next to no energy. I nodded, mouth still full of pancake. Olivia mirrored my response, her own face stuffed with eggs.

"And seriously? I forgot to mention this, you guys, but this hospital food is way better than any other hospital food I've ever had. I've had to stay overnight a few times at different hospitals for observation for previous shit, and their food sucks. This is damn near gourmet in comparison. Have you guys had a cheeseburger yet? Delicious." Veronica added.

I saw from the other table out of the corner of my eye that the middle-aged man with the hollow cheekbones, Lucien, seemed to be getting fed up with his meal. I overheard him talking about how his eggs weren't seasoned to his liking. He sounded really pissed off over it. Suddenly, he was out of his chair, heading back for his room, his food nearly untouched. Apparently, under-seasoning was a reason to up and leave breakfast. Got it.

Just as I returned to eating the last few bites of my pancakes, I noticed my roommate made a brief appearance, asking a nurse for her breakfast tray. I was wrong about her hair color before. It wasn't brown but a pretty auburn color. No roots. It had to be natural. I saw her meet my gaze briefly and then put her head back down, her hair hiding her face in a curtain of auburn. She took a seat at a table alone, and a tech brought her the food that was waiting for me, one I didn't recognize. I guessed it was time for a shift change, and I hadn't noticed. I wanted to go to her and talk, but something told me that wasn't a good idea. I hadn't breathed a word to her last night, but then again, she hadn't been awake. Or at least, I didn't think so. I could've sworn I heard her breathing harder, with more strain, as if her chest was tight, like she was trying to hold back tears at one point. But otherwise, I didn't hear anything from her. I decided against going and talking with her, at least for that moment. I promised myself I would speak with her eventually. I didn't want her to feel isolated in that unit.

After having finally finished my pancakes, I turned to the orange juices I had been waiting for. I preferred eating and drinking my foods and drinks in order of least-to-most looking forward to. For me, that was the pancakes, then the orange juice. I knew that the way I ate was weird, but I didn't care. Not the way itself, but the way I've tried to explain it to others. People pointed out that they normally just ate whatever was on their plate in a seemingly random order. I couldn't wrap my head around that.

"Earth to Brina!" Veronica yelled loud enough for her voice to carry around the entire ward. Nobody could have mistaken her voice anywhere.

"Sorry, lost in thought. What were you saying?" I replied, a bit shocked that she just shouted at me like that.

"I was asking what you wanted to do the second you got out of here. I said I wanted to go out to eat with my husband and kid. What about you?" She asked me, expectantly.

"Oh. Hmm. I hadn't really thought about it. Maybe get some pizza?" I offered, hoping my answer was satisfactory.

"Seriously? I've been thinking about what I want to do when I get out since I got in. I want to go see a movie, and then go to dinner with my husband and kid. Maybe get a good steak," she said, making me feel my answer was inadequate. Normally, I would've shut down a bit at the perceived rejection, but right now, I just felt annoyed. Angry even. That was a dangerous emotion for me. I never knew how I'd react if I let go of any control when I was angry. I could feel my jaw clench and my breathing quicken ever so slightly.

I pushed myself out of my chair, saying I was full even though I wasn't and still had another juice in front of me. I needed a bathroom break. I hurried back to my room and used the bathroom, thanking whatever god that existed that my roommate wasn't back in the room already. I knew my anger could be volatile, and all I could do to handle it was isolate and wait for it to subside, kind of like some people did for an anxiety attack. I didn't want to be a public spectacle.

I guessed breakfast was a place where people showed their anger. First Lucien, then me, however privately. Who was next? These kinds of things usually happened in threes, but that place seemed to run differently than the outside world, like it was its own separate reality from the outside world.

I breathed through the heat I could feel rising up my belly and to my face. Not wanting anyone to see my reaction. I stayed hidden in the bathroom for about ten minutes, just breathing until I felt calmer. No longer ready to launch into an argument with Veronica. That was something I had to deal with even when I was no longer manic. My ever-present, easily triggered anger. I felt like a walking contradiction—something that shouldn't exist but did anyway. I felt that way about myself for several reasons, but this was just one of them.

Once I was ready, I splashed some water on my face for good measure and went back out to the main living area, looking back at the dining and recreational area that had been cleared of all food remnants by someone unseen to me. Probably one of the nurses or techs. That's another thing I didn't like about this place. People were cleaning up after me. I was used to picking up after myself and others.

The other patients were all spread out, doing their own things. Killian and Lucien were on the couch in the main living area, watching some movie I didn't know. Veronica and Alice were walking in opposite directions, doing laps around all the common areas. It seemed like they were either needing to expend some energy or were just bored out of their minds. Renee was reading a book with a religious title. I had no clue what to do just then. I decided to walk up to the nurses' station once more and ask them about a schedule.

The nurse on duty, whose name was Rachel, as I could see from her badge, cocked her head to the side, questioning my question.

"What do you mean by schedule? Visitation hours? Meal times? Group? I mean, they're all pretty much listed in the corner by where your names are written, but they're all guidelines. You're free to pretty much do whatever you like within the rules here. You can watch a movie as long as it's PG-13 or under. You can listen to music on the TV if nobody else is using it, following the same general guidelines. No excessive profanity or obscene scenes allowed. We have word searches, coloring pages, and journal pages you could fill out. We've also got blank paper up here behind the desk if you want some. There are games in the closet, but you do have to ask for access to them. Pretty much anything that isn't laid out for your use, you need to ask for. I know, it can be a lot to adjust to," she stated clearly.

"Wow. Okay, I was under the impression that there would be a routine here," I replied, frustrated at the lack of a real schedule.

"Sorry, not really. The visitation schedule is above the phone to your right, my left. The group is from 8 AM and 2 PM. It is twice a day on weekdays only. Weekends, we kind of let you guys sleep in if you don't mind missing breakfast. You also have shorter visitation on weekends than weekdays, so sorry about that, too. That's mainly because most visitors come on weekends, and we divide them into groups so different patients can see their loved ones while others get visited by the psychiatrist on rotation," she added, annoying me further about the shorter visitation on weekends.

I nodded at her and asked for the list of my contacts so I could call Alex, my mom, my sisters, and my mother-in-law. I wanted to let them all know I was doing alright. I didn't want them to worry. The nurse, Rachel, was kind enough to get me the handwritten list Alex had made up for me since I wasn't allowed a pen or pencil here. It had six numbers on it: my mom, my mother-in-law, both my younger sisters on my mom's side, Alex, and one of my best friends, the one who had been there since high school, Montana. I called her Monty. I was the only person allowed to do that.

I dialed the number for my mother-in-law first, Rebecca, knowing she'd most likely be up at this hour. I was met with a busy tone. I figured she was on a call with her job or a client. So I hung up and dialed the one for my mother. Busy once again.

"Excuse me, I've tried a few numbers, and all I'm getting is a busy tone. Do you know what's going on?" I asked Rachel at the desk. She turned her head towards me and then to the clock on the wall, my only way of telling exactly what time it was in there. It read 7:55 AM.

"The group is about to start. Phones are off when the group is going. We'll turn them back on afterward," she explained shortly.

I hung up the phone with a sigh and perhaps a bit more force than necessary. Group. Maybe then we could start deep diving into why we were here, and then we could at least have some homework to do before the next one. It was something, I thought.

I saw a man in a white shirt walking towards the back of the hall, to the room next to mine. It said it was the therapy room on the plaque next to it. The man in the white shirt unlocked the door and held out his arms in a gesture I interpreted as wanting us to go into the room. All eight of us, including my roommate, went in and gathered around the awkwardly long table and took a seat. At the far end of the room, there was a window, and the walls around us were surrounded by cheerful-sounding affirmations painted onto them, things like "I am kind." "I am patient." That kind of stuff. Things you'd expect to see in a kid's classroom. I immediately felt patronized.

The room felt stale, like it was hardly used, but I knew that wasn't the truth. Unless the group was normally in the common area, which I kind of doubted. It smelled far too sterile, like somebody just wiped the tables down with an alcohol wipe and then Febreezed in there. Nothing in that room felt dynamic. It all felt very static. This didn't give me hope for moving forward in healing.

"Alright, is this the group for today? I thought there were supposed to be eleven of you, but we can work with eight." The man in the white shirt announced. I guessed three more people weren't coming out of their rooms, but I wasn't going to go looking for them.

"Right, my name is Ryan, and I'm a student here. It's my last week as a student therapist. How about we go around the group, introduce yourselves, share a fun fact about yourselves, and your favorite color? I'll start. You already know my name. One fun fact about me is, again, this is my last week as a student in this program. And my favorite color is green. Who's next?" He said as he looked down at the papers in his hands. I figured this was an icebreaker opportunity and took it, desperate for connection.

"I'll go next," I announced, reserved but eager. The heads of everyone in the room turned to me expectantly. I took a breath. "Hi, I'm Brina. A fun fact about me is that I like doing collaborative paintings with my daughter, Luna. And my favorite color is red."

"Thank you for sharing, Brina. You, next to her, have blonde hair. Care to share?" He indicated Killian.

"Sure, it's whatever. I'm Killian. Fun fact: I can't wait to get out of here. My favorite color is green." He shared rather curtly. He really didn't want to be there.

"I guess that makes me next. I'm Olivia. A fun fact about me... hmm. I guess a fun fact about me is that my special interest is rap, specifically Eminem. And my favorite color is pink."

"Oooh! I'll go next. You guys already know me. It's Veronica here! Coming at you live from the nut house. A fun fact about me is that I'm more qualified to run this group than a student therapist. I have a fucking master's degree in social work! And my favorite color is purple. I know pink hair throws people off when I say my favorite color is purple, but I kind of love watching their reactions. It's hilarious!"

There was an awkward pause after Veronica's introduction. The rest of the group was more reserved than us.

"Thank you for your... contribution, Veronica. It was very enlightening. Who's willing to go next? How about you there?" He gestured with his whole hand to Lucien, who had been looking barely conscious since breakfast, after he stormed away from his unseasoned eggs.

He sniffed and looked at Ryan. "Fine. I'll share. It's Lucien. Not-so-fun fact, I'm here instead of jail. The next step is rehab after this place, so I fully intend to get the most out of my time here. Oh, and the color is green, too."

The remaining three people looked amongst themselves and Renee went next.

"Hi, I'm Renee. Something fun about me, I crochet. Mostly blankets. I really just like doing things with color in general, so I don't really have a favorite. They're all pretty." You could see her face light up a bit at the end. I smiled a bit, happy to meet someone so optimistic. The next person to go was Alice.

"I'm Alice. I like to read. Mostly the Bible and other books about devoting myself to Christ through the act of helping others. My favorite color is white," she said, rather quietly.

That left one person left to share. My roommate. I didn't even know her name. She looked about as red as her hair, tissues still stuffed in her nose. I waited intently to hear her answer.

"Sorry, I'm really shy. I don't really like talking about myself much. I'm Elise. I guess a fun fact would be that I like to doodle. And my favorite color is also pink. Soft pink," she barely whispered. I wouldn't have heard her if she hadn't been directly across from me. She was practically trembling as she fought to get each word out.

I was glad that Elise finally opened up. And then I could stop calling her just 'my roommate'. Now she felt much more real to me. Elise was like everyone else in there, like me. Someone who needed help. Not some random recluse.

Ryan let out a soft sigh and clapped his hands together. "Right, you guys, I'm so proud of you all for opening up and sharing that little bit of information with me. Today, I'm going to pass around these worksheets and have you each fill them out. You can use your favorite color of either a crayon or marker in the bins in front of you." Ryan passed me the worksheets. I took one and passed the next ones to Killian, and they eventually made their way all the way to Elise. She handed the rest back to Ryan, and I listened intently, hoping this would be us all doing some deep diving. I was seriously wrong.

"So, as you all can see, this is a worksheet about emotions. You can see they're in alphabetical order." He pointed out. I looked at my own worksheet. It looked like something you'd give to a little kid, practicing which emotion was which and what made them all distinctly different from each other. I felt this was trivial at best. How was naming emotions going to help any of us? We all knew what sadness felt like. What anger, frustration, glee, and remorse felt like. I already knew I wasn't going to like this assignment, but I decided to participate. I was willing to try. Anything to hurry my release.

"Who here has been feeling an emotion they're willing to share?" Ryan asked.

Veronica's hand shot up so fast, I could see the wind coming off her arm through Olivia's stray hairs. "Oh, me! Okay, I feel frustrated because this exercise feels beneath us. I also feel excited because I'm supposed to be going home today and I won't have to participate in these anymore. I think you'd benefit from getting people to open up more. Not to play some little word game and have people realize that other people have felt the same emotions as them. Come on. We're all adults. This is something you do with kids," she ranted at Ryan. Way to say the quiet part out loud, V. I thought, genuinely happy she said something. I let a small smile show on my face and I snickered to myself. I wished I'd been brave enough to call him out like that. Nothing against Ryan. He was probably just trying to play this safe, but I did agree with Veronica. I was thinking we'd be talking about what brought us all here and how we could move forward from that.

"Oh my god, Veronica, you can't keep doing this every session," Killian groaned. "You just take over and rant all crazy like. I get it. We all get it. You want the fuck out. So do I. So does everyone else here. Could you just try to chill, please?" He begged. I think that was the most I'd ever heard him say.

Veronica looked like she wanted to rip his head off then, her face red, brows furrowed, mouth agape. Before we could say anything further, Ryan interjected.

"Okay, got it. This clearly isn't the vibe you were anticipating. So let me shed some light on things. I'm trying to avoid triggers for any of you. I want this to be a welcoming space for all. Some of you may find it childish. But some people are just this out of touch with their emotions. For example, Veronica, can you tell me where in your body you feel anger? Or excitement, as you said earlier?"

Veronica didn't miss a beat. "It's mainly in my head for anger. I get hot, my head throbs, but not with pain. Excitement feels like electricity buzzing everywhere in my body, but mostly in my head, once again. Now that I know my feelings are in my body, can we actually talk about what brought us all here? I feel like that'll be more healing for any of us than talking about all our little 'feewings,'" she stated, holding her hands up to her face, pretending to wipe away tears exaggeratedly at the last word.

34

I was trying not to laugh. This was something I found absolutely hilarious. One under-experienced mental health professional was kind of up against a much more seasoned one, even though she was manic. Clearly, she knew what was up and wasn't going to concede to him trying to redirect her. She knew the techniques. She was trained in them. Exactly why they wouldn't work on her. I felt strangely akin to Veronica, despite her intensity.

"Well, if you don't feel like sharing, you don't have to. Though I have appreciated your willingness to share up until this point. It is a net positive. Thank you for your valuable perspective." Ryan replied rather skillfully for a student. I saw what he was trying to do. Get her to stop, but also made sure her input felt valued. "We will, however, continue talking about our emotions. Does anyone else have something they're feeling that they'd like to share? Maybe even share why you're feeling that emotion, if you'd like." Veronica huffed at that and sank back into her chair, fidgeting with her assigned jacket. Where was I supposed to go to get a jacket? Wait. Let me guess. I'm gonna have to ask for one. Lovely. I shook that thought out of my head and decided now was a good time to participate.

I blurted out, "Amused. Because of that interaction." Ryan looked at me like I just sprouted a second head before nodding along, glad that I was at least sharing something in a way different from Veronica.

I happened to look over and saw the only other clock I've seen here. Another analog clock. We had already been there for about 35 minutes. How long did these sessions tend to last? I wondered.

The rest of the group all shared their emotions, but none of them really gave a reason as to why they felt them. Killian said he felt annoyed, which was entirely fair. Olivia said she was anxious, probably because she was afraid of Veronica. Renee said she felt grateful, which I guess was a good answer. To me, it felt like she was being insincere. Alice blushed but eventually said that she felt embarrassed. I had no idea why she might have been embarrassed. Elise said she was feeling tired. I suppose that made sense. Being there in the behavioral health unit, where we were all on medications that made us all tired.

Ten minutes passed, and then we were dismissed from the group. I got up quickly and headed straight for the phone, not picking up my worksheet that I didn't even bother to fill out, as I was more focused on the group and the discussion happening at the time. Hopefully, the phone would be turned back on then. I really wanted to talk to my mom.

4

Waiting to get Shrunk

As I reached for the phone and grabbed it once again, I pulled out my list of phone numbers and dialed my mom's number, not that I needed a list for that. That was one of the three phone numbers I had memorized. Mine, Alex's, and hers. I heard the phone finally ringing. I turned my head to get a look at the group exiting the therapy room and felt a sharp yank from the phone. I turned back and noticed for the first time that the phone cord was extremely short. I had to stay right by the wall and the nurses' station to talk to anyone. Well, that sucked, but at least they had a chair set up back there.

After a series of rings, a groggy woman's voice answered the phone. "Hello?"

"Mom? It's Brina. I just wanted to call you and let you know I'm alright," I spoke carefully, not wanting to shock her awake. My mother was not a person you scared or shocked awake.

"Sabrina? Oh yeah, the psych ward. How are you doing, honey? Are they treating you well there?" She asked.

"I mean, nobody's been outright a dick or anything. There's one woman in here who is actively manic, and while I agree with a lot of the points she's making, she takes them to extremes and she seems like she kinda sets off other patients. But, from what she's told everyone who will listen, she's getting out today," I replied, not wanting to give out too much information; however, I was dying to talk about what had been happening there.

"Huh. At least you're not the one being an asshole. You know when I was in the psych ward as a teenager, there was literally a guy there who thought he was a box of juice and kept trying to put himself in the refrigerator. I chased him around with a straw, saying I was gonna drink him." She laughed and so did I. That was awful, but hilarious. My mother was a mean-spirited person as a teenager, but at least she had funny stories about back then.

"Well, I don't think anybody here believes that they're a juice box and it's not like I have access to a fridge or straws. I swear, they took those things away from us because of people like you." I joked with my mom. We had a unique dynamic. We communicated mainly through dark humor, but I knew she cared about me, no matter what.

"But seriously, Sabrina, are you okay? I know you. You've always been resilient, but this isn't the time for that. You don't need to pretend to be okay right now. So, please, tell me the truth, are you genuinely alright?"

Well, damn. She was almost never that direct with me. I knew I was resilient, but I didn't think she saw it. I thought I was just doing what a good daughter would do and getting through everything without complaining too much. I didn't really put much thought into my overall state of mind right then. It wasn't manic, but not depressed either. However, I still didn't feel quite like myself. Maybe it was just being in that ward. I wasn't sure how to answer my mother.

"Honestly? I don't know how I'm doing. I don't feel the high energy or anything like that anymore and I'm not depressed, but things still just feel, I don't know, off or weird. Something," I replied, giving her as much honesty as possible. My emotions were something I didn't like talking about, mainly because it took me a while to realize what I felt if things were complicated or not straight-forward.

"I get it. Being locked away from other people is weird. Do they at least have activities or stuff you can do in there? Back when I was in a unit, there really wasn't a whole lot you could do. Or has that changed?" She asked, not prying. She knew firsthand from my years of growing up under her roof how bad an idea it was to pry into things I didn't want to share. Far too many screaming matches. I shuddered, remembering that turbulent part of my adolescence.

"I mean, yeah, they have coloring and worksheets you can do, but their only schedules revolve loosely around food times, vital checks, med distribution, group, and lights out. We have far too much free time here. They won't even let us clean up after ourselves or have trays for meals. How weird is that?" I wondered out loud.

"Actually, I can get that. People could use the trays as weapons. Smack other patients with them or something. I probably would have if someone pissed me off," she remarked far too casually.

"Mom, inappropriate. I'm pretty sure they listen to our calls here," I pointed out.

"Oh, so the tray thing is inappropriate but the thing about the juice box guy was perfectly fine, then? Make up your mind, kid. As long as you're not actually planning to hurt yourself or anyone else, we can pretty much talk about whatever," she replied, more knowledgeable about the phones than me.

"Okay, if you say so, but don't be surprised if you get removed from my call list after all this," I laughed, making it clear that it was a joke.

"Alright, baby, listen, I'm very glad you're doing okay, but I have to get up and get ready for the day. Can you call me after dinner tonight and we can talk more? I love you."

I sighed, not quite ready to get off the phone with her. "Okay, yeah, I can do that. I love you too, Mom. Bye." I hung up and pressed my forehead to the cool wall, the headache having barely subsided. The tylenol barely made a dent in it. Maybe I should've just given it more time.

I didn't let that get me down. I needed to make at least one more call to Alex. I needed to know if he was going to make it for visitation time in a few hours, but I didn't want too share much with him either, determined to have something to talk about when he got there to actually see me. I felt a shift in the air behind my back and saw Lucien behind me. I just looked at him.

"You got any more calls to make? I gotta start setting up rehab shit. Take your time, but not too much of it," he said, a bit flustered and blowing out his cheeks. I decided to forget about calling Alex and let Lucien have the phone. I didn't want to see what would happen if I took too much time. Despite my

39

own anger issues, I couldn't stand being yelled at. And he seemed the type to yell if things didn't go his way. I moved out of his way and was met with a brief word of thanks as he pulled a crumbled piece of paper from his jacket pocket.

That's right. I still had yet to ask about getting a jacket. But that required asking a nurse or a tech for it and I felt like I'd already asked them for multiple things, like the meds and a bunch of other questions. I didn't want to bother them over minor things. Besides, it's not like I was cold just then. I just wanted one for later. I decided I'd ask if I got cold. If anything, I was hot at the moment, nearly sweating. Everyone else was wearing a jacket, though, so I assumed it was cold in the ward. Why was I the only one that was hot?

I looked back over at the clock at the nurses' station. It was just shy of nine o'clock in the morning. We didn't have anything to do until lunch, which I didn't know what time it would be at as everything seemed to follow a very loose schedule there. *Now what?* I wondered.

I scanned the room. Lucien was obviously on the phone calling different rehab facilities. Veronica was talking poor Killian's ear off once again. About what, I wasn't sure. Alice and Renee were walking laps around the common area and chatting quietly. Olivia was watching a recorded Eminem concert on the TV, and Elise was nowhere to be seen. Probably back in our shared room. I decided to see if I could try and talk to her. She's the only person I hadn't talked to in there.

I went back to my room and found her huddled on the bed. I decided to lead with an easy question.

"Hey, they really gave us the world's thinnest pillows. Do you want me to go ask for an extra for you?" I offered, hoping this would be an in, wanting to get her to open up.

"No, thank you. I'm fine," she replied quietly and politely. I figured this was my cue to let her be. If she wanted to talk, I'd be here. I moved to sit on my bed for a while, as it was the most comfortable piece of furniture there. I stared off into space, really thinking about how I felt about being there.

I still felt the incident with the blowtorch wasn't that big of a deal, but everybody else thought so. I tried to put myself in the shoes of literally anyone

40

else. If one of my close friends or loved ones were playing with a blowtorch and ranting and raving, sounding completely mad, would I be concerned? Yes. But this was me. I'm different. I wouldn't have let things go too far, as was clear by my unscorched face. I was still in control then... right? I must've been.

The idea made my chest tight, almost like I wanted to cry, but no tears came out. Instead, I just felt heat rising. My face felt aflame. I was angry. Not hurt, or upset, but angry, once again. Unacceptable, I told myself. I had no right to be angry. I was the reason I was there. Nobody else. I didin't get to get angry and take it out on other people. I needed to deal with it alone and make it stop.

I turned and flopped my face into my mattress and let out a frustrated groan. I wasn't going to scream into my pillow with it being so thin and I didn't want to disturb Elise too much, but I needed to let it out somehow. My normal coping method for dealing with self-hatred would be to sing loudly or dance to music, but that felt very much not okay to do here. So, I would have to deal with just making angry sounds into my mattress.

"You okay?" I heard a soft, timid voice ask. I looked up, and saw that Elise had turned over. Where her back was originally turned to me, it now faced the opposing wall. Her eyes were on me, not as shy now.

"Yeah... no... I really don't know. Emotions are hard," I explained poorly, not wanting to drag her into my personal soap opera.

"You know you don't have to bottle things up, right? That's really bad for you. Can actually make you sick. Physically." She pointed out. That woman was much more astute than I originally gave her credit for. I thought she kept to herself entirely. I guessed not. Another person in here that could see right through me.

I nodded and said that I knew that. It was easiest to just pretend though. To pretend that I didn't feel that way. To put up a front for others. I didn't like what I'd seen from people when I fully opened up before. I wasn't understood. I was told I'm too much. That I'm too intense. Too weird. So, into the bottle everything went.

"I appreciate you looking after me, but I'll be okay. As I told the nurse downstairs, it's all just screwy brain chemicals that brought me here," I joked, hoping to have diffused some of the tension there.

I saw a smile play across her lips. I think that was probably the first time she'd smiled since she'd been admitted here. I was glad I could provide that for her. A reason to smile.

"Well, you don't need to worry about disturbing me at least. I'm pretty easygoing," she said softly once more, her red hair falling back over her face. She didn't bother to move it.

I nodded and moved to get off my bed, thinking I'd finally made a connection with Elise and wanting to stand up and move then.

"Do you wanna talk about anything?" I asked her.

"Sorry, not really. I just wanna take a nap, if that's okay. Do whatever you want, but I'll be up for the group when it's time again," she informed me. Damn, I guess I didn't break through like I thought. Or maybe she was genuinely tired. I remembered her eyes just now. How they looked almost bruised. She must've not been sleeping well before she came there.

I only just became aware of a dull throb in my head, starting to grow worse, but I still didn't want to go ask a nurse for more tylenol. I wanted caffeine badly, but knew I wasn't going to get any. I strolled back out of my room and started pacing up and down the hall, not knowing what to do. I had a bit more energy, but no direction to point it at. I looked out of the corner of my eye and saw Veronica talking with a man; a doctor. I could tell from his white coat. Probably the psychiatrist. I looked back at the nurses' station. Somehow, between my time in my room and the pacing I was doing, an hour had passed. It was now 10 AM. I was waiting until 12:30 so I could see Alex. I felt that was going to be a long two and a half hours. Especially with my reluctance to ask for help.

"Brina! Your turn with the shrink!" Veronica called out, her voice piercing through my head like nails on a chalkboard. That headache wasn't gonna go away on its own, but I was determined to get through it.

"Okay. Thank you!" I replied, not letting on that my head felt like it was momentarily going to split open. The doctor from earlier walked over to me, confirming my identity and leading me to the consultation room.

I entered that too bright and sterile room and took a seat on the cold, hard plastic gray chair that was placed across from an identical one in between a desk. The room was entirely blank aside from the gray tables and chairs and smelled sharply of antiseptic. I felt this room was somehow more dynamic than the group therapy room, like real discussions happened here, not the fluffy emotional bullshit that I felt was aimed more at a group of kids rather than adults.

"Hello, Sabrina. How are you feeling today?" He asked with a light accent I couldn't place and a professional smile planted on his face.

"Fine. Or, as fine as you can be here," I replied shortly, omitting the details of headache.

"That's very good to hear," he replied as he wrote notes in his clipboard that I didn't really notice until then. "And how did you sleep last night? Did you get woken up by the outage?" He asked me.

"Up until the outage, I was sleeping like a log. Out. But that was probably due to the trazodone I was given. I have a thing about sleeping around other people that I don't know," I blurted out, giving way more information away than I meant to. I mentally kicked myself.

"I see. Well, I am sorry the outage woke you, but I am glad you did get some rest. So, down to business. I'm here to discuss the details of your case, like your new medications and your treatment plan upon discharge. From everything I've reviewed from your intake, you're simply here to be monitored, to make sure you don't slip into a depressive episode, which you already are aware of. Now, there are several medications I'm going to be putting you on. I did provide a list for your personal use." He took a page from the clipboard and handed it to me.

I saw a list of six different medications. Six diagnoses, six meds. It made sense. But that still felt like a lot to me. I read through the list as he was speaking, describing what each medication did and the most common side effects I could experience and side effects I needed to get help for immediately.

"The nurse already explained some of these to me. I just need information about this last one as I was already on anxiety medication before I was admitted, so I'm familiar with buspirone," I announced, already a bit ahead of the game there.

43

"Ah. I understand. I'm glad you're already so well informed, and, well, that last one is mirtazapine. That one is for depression, which we are trying to prevent. This can make your metabolism slow down, so you might gain weight with this and you might feel a bit drowsy, which is why I want you to take it at night before bedtime." He concluded with the list of medications firmly in his hands.

"Now as for your discharge. If you're still feeling fine by Monday, I am 90 percent confident you'll be out by then. It won't be up to me, however, but another colleague of mine. I'm just here through the weekend. Do you feel comfortable seeing one of the therapists here at the hospital in our outpatient center? If so, we can go ahead and get you an appointment set up for a med check and a first meeting with your psychiatrist. We will be sending out refills of all the medications that have been prescribed for you to your chosen pharmacy and we want you to pick them up the day you get out so there's no break in the medication," he added. I guessed it was really up to how I acted and felt that determined my release. Hopefully, his colleague felt the same way about my condition as he did.

"Do you have any questions for me?" He asked, raising his eyebrows.

I did have a question about getting more tylenol, but I didn't raise it, choosing to appear strong. "No, you summed things up pretty well. Thank you," I replied politely, effectively disguising the ever-growing throbbing in my head.

He rose from his chair and led me back out to the common area where nearly everyone but Elise had reconvened to do various tasks. I remembered it was only Friday. The incident with the blowtorch happened on Wednesday. Everything felt like it was both dragging along but also happening so quickly. A weird contradiction once again. This was incredibly common for me. Not that I liked it. It just seems no matter the situation, I'm always at the end of some contradiction.

I stepped back out to the less bright, less abrasive main living area. I'm glad not to be in the consultation room anymore. Despite getting more useful information about my medication and when I was expected to get out of there, I felt discouraged. I knew I was going to be stuck in here through the weekend.

I'm going to miss my daughter's 7th birthday party. *Damn it. Damn it. Damn it!* A scowl appeared on my face as my hands raked through my hair, showing the contorted features to anyone who was looking. I couldn't hide my frustration right then and headed back to my bedroom, quickly, shutting the door and pacing, the heat rising to my chest once again. Nobody needed to see all this. Elise was snoring, so I wasn't worried about disturbing her as long as I stayed quiet.

I paced furiously back and forth across the floor of my room. It was a few minutes before a tech came by and looked into my room. He saw me pacing, but I didn't think to acknowledge his watchful gaze until he opened the door. I spun around to look at him, irritation clear on my face.

"Sorry, during the daytime, doors have to stay open unless you're showering. Are you feeling alright?" He asked, referring to my clearly angry state.

"I will be. I just wanted a bit of privacy to work something out. That's all," I said as coolly as I could manage, giving away only a little bit of information.

"Okay, well you're free to walk around the common areas too. You don't need to stay shut up in your room the whole time you're here. Honestly, it looks better if you're out of your room more than in it. It'll help you get out as quickly as possible. Interacting with the other patients helps too. So participate in a group and eat the majority of your meals." He added, giving me some useful information to try and get through my stay here as painlessly as possible.

I nodded and became reacquainted with the now absolutely clear pang in my head. I couldn't hide the pain from my face anymore. I needed tylenol. Right then.

"Um, I'm sorry to bother you, but could I get some tylenol? My head is splitting," I requested, the heat in my face then having nothing to do with the anger that was absent, replaced by a warm sensation of fear and embarrassment. Asking for something as small as tylenol felt like showing weakness and took monumental mental effort.

His face softened and he left to go and get a nurse. Minutes later, a woman in red scrubs came to my room, where I had moved to sit back on my bed and willed the pain to go away. She looked at me and smiled, handing me the cup

45

of water and the other smaller one with tylenol. I took the pill and swallowed it with the water supplied to me and thanked the nurse, stacking the smaller cup into the bigger one and then handing them back to her for her to dispose of. She asked if I needed anything else. I asked her what time it was. She looked at her digital watch on her right wrist and said it was about 10:35. I'd only been back there for about 20 minutes, but it felt so much longer. Time was really going to drag there.

I laid back on my bed, trying to block out the background noises of people chatting and watching TV in the common area. I closed my eyes, hoping to filter out some of the light that wasn't helping my head any. I focused on my breathing for a bit and then I lost time. I think I fell asleep, but wasn't sure. My limbs still felt heavy and achy. I must've stayed really still. I blinked a few times, my head still hurting, but not quite as much as it was earlier. If earlier was a six, it was then a five. Only a small, marked improvement, but still ever present. I knew I was going to go through caffeine withdrawals as soon as I heard there was no sugar in the syrup. That was going to suck, for me and for those around me.

I moved to stand slowly and regretted it. My head felt even worse than before, but I knew visitation had to be soon. I wasn't willing to miss my one shot to see my husband this entire weekend over a fucking headache.

5

Pouring From Empty Cups

I walked out of my bedroom as calmly as I could, my head still throbbing and angry with me for moving in the first place. I looked at the clock and saw it was nearly 12:30, mere minutes before visiting time. I was glad I woke up in time for it. I had no clue if anyone would have woken me if Alex got there and I was still asleep.

I wandered to the entrance of the ward, eagerly waiting for my single visitor. I assumed he would only visit that day since he was alone with our daughter and preparing for her party on Sunday. The only reason he could see me then was because Luna was in school. I wondered what all had happened with him and Luna while I was there. How he was holding up. If Luna had missed me at all. Had he looked to family for support while I was there? I wanted to know it all.

I heard a loud buzz from the door at the front of the unit and I stepped back, ready to allow visitors in. I saw a small group of people enter, maybe three or four people with Alex's tall head following them at the back of the group. He was a foot taller than me, and he was normally the tallest person in the room at nearly every place he went. I could see his chestnut colored hair, tied back as normal. As the group dispersed, I felt my legs moving towards him before I could ever begin to think of how I wanted to approach. I found myself wrapped around his torso, giving him the biggest hug I could manage. I really had missed him, even though it had only been a day.

I felt him hesitate, but his arms were around me quickly, giving me an equally strong hug in return. He was slight in build, as I was accustomed to. He weighed as much as I did, but on him, that meant he was nearly underweight. I felt like I was going to break him, but I didn't let go. Latching on to one person from the outside world that felt normal. One person who I knew loved me unconditionally and would never let me go.

"Hey, Hun," he said, bowing his head into my hair, giving me a kiss on the top of my head.

I replied, "Hi, Honey," and then led him by the hand to the quiet social room, the one with the weird rubber cement furniture so we could sit and talk. It was mostly unoccupied except for Alice and her two visitors on one far end. We occupied the other, giving them space. We had half an hour to talk. It didn't feel like enough. As we both took a seat, I leaned my head on his shoulder and asked him how he's been doing.

"I'm- I'm doing my best. It was so hard leaving you here yesterday. I didn't even make it out the door before I broke down. A nice nurse met me with a box of tissues and asked if I needed anything, but I had to leave and get Lulu, so I took the tissues, thanked her, and left. I got dinner done, got her in bed, all the nighttime stuff done and I tried not to think of all that happened then before crashing out for the night," he replied, sounding like he might break once more. I didn't want that to happen.

"Have you considered getting a therapist to help you through all this? I know I'm getting a psychiatrist appointment after this. That's what I was told. It's probably just as hard on you, if not harder, since you're the one who has to sit back and watch it all unfold, not able to do anything to stop it," I pointed out. Perhaps a bit direct, but I didn't think I said anything wrong.

"I don't know, hun. I'm not sure. I promise I'll think about it, but my focus is on you and Lulu right now. I promise we can talk more about it when you're out of here. Deal?" He requested.

I sighed. I knew him all too well. This was him trying to get out of something he doesn't want to do. He's changed his tell over time, no longer running his hand over his face, but the way he sounded too desperate to change the topic, promising to return to it later... I knew what that meant. "Fine, but you're actually following through with the talk this time. Promise me," I demanded of him, my eyes locked on his, my head lifting off his shoulder, not taking no for an answer.

"I promise, Brina," he replied, no hesitation in his voice. *Good. Maybe I won't have to beat it into his stubborn head,* I joked to myself darkly. Despite being stubborn, my husband responded to logic.

We sat in silence for a long moment. I suddenly had nothing to share and just wanted to enjoy leaning on my husband. He started to shift a bit. "I wanna know how you're doing here. Enough about me. Tell me everything," he stated. Not allowing the wiggle room a question might have.

I panicked, suddenly forgetting everything about the behavioral health unit. I knew he needed an answer from me, but I found myself unable to give one.

"Um, I don't know. It's weird here. No clear schedule. The staff are nice enough. The pills make me tired at night. There's no caffeine for us-" I started listing off things from my experience, purposefully not talking about the other patients, not wanting to violate their privacy. Alex interrupted me when I got to no caffeine.

"No caffeine? Knowing how much pop and coffee you drink, that's not good. How's your head?" He asked, remembering the single time I tried to quit drinking any and all caffeine cold turkey. It really hurt. I had a near migraine the whole time and was irritable with everyone, including Luna, who was only four at the time. Bad times all around.

The throbbing in my head made itself known once more. I hated how well Alex knew me at that moment. "Fine. I took some tylenol a bit ago," I half lied. The whole truth would have been that Tylenol wasn't touching it. It'd only gotten worse.

"Oh really? Is that why you look ready to rip somebody's head off?" He joked humorlessly at me.

"Alex, I'm fine. I can deal. It'll be okay. If I need something, I'll ask," I blurted out, letting my annoyance get the better of me, my tone clipped. We were both far too similar in this regard. Neither of us wanted to get help ever and were quick to help others. We both 'pour from empty cups,' as Alex called it.

"Fine, but I swear if you're just trying to put things off again, I'll be upset with you. I want you to get better. I want what's best for you, but you've gotta be able to ask for help, Hun," he said, unaware of the irony.

"I promise I will ask for help if and when I need it. I already asked for tylenol, remember?" I pointed out, showing that I was actually trying. My head pounded further. It was going to get worse. I just knew it. I decided to try and distract myself from it and asked Alex about how Luna was handling all this. If she missed me for bedtime the previous night.

He looked down at me, studied my face and gave me an answer. "Luna was asking where you were. 'Where's Mommy?' She asked me over and over again. I told her you were sick and getting help. She tried to ask to visit you in the hospital, but I told her only grownups were allowed in the area where you were. I told her you had a special kind of sickness," he got out, looking pained while doing so. I felt bad for him, having to try and remain strong not only for me, but for our daughter as well. I reached for his hand and gave it a squeeze, offering him my silent support.

He squeezed it back and gave me a small smile, making some of the physical pain in my head more bearable for a moment. "Did she accept the answer or did she pull a Luna?" I asked, trying to bring some levity to the hard conversation.

"She pulled a Luna. Crying for a bit, demanding she have uppies and wanting her special blanket. She went down easy enough, though. I told her pretty much right after we got home from picking her up from school, so bedtime wasn't too chaotic." He knew exactly what I wanted to know and gave a satisfactory answer.

I snuggled closer to him and glanced over at Alice and her two visitors. They were all sitting across from one another, seemingly discussing something serious. I couldn't make out what, though. The warmth from Alex's side was a welcome comfort in a ward so isolating. I leaned into him and he wrapped his arm around my side, pulling me in closer. He wanted me close as much as I did.

I heard a nurse call from the main social area. "Visiting hours are over. Please make your way to the exit, visitors." I frowned. Had it really been half an hour already? I felt like we barely got to speak. Alex's grip on me tightened for a brief second. He made eye contact with me.

"It's just until you're able to go home, okay? I'll be back Monday to pick you up. You can call me later if you want. I'll have my phone on me at all times," he told me, before planting another kiss on the top of my head and releasing me, walking towards the entrance without another word. I watched him go. Another throb hit my head, harder than it had before, while a simultaneous pang of sadness hit me equally as hard in the chest. Alex's physical absence left my side feeling cold and suddenly, I wanted a jacket. I figured this was it, the moment all the tears that had been dried up would come rushing out. I waited and waited, but no tears came. How annoying. Why couldn't I cry?

I let out a huff of annoyance. A headache that wouldn't leave me alone, Alex having to leave, and then, I was left to my own devices once more. It was an hour until the afternoon group. I didn't wanna try and ask for more meds before the group, so I decided to do so after. I also realized I hadn't eaten since breakfast and wondered when lunch was. I might've slept through it. *Oh well. What's one lost meal?* I thought to myself, not wanting to bother anyone with a request right now.

I decided to go to one of the tables and just put my head down. I got up, and the world spun for a moment, but I quickly got my bearings and headed over to the table to do exactly as I planned. The table was a cool, firm thing I could ground myself with. I laid my arms down and then my head, pressing it downward into the smooth surface. It felt good. After a few minutes of just sitting there, I saw socks and pant legs approach and sit at the other end of the table. I looked up. It was Killian. I guessed he wanted to talk. I was open to that as long as it doesn't make things worse.

"'Sup?" I asked casually.

"The lack of caffeine getting to you? It's obvious," he stated bluntly, sitting across from me. I immediately felt defensive. I hated when my internal feelings were obvious to others. I started to feel that familiar angry heat rise, but I let it go, in too much pain to maintain it over something that small.

"You got me," I said as I laid my head back down. "Already got tylenol, but it isn't doing shit," I mumbled, my head down, muffling the sound of my

51

answer slightly. I could feel my leg start to tap in annoyance. Shouldn't the tylenol have kicked in by then? I guessed that wasn't going to cut it.

"Could you stop that? It's kinda annoying," Killian requested lazily.

I looked up at him, my face contorted with pain, and my leg still tapping. "Dude, I've got a killer headache, I just watched my husband leave, and they took me off my ADHD medication. It's one thing I could control right now," I said as I put my head back down, gripping the table, feeling the annoyance spread through me, but I was prepared to let it go.

"Don't tell me you're one of those people who uses their diagnosis like a crutch," he said, his tone still lazy, but a bit more clipped, like he was annoyed with me for mentioning my neurodivergence.

I snorted at him, humorlessly. "Says the man who can't even keep his roots dyed. Or are you gonna say it's because you don't care how you look? Are you just that apathetic?"

He just looked at me, for the first time making eye contact, and shrugged, slightly lifting his eyebrows while rolling his eyes.

The rage was about to pop out of the bottle I had stuffed it down so far in. I could feel it. It didn't come out in physical violence, but in a way meant to break a person down verbally and intellectually. I've made so many people cry before, and many others have walked out of my life over it, and I always felt horrible about it immediately after. I didn't know why I'm like that, but it was about to happen once again.

"You know what Killian? You're so fucking judgmental for somebody in the same place as me. You act like you're above all this, acting so laissez faire, but the truth of the matter is you're a suicidal drunk who landed himself in the nut house. You can't even manage to find the will to live without a bottle in your hand, am I right?" I practically yelled for everyone to hear.

"Hell, at least when I was out in the world, I didn't give neurodivergent and disabled people a hard time for not being able to keep up with household tasks. Life is already hard enough and people like your ungrateful ass make it that much harder for them to keep it all together. Fuck, I'm bipolar and I've even managed to never let my daughter see the worst of my symptoms! You can't even keep it together for yourself," I added, radiating fury, as I stood up so quickly, my head spun, sending dark spots into my vision and making the pain so much worse that it grounded me. I didn't fall over, but my hand did have to hold me steady on the edge of the table, the other flying straight for my head, cupping the worst of it. I'd easily say that rated seven on the pain scale.

As I stood there, the black spots retreating, I could see the damage I had done. The nurses behind the counter were staring at me, as were the rest of the patients on the ward. I felt the heat in my body quickly turn from anger to embarrassment. I couldn't believe I just let it all out on Killian like that. How I spoke to him. Used his recent trauma against him. I instantly hate myself for it.

"Killian-" I said, calmer then. He didn't look at me, just left his chair and went to say something to one of the nurses that I couldn't hear. I looked around further. People were all either looking at me with either fear, disappointment, or they avoided my gaze altogether. I noticed a face missing. Veronica wasn't there. At least, I didn't see her.

After a moment, a nurse left the station and approached me with caution, stating that she could find something else to get me for my headache, but she needed to call a tech to get my vitals again to confirm what could be done. I agreed verbally, not wanting to move my head much. I asked if it'd be long. She confirmed it'd be just a few minutes. She left and went back to the nurses' station. She spoke with one of the techs there.

I looked at the analog clock. It'd only been about 15 minutes since Alex left. 15 minutes and I already flipped out. It was only my first full day on the ward and everyone was avoiding me like the plague. How could I have messed up that monumentally so quickly?

A few minutes went by and a tech came from the nurses' station followed by the nurse from before. The tech greeted me and asked for my arm. I offered it willingly, the movement making my head throb more, returning the black spots that danced across my vision once more. The cuff inflated, my temperature was taken, and we waited for the results.

"140/87," the tech remarked.

The nurse's face looked grim. "I'll let the physician on shift know and then we're gonna get you started on a migraine cocktail. Sound alright to you?" She asked.

I knew what that was. I've had it once before for a really bad headache when I was a teenager. That meant I needed to have an IV inserted. I really didn't want that. I hated needles.

"Sure, but does it have to be an IV?" I asked, hoping to avoid it.

"I mean, we can give you oral medication, but it won't work as fast. The IV will get it going through your system more quickly, but either way we do it, the side effects remain the same. Mostly drowsiness, you might develop low blood pressure and nausea, but we can give you something to prevent the nausea as well," she explained.

"Okay. Would it be alright if I skipped the second group today to deal with all this?"

"Of course. Group is optional and with how you're feeling right now, it would probably be in your best interest to opt out today. But I recommend making your best effort to make both of your sessions on Monday if you want to get out then."

Get out. If I want to get out. Veronica. Had she already been released? Did I miss it when I napped? I could've sworn she was still there when I woke up, but I didn't really check. It was weirdly quiet, but that might've been from my outburst. I looked around and saw a familiar head of pink at the edge of her doorway, not in scrubs, but in a black crop top with a smiley face on it and torn jeans with a pair of Converse. Those must've been her street clothes. I liked her aesthetic. Very punk. Like her. I wondered if she'd overheard my outburst earlier.

I looked at her, trying to gauge her reaction. She back looked at me, but only nodded in response. None of her manic energy from before was present. Only a cold sense of seriousness. I had really screwed up. I felt like she was someone I had established some camaraderie with, but now, she was leaving. And I had just lost my chance at having any friends while I was in there from losing it with Killian over a disagreement at most.

The nurse who was nearby left with the tech and headed back to the nurses' station. She reached for a phone, probably to call the doctor to order my meds.

I shuffled, head down, back to my room. Elise was awake, reading a book on her bed. She looked up at me, then back to her book, sighing.

I looked at her and asked "What?" My head was killing me.

"You know what. The way you just flipped out on that guy earlier. Not okay," she said to me, pointing out the obvious.

"I know. I tried to apologize, but he walked away before I could," I started as I sat down very carefully on my bed, hand still on the side of my head. "I know it's not an excuse. I just get so angry sometimes, often over the smallest things. I thought I had a better handle on it than this," I explained before she simply opened her book again and began reading, ignoring me. I felt ashamed, and slowly sank down into my bed, laying there, waiting for the nurse to come with the migraine cocktail. Anything to take that pain away.

A few minutes passed and eventually a nurse came in with a tray and an IV pole, setting it up near my bed. That got Elise's attention and she looked up from her book. I laid there, wishing I had thought to turn off my overhead light, as it made the headache that much worse.

The nurse, already gloved, opened the equipment and started to scrub my arm with disinfectant before she gave me a knowing, kind look. She had seen my outburst earlier and was still treating me with kindness, not asking anything about it. I wondered how much she had seen working here. Did people ever escalate beyond what I had? It was a thought I wanted to ask, so I did.

"I know you saw what happened earlier. I'm sorry about all that. But I need to know, is it common for patients to escalate like I did?"

"Well, I can't name names, but I'm surprised it was you who did and not somebody else. And yeah, it happens from time to time. It's only if you're building up and not relenting or escalating to physical violence that we tend to step in. I've had to break up a few fist fights here before. Trust me, you're not the worst I've seen and you seem genuinely remorseful," she said as she started to prick my arm with the needle, before skillfully switching it out with the medication and the actual IV. I flinched a little at the needle going into my arm, but the small prick couldn't hold a flame to the pain in my skull.

Elise had continued to watch us and listen. I felt the headache start to throb less urgently. The medicine started working nearly immediately.

"There. Your headache should be gone very soon. Try to get some rest. Don't be someone who fights the meds, please. You won't like it. It'll just make you dizzy and exhaust you further," she said. She had caught on that I was stubborn, but in that moment, I didn't care how well she could read me. She turned to leave and gave me a final warm smile, saying it'd all be alright.

I could feel my head getting significantly lighter and less painful than before. The edges of my vision were getting blurry and my limbs were becoming heavy, as were my eyelids, but I didn't want to sleep right then. I had a nap already and it was the middle of the day, when my sleep wouldn't count anyway. I fought it a bit and tried to lean over to get up.

"Don't. Just stay put," Elise said, as she moved out of her own bed to try and physically stop me.

"I just wanted to turn off the light," I lied, not very convincingly.

She moved away from me and flipped the switch for the light that was over my bed. The room was a little darker, her reading light still on over her bed. Much better, but I still wanted to get up.

"There, now you've got no real reason to move. If you need to use the bathroom, do it now. Before those meds kick in anymore. I've had migraines all my life. I know how this works," she stated, confidently. Her earlier shyness from the group was gone.

I started to get up and gripped the IV pole for dear life, my body threatening to give out under its own weight. I moved towards the bathroom, got to the toilet, and did my business. I felt my head getting even heavier and more clouded, moment by moment. Outside, Elise sat waiting for me on her own bed. I knew because I saw her move before I made it all the way to the bathroom. She looked ready to catch me if I fell earlier, but luckily, I didn't need her to.

I finished up on the toilet and stumbled over to wash my hands, feeling like the weight of the world was pushing me down, but still not falling entirely. I looked at my reflection, my eyes, normally blue with clear whites, were tinged red around the edges, showing my current medicated state to anyone who looked. I hated being this vulnerable. My long dark hair was unwashed and unbrushed. I suddenly wanted to get a brush and get the knots out before they got worse. To ask for a hair tie so I could braid my hair and keep it out of the way. I pondered the possibility that I might be able to request a brush and hair tie from up front, but I knew Elise wasn't going to let me leave the room. So, I was gonna have to suck it up and ask her. I could feel my head start to droop. Darkness threatened to pull me under, but I fought back. I left the bathroom and headed back to my bed, sitting, not laying. Elise looked at me expectantly.

"Okay. The light is off. You've used the bathroom. Now, you need to lay down and let the meds work," she insisted, folding her arms.

I looked at her and pouted. My head felt very foggy, but I still wanted to do something about my hair. It was starting to bug me.

"I will, but there's one thing I want to do first. Can you go ask the nurse or a tech for my hygiene bucket for me and a hair tie? I just wanna get my hair brushed and braided and then I promise I'll lay down," I told her, my voice quiet and somewhat unclear.

She huffed at me and wordlessly got off her bed slowly, leaving the room. I remained sitting up, lost in my thoughts. My head and eyes started to droop again. I was thinking about how I had messed up with Killian earlier and how I hoped he'd let me apologize and explain. I thought about Alex and Luna, and how I must've disrupted their routine at home with my absence. I thought until I heard two sets of footsteps approaching. My eyes snapped open and I felt my body sit straight up. I had no clue who the other person was but it sounded like a man's footsteps. The way the weight shifted told me so. It was somebody who walked with a lower center of gravity, so I assumed it was a man. The other was obviously Elise, her steps light and purposeful.

The tech came in and unlocked the closet door. He told me he brought me a hair tie and to just leave the hygiene bucket at the foot of my bed and someone would put it up for me when I was done with the brush. I thanked him quietly, my voice a bit slurred from the exhaustion that replaced the pain.

I opened the brush from its protective plastic container and started slowly working my way up my hair, starting from the tips of my hair, up to my roots. Something my mom taught me to do in order to avoid catching too many tangles. The brush itself felt like it would break in my thick, dark hair, but somehow, it didn't. The strokes of my brush got slower and slower as the medication tugged on the edges of my consciousness, demanding that I hurried up and finished. I shook my head some and tried to speed up and got to work braiding my hair rather clumsily. I couldn't get a grasp of the three strands evenly and then I heard another sigh from Elise on her bed.

"Here. I can do a basic braid," she said. She walked from her bed to mine and sat down behind me, grabbing my hair without asking. I normally would have been taken aback, but I was grateful then. A moment later, there was a knock at our open door. It was a familiar flash of pink.

"Hey, just here to let you know I'm leaving. My husband is here to bust me out. Look, the thing with Killian was super fucked up, but I didn't hear all of it. I was changing in my room after they gave me my things for release. I hope you get the chance to apologize, but I'm out. See you never!" She exclaimed as she cheerfully left, less rapid than she had been the entire time she was there. Or maybe that was the meds making my brain slow.

"Good. She was a lot," Elise mumbled. I wanted to come to Veronica's defense, but Elise braiding my hair and my exhaustion kept me from doing so. I managed a small 'hmm' and let her continue.

Once my hair was fully braided, I handed her the hair tie I kept on my finger and let her secure it. It felt nice and taut on me. Not too loose or too tight.

"Thank you," I managed before flopping back on my bed.

"You can thank me by shutting up and getting some rest. No more talking," she replied curtly, a distinct difference to her shy persona from before. Maybe it just took someone pulling her out of her shell to see beyond the shyness, I thought before my eyes fluttered shut. I wasn't asleep yet, but I was very close to it. I could hear her move and suddenly felt a blanket over me, my breathing deep and even. And then nothing.

6

Breakthroughs and Breaking Fast

I felt heavy everywhere. My arms, my legs, my torso—my entire body, especially my head. But at least I didn't hurt anymore. I fought to open my still heavy eyelids, but won in the end. Although things were still blurry, I could at least tell time had passed by the difference in lighting. Was it sunrise? Or sunset? I couldn't quite tell. I turned over and saw my IV had been taken out, replaced by a wrap of medical tape around my left arm. I wondered when they took the IV out and how it went unnoticed by me. Then again, I knew from experience that a migraine cocktail would put you out for a while.

I made my best effort to get up, but my movements were slow and awkward, my joints stiff from not moving for an unknown amount of time. I blinked my eyes several times, trying to clear away the blurriness. Elise was asleep in her bed, facing away from me. Maybe it was dawn after all, but I couldn't judge the time off of her sleep schedule. It was so sporadic that it still might have been dusk.

Once I had finally made it to a sitting position, I heard a knock at the door and a tech walked in, informing me it was time for vitals. I asked him what time it was and he said it was nearly 7. I wondered out loud whether he meant AM or PM. He clarified that he had meant AM. He wrapped the blood pressure cuff around my unbandaged arm and took my temperature as the cuff inflated. He waited, and as the cuff deflated, he announced my blood pressure and temperature were within a normal range. He then asked if I was feeling better, as he was informed about my killer headache.

"I'm doing a lot better. Just still really tired," I mumbled.

"That's to be expected. Do you think you could do some breakfast today? I saw on your chart that you didn't have lunch or dinner yesterday. You must be hungry," he requested of me.

I sat there for a second, assessing my physical state. My stomach did feel empty and there was a dull ache there, probably from a lack of food.

"Yeah, I could eat," I replied, still worn out from the meds of the previous day. Then it hit me. I never got a menu to order what I wanted from the previous day. *Damn it. More generic meals.*

I sighed and moved to get up as he woke Elise to get her vitals as well. My legs felt like lead as I shuffled toward the bathroom, wanting to brush my teeth and comb through my hair. I looked around the room and noticed that there were no toothbrushes in there. Or toothpaste. I remembered I needed to request my hygiene bucket in order to get access to those things. I'd put it at the edge of my bed yesterday, but it wasn't there that morning. Hoping the tech was still there, I poked my head out of the bathroom door. He was, having just finished taking Elise's vitals.

"Excuse me, but could you unlock the closet so I could get my hygiene bucket? I want to brush my teeth before I go to eat," I requested of him.

He smiled at me. *Why were all the people who worked in this unit so damn smiley?* I thought, remembering that everyone I had made a request to had smiled at me whenever I had done so. He moved swiftly to the closet and unlocked it with a key connected to his name badge.

"Here you are, Brina," he said while handing me the medium-sized bin with assorted toiletries inside. I was a bit shocked that he knew my name. Was he a tech I had before? I wasn't great at remembering people. I didn't really get a good look at the bin last night, as I was very much out of it. It had quite a few things, all wrapped in individual bags that I would need to rip open. A toothbrush, toothpaste, lotion, deodorant, a wash cloth, shampoo, conditioner, body wash, lip balm, and lotion, as well as the hairbrush I opened the night before. Or rather, the afternoon before. I vaguely remembered how fragile it felt brushing through my tangled mess of hair.

I grabbed the toothbrush and toothpaste and put the rest of the tub on my bed as the tech left. I figured I could brush my teeth, eat some breakfast, and then get a shower. But then I additionally remembered I had to ask for more scrubs if I wanted a shower. I weighed that against the fact I haven't showered since I was admitted Thursday, and it was then Saturday. I really needed one, or I was going to start smelling very soon.

I opened the toothbrush and toothpaste and got to work cleaning my teeth. I wished I had thought to ask for them the day before, but everything felt so odd. My normal routine of just going and brushing my teeth and hair was thrown off. I had extra plaque build-up I had to deal with. I spent the whole two minutes brushing my teeth, dancing to a two-minute song I knew by heart and hummed while scrubbing hard with the brush. I finally finished the song and spat out the then frothy concoction from my mouth. As I opened the door, I could see Elise had gotten up and left the room. Probably for breakfast herself.

I headed out to the main common area, feeling less heavy and more like myself. I noticed eyes on me from the other patients and thought it was odd for a moment, temporarily forgetting about my outburst the day before. Once it came to me, my face flushed scarlet, embarrassed once more. I could see everyone was eating their breakfast and all the tables had at least 1 person at them, so I decided to ask a nurse for a set of scrubs for my shower, determined to wait until I could eat alone, not wanting to deal with the awkwardness of trying to see who would allow me to eat with them. I could see the back of Killian's head, and he was talking casually with Olivia about something I couldn't make out. He didn't seem upset or angry about what happened. It didn't change that I still felt awful for what I said to him.

"Excuse me, can I get a fresh set of scrubs? I want to grab a shower. Also, would it be possible for me to eat after my shower? I just want to feel clean first," I said, telling a small white lie. I did want to feel clean, but I also wanted to avoid talking with my fellow patients right then.

The nurse in front of me nodded and got up to go and unlock a closet near the opening of the ward, where I could see a shelf full of scrubs, underwear, socks, and towels. In the middle of the shelves was a stacked washer and dryer combination. I guessed this ward did its own laundry. I always assumed all the scrubs and gowns patients wore automatically went to a laundry room in the middle of a hospital. Maybe this ward was different.

I thanked her as she handed me everything and she told me to let her know when I was ready for my breakfast. I didn't think she was the same nurse on duty yesterday, but I did wonder if she knew what I did and why I was avoiding everyone. Did the techs and nurses gossip about us? What if they all knew what I said to Killian? Then again, why did it matter what they think of me? I shut that thought down quickly. It didn't matter what anyone there thought of me. I was there to get better and avoid a depressive episode. Not to make friends with the other patients, although things would be a lot easier if I could let them see I'm not as volatile as the day before suggested. Those were extenuating circumstances. I sighed, wondering what my next steps should be.

I walked back to my room, scanning the main common area and dining area. Killian and Olivia were still talking calmly, Renee and Alice were reading their respective books about their faiths while eating. Lucien was alone at one table, eating some scrambled eggs that I assumed were seasoned closer to his liking. And Elise was also eating alone, tackling some cereal.

As I reached my bedroom, I saw my hygiene bucket still out, so I went and grabbed my hairbrush, shampoo, conditioner, body wash, and a washcloth from the bin. The bottles of cleansing fluids were all tiny, like the bottles you'd bring on an airplane. I guessed they didn't want to supply bigger bottles in the bathroom itself, so nobody tried to drink them or something. But what if they tried to drink from the little bottles? I shook my head. That was neither here nor there. I wasn't going to drink a bottle of shampoo. I just wanted to get cleaned up.

I slowly stripped off the scrubs that I had been wearing for the past 2 days, feeling a bit gross. I was told at intake I couldn't keep my bra, even though it was a sports bra with no underwire, so I had no chest support in there. I hadn't looked in the mirror at all other than the single time yesterday, remembering my red-tinged eyes from the medication given to me for that awful headache. I looked terrible then. I wondered if a shower now would make me feel better about the way I looked.

I pushed the single button for water. It came out cold initially and then heated up rather fast, basically to scalding. Just like I liked it. I stood under the running water for a moment, letting it soak my unbraided hair, allowing it cascade down my shoulders and back to the rest of my body. I looked down and saw all the stretch marks I had. The ones on my breasts, the belly, my thighs. I turned to look at my back, where I knew they were on my bottom as well. I sighed, frowning at the permanent marks that signified the weight I had gained and how much my body had stretched. I didn't regret having my daughter, but the pregnancy itself took a large toll on my body.

I thought back to my pregnancy with Luna. I thought when I was pregnant, it was relatively easy, other than all the weight I had gained, well over what was recommended for a singleton pregnancy, or even a twin pregnancy. I had gained fifty pounds by the day before my C-section. I was nearly two hundred pounds, about two pounds shy of it. I started at around one hundred and forty-five pounds, give or take. I was an average weight for my height and build. Before my pregnancy, I had just begun to like my body, as I was no longer a stick of a girl, but was finally getting womanly curves.

I didn't dislike being pregnant or that I was going to have a baby girl, but I did dislike how uncomfortable I was all the time. My discomfort was often the catalyst for a lot of fights between me and Alex, as well as a variety of my family members, since we were still living with my mother at the time, trying to save money to get our own place with at least two bedrooms for ourselves and our little one. I was so enthusiastic about it in the beginning of my first trimester. So excited, but it didn't feel like anybody else was matching my enthusiasm, especially Alex. That threw me through a loop and caused me to kinda spiral into a depression. I wanted other people to be as excited for my baby to come into the world as I was. The only person who seemed to be as excited as me was my mother-in-law, but she was in a different state at the time. Alex had moved to be with me before we moved to be closer to his family.

I was depressed about people's lack of enthusiasm for at least two months. I didn't want to eat much and mostly laid around the house, not going out. Not having the energy to argue with Alex or anyone. Not seeing friends. I wasn't working, so I didn't really get to see many people outside of my mom, my youngest sister Zoe, and Alex every day. I did see my middle sister, Abigail, occasionally, as she popped in and out of our mother's house sporadically during her own, simultaneous pregnancy.

She was due 3 months after me. I was initially annoyed that I couldn't have time to myself to be the only person pregnant in our family, but got over it rather quickly, excited to have a niece or nephew. By the time she found out she was pregnant, I'd already done a gender reveal at fourteen weeks, hoping that by doing the reveal, it would make it more real to my family members, rather than just seeing a picture of a little weird-looking peanut thing from a sonogram. It worked to an extent, and I was elated again, but still picking fights with Alex over what I thought were normal things, like wanting him to help me build the crib, but I was still only fifteen or sixteen weeks along. I hated being idle and needed to build something. I wanted to be productive. I was pretty sure that I was manic for several months of my pregnancy, but I didn't know I was bipolar back then.

Alex suggested something I hadn't done in months that would take some time to make, and it could be a gift for the baby when she arrived. He suggested I crochet a baby blanket. I thought it was a stroke of genius, but then he regretted suggesting it when he saw the price of the yarn. He bought several skeins of it for me, but told me I had to make due with what he bought. I looked at the amount he got for me and thought it should be enough, considering I had made baby blankets before for friends who had kids. It was a blue and pink variegated yarn that he bought for me, wanting me to make a traditional baby blanket. I was furious and screamed at him because I wanted to do something non-traditional for the baby, but I forgot to tell him that. Back then, I still felt bad immediately after yelling and was able to cry thanks to pregnancy hormones. He spent an hour and a half comforting me during that spell. I hated thinking about it.

The water was cut off after about three minutes of being on. I realized I had been lost in thought and pushed the button for water again as I got the shampoo bottle and poured some into my hands, rubbing it thoroughly across them, sudsing it up before putting it on my hair and rinsing it out. I repeated the shampooing process once more before moving on to conditioning my hair while I washed my body with the body wash I was provided with. None of it had any floral or honey scents like I was used to. It all vaguely smelled neutral or even antiseptic. *Great. I was going to smell even more like this place.*

I hurried along with cleaning my body and quickly scrubbed everywhere, especially my feet, which I hated touching. I hated how rough they were from my childhood of running around barefoot. Sure, it built resilience and endurance, but I'd much rather have softer feet.

I let the hot water continue to cascade around me, letting it take away the ache in my back from being still so long in the bed. I didn't think I moved once. I woke up still laying the same way I was the day before. No wonder I was stiff. I slept nearly eighteen hours straight and didn't even toss or turn. Lucky for me because I might've ripped the IV out if I had.

Once the water had run out, I stepped out from under the weird shower head and turned to face the toilet directly behind me and the sink and mirror directly across from it. I walked over to the mirror, letting the water on the floor drain into the weird central drain in the middle of the room, wanting to get a good look at myself. My face looked drained of color. Dark circles under my eyes indicated the lack of sleep I had before I arrived there. The skin where my stretch marks were sagged ever so slightly. All things considered, I could've looked way worse. I still had a good body, almost an hourglass figure with a rather defined waist despite a little sagging and a few stretch marks. One positive thing pregnancy had done for my body was that it made my hips wider, which Alex seemed to love. And, of course, I got Luna out of it. My brilliant little girl.

A small smile played on my lips as I started to dry off, resigned to accept what I saw reflected back at me. I didn't look horrible and that was enough for me.

I grabbed a towel off the floor where it was dry on top of my scrubs and wrapped it around my body the best I can. It's a bit shorter than a standard towel, so it doesn't reach all the way around me. I just use it to dry myself instead when I realize I wouldn't be able to wrap it all the way around. After the majority of my body was dry, I grabbed the 2nd towel I saw in the pile, originally thinking it was part of the first towel, and used it to wrap my wet hair up, letting it dry inside the towel cocoon on my head. I pulled on my mesh hospital underwear and the scrubs that I swore were bigger than the ones I had before, but I wasn't complaining. Bigger scrubs meant they'd be more comfortable to sleep in. I pulled my yellow extra-large grippy socks on and took a breath, preparing to leave the bathroom where I knew I'd have to see everyone once again and eat breakfast.

I exhaled and opened the bathroom door to see Elise returned to her place in the room, on her bed reading a book I wasn't familiar with. She briefly looked up at me and went back to her book.

"Feel more human?" She asked, eyes still firmly on the page she was reading.

"Yeah. Definitely. Thanks, by the way, for yesterday. It helped. And thanks for giving me some grace. I know I probably didn't deserve it, but I appreciate it, regardless," I said, wanting to make my gratitude known.

She didn't look up at me. She just raised a single eyebrow before saying, "Don't thank me. I saw somebody in need and just acted. It's what I do. And I've had migraines before. I know how bad a headache can get, and I'm all too familiar with those cocktails. I'm honestly surprised you remember anything." She sounded so quiet, but very matter-of-fact. Not letting a lot of emotion show in her voice or her face.

"But still, it wasn't cool of you to go off on that guy. Killian, I think his name is. I did talk to him briefly. He didn't acknowledge anything I said about your weird outburst, but he did admit he spoke to a nurse to get you meds for your head. If you should be thanking anyone, it'd be him," she added.

I looked at her blankly. I knew he'd approached a nurse after I yelled at him yesterday, but he was the one who asked for help on my behalf? After I just verbally lashed him? I felt my body sag. I couldn't believe after all that, he helped me. He didn't break, cry, or judge. He just... helped.

"I'm going to. And I'm going to apologize. He didn't deserve all that. I know I can fly off the handle sometimes, but I swear, I always feel so awful after. It's like I'm watching myself outside of my body sometimes, tearing into people over what most would consider minor issues," I explained to her. I'm not sure why I was sharing my anger issues with her, but it did feel good to tell someone. "I don't want to be like this forever."

At that, Elise looked up from her book. "Then don't. Grow. Change. Try. That's what you're here for, right?" She asked, her gaze meeting mine, unwavering.

I nodded. She made it sound so simple. Like all that I had to do was flip a switch in my brain, but it wasn't that simple. It was undoing years of what made me like that, which I still wasn't sure why. I knew bipolar was genetic. I got it from both sides of my family. My maternal grandfather had it, and my father had it. I really didn't want to think about my father right now. But what about the anger? It felt like it was almost always there, under the surface, even now. Just waiting for someone to say or do something that would make me snap. Of course, under normal circumstances, I had some control over it. I could separate myself from others and breathe through the rage I felt. But yesterday was different.

Killian came up to me and started talking about people using their diagnosis as crutches. I hated when people used that rhetoric. They had no clue what people like me went through every day, just to try and fit in. To pretend to be okay and normal. It was hard. So freaking hard. Even with medication.

My stomach rumbled, empty. I'd gone pretty much a day with no food. That was the opposite of what I was trying to do. During my latest manic episode, I stopped eating almost entirely. Dropped ten pounds in three weeks. A dangerously fast rate. And I didn't have much spare weight to drop then. I needed to get some food now. I broke eye contact with Elise, and she returned to her book. I walked out of our shared bedroom, any grogginess I had felt before was gone now. I strolled past everyone and went right up to the nurses' counter, my hair still wrapped in a towel. I asked the nurse from before if I could get my breakfast now. I looked at the clock behind her and could tell it was 7:30. Everyone else's breakfast had been eaten and the tables cleared, but I wasn't going to ignore the physical demands of my hunger.

The nurse left the nurses' station after going to a room closed off behind the station itself, where I assumed they kept snacks and food and such for us. She returned and in her hands was a grey breakfast tray with a white styrofoam container with a pint of juice for me on the side. The nurse pulled my food off with the liner on the tray then being on the table containing all my food. I sat down, alone at the table. I thanked the nurse and opened my container, ignoring the annoying sound of the squeaky styrofoam. Inside was cereal, milk and some more pancakes. I guess somebody got the memo about me and eggs not getting along. I dug in on the cereal and found it surprisingly good. I checked the box and thought it was just Life cereal or something similar. It tasted good, at least. Something to fill my empty belly.

I didn't even get a chance to think about how lonely I was about to be because I was so focused on devouring the meal in front of me. Suddenly, the cereal was gone, and then I started on the pancakes which I also finished quickly and then downed the orange juice. I had no clue how hungry I truly was since I didn't have anything to eat since breakfast yesterday.

I looked up from my recently finished meal and took in my environment. Nobody was looking at me. I couldn't tell if this was intentional or if the other patients were so wrapped up in what they were doing that they didn't notice me. I knew meds were due to be distributed soon, that I had maybe 20-ish minutes, as that's about how it worked yesterday, when I was talking with Veronica, when a nurse gave me tylenol and a handful of other meds for my various conditions.

I noticed Killian, Olivia, and Lucien were all having a conversation of sorts on the couch. About what, I wasn't sure. Renee and Alice were both talking while working on the pages they were each coloring. I considered seeing if they'd be willing to let me join them, but decided against it, remembering both of them being religious, and I really didn't want to participate in a conversation about something I didn't share or have much interest in.

I decided I'd work my way up to trying to talk with someone on the ward. For the time being, I thought I'd rather talk with someone familiar. I walked back up to the nurses' counter and asked for a number out of my contact list. She handed me the sheet with my contacts, and I cleared the short distance to the phone on the right side of the nurses' station.

I started to dial the number and realized I was shaking. Was it nerves? I wasn't certain. I took a deep breath as the phone started to ring. "Hello?" A woman's voice asked, high and clear. "Hey, Mama. It's Brina. Can we talk?"

7

A Stupid Red Crayon

My relationship with my mother-in-law was strong; at times, we got along better than my own mother and me. Not to say my mother didn't love me. I was just that things with my mother-in-law just felt different, as it filled a different hole.

"Yeah, I've got time. I'm off this weekend for Luna's party," she said, and I could feel a pang of ice in my chest. I was going to be missing her party. People would talk. *What kind of mother misses her own child's birthday party?* I thought. "Of course, if it's still happening?" She questioned.

I cocked my head in confusion. "Why wouldn't it still be happening? Did the venue fall through?" I asked, completely missing the obvious.

"Umm... sweetheart, I love you, but with you being where you are, I kinda figured we'd have to reschedule. I can call the venue after I get off with you-"

"No! Don't cancel. I don't want to be the reason her birthday gets rescheduled or canceled. Like my mom told me, 'it's better to miss one birthday and be there for the rest,'" I stated firmly. I truly wanted my daughter's birthday to happen as planned and for her to have a lot of fun. I was just sad that I wasn't going to be there for it.

"Well, that's really mature of you. I'm proud of you for saying that. You know you're a good mom, right? The fact that you're in a behavioral health unit means nothing about your parenting," she pointed out, knowing my insecurity about my role as a mother already. We had talked about it several times before.

I often felt I wasn't enough for my daughter. Before her autism diagnosis, before my own one of ADHD, I felt like I was operating complex machinery without an instruction manual and being expected to make it work perfectly. I still didn't have a manual, but I had experience and a few tools.

"Aww, thank you, Mama. I was calling to ask if you think you could visit me today? I know it wasn't talked about before. I wanted to call yesterday to set it up, but, well, I don't want to get into it over the phone, if that's okay. I'll be honest and say it was ultimately my own fault. Hopefully, no permanent damage, as nothing physical was done, but I told someone off. It was bad," I admitted, my cheeks flushing scarlet once more.

"Brina, I'm glad you told me. However, I wish it hadn't happened, but at least you didn't keep it to yourself. I'll definitely be there for a visit. You're really wanting to try, aren't you?" She asked.

"Yeah. Also, can I ask a favor? Could you bring me some books? I'll call Alex and have him put together a list of what I want to read. Gives you a reason to stop by and give your favorite granddaughter some attention." I smirked, knowing how much my mother-in-law loved my daughter.

"My only grandchild, thank you very much. You've made it very clear you're not having any more, which, I think, is the right decision for you, Sweetheart. Not that you aren't a loving mother, but with what happened last time... sorry, I know that's still hard to talk about," she said quietly, bringing up a rather painful memory for me.

"It's fine. You don't need to apologize. What happened was nobody's fault, and I knew something was wrong the entire time. I just wish somebody had listened to me before it finally happened," I said, speaking around the agonizing event I didn't want to think about. I never processed it. I just kept going and pretended things were normal when they weren't. Sure, I had a few bad days where the thought would cross my mind and I couldn't leave bed beyond caring for my daughter's basic needs, but who hasn't had days like that? Non-bipolar people, that's who.

I didn't want to linger on such a gut-wrenching topic, so I decided it was time for a change.

"Didn't you have a book you wanted me to start, too? I know I've got time in here. Feel free to bring that," I said to her, giving her an out.

I heard a soft sigh on the phone, probably of relief. "Of course. I think you'd love it. I know how much you like romantasy novels like I do. Just another reason I'm glad you're my daughter-in-law. Someone to read with. Or give and get recommendations," she said rather enthusiastically. I swore, between her and my own mother, I was drowning in sentimentality.

Why couldn't they act like things were normal? That's all I wanted. The mundanity of life outside the psych ward, excuse me, behavioral health unit. I had no idea what to call it. I just felt like I might be both starting to lose it and also starting to gain some insight into a few things about myself, thanks to a few people here.

"You're absolutely right, Mama. I'm gonna let you go and call Alex. I told him I'd call him last night. That didn't exactly end up happening," I said, a small flush rising to my cheeks.

"Alrighty then, Brina. I'll talk with you later. Love you. Bye," she said and hung up. I found myself looking forward to her visit later that day.

I then hung up the phone before picking it up again, both to call Alex about the books and to explain about last night, in addition to avoiding talking to any of my fellow patients. Avoiding any potential awkwardness. *I really, seriously fucked up with Killian yesterday*, I thought to myself, sighing and closing my eyes for just a moment before I dialed my husband's number. His was one of the few I had memorized.

It rang a few times before going to voicemail. I guessed he was either sleeping in, busy with Luna, or mad at me for not calling last night. I left a voicemail anyway and read off the callback number listed on the piece of paper taped above the phone.

"Hey, Honey, it's me. I was just calling to try and explain why I didn't call back last night. Could I also ask a favor of you? There are two books on my nightstand, one with a purple cover and one with a green cover. Can you put those together and get them to your mom today? I asked her to visit, and she said she'd bring me things if I wanted them. I love you. This is the callback number. 555-6428. Call me back soon, okay?" I said and then hung up, my words just lingering in the air. It's too early for anyone back around my side of the family to be up, so I don't bother calling them, and I knew my best friend, Monty, would be at work by now. I sighed, letting my head fall back, a little harder than intended, against the desk of the nurses' station.

"Sorry, didn't mean to do that," I said out loud, to nobody in particular.

Just as I hung up the phone, I noticed the nurse at my side with medication and a cup with water in it. I nearly jumped out of my skin. I got myself under control and saw her chuckle a bit to herself, clearly amused by startling me. I accepted the medicine and noticed an extra familiar pill. Tylenol. I guessed it was to prevent the headache from coming back. I put all the pills in my mouth, chased them down with the water, and handed both cups back to her. I gave her a small smile. She returned one of her own and left to give Lucien for his medication.

I got up and went back to my room. Maybe I could hide until lunch time. The problem with that would be that I have literally nothing to do, and I don't want to spend my whole day asleep. If I were gonna be stuck there, I was gonna make the most of my time, damn it. I grabbed a stack of word searches and a red crayon. I went to my room, turned on my reading light, and went to town.

The first one's theme was the circus. I looked around and found 'clown' and 'ice cream' intersecting immediately. What was the age rating on these? Were they meant for children? I found three, then four more, and then the word search was done. I got it all in under four minutes. I truly believed that one was for elementary school kids. Honestly, it probably was. I looked over and saw Elise in her bed, still reading the same book. She didn't look at me. I returned to my next word search. That one's theme was vegetables.

I saw 'tomato', and my mind went back to that old debate I had with a friend once on whether or not a tomato was a fruit or a vegetable. I was certain it was a vegetable, because it had seeds. He was certain it was a fruit because of the way it was made up. We never did look into that. That friend was Alex before we started dating the first time. I figured this could be a good in with Elise.

"Hey, I'm doing this crossword, and the theme is vegetables. Tomato is

73

listed. It is a vegetable, right?" I asked her, genuinely wanting to know.

She looked up at me, her face contorted with confusion. "Um, I think that page is misprinted. Tomatoes are fruits. They're in the same family as peppers, too," she said, returning to her story.

I shrugged my shoulders, grateful for the small amount of words spoken. I didn't expect her to actually answer me in the first place. I returned to my potentially inaccurate word search, making a mental note to ask a tech or nurse if they could look up whether a tomato is a fruit or a vegetable. I find a series of words back to back, once again completing the word search quickly. I huffed.

These aren't challenging enough, I thought. I flipped the page over and just started writing everything and nothing. What I was thinking, how I was feeling. What I had for breakfast. My outburst with Killian. The hard conversation I didn't want to have with my mother-in-law. Everything. By the time I was done, I had filled out the backs of about five or six word searches. My writing was also large print and clunky because of the crayon that I couldn't sharpen as it dulled with more wear. I read through everything, not caring about anything else but what was directly in front of me, my focus entirely on what I had written. I couldn't stand it. My clunky handwriting made it impossible for me to enjoy it. I stood up off the bed quickly and made two long strides before entering the bathroom, still holding the short list of my thoughts and feelings.

"What are you doing?" I heard from the other side of the door. What I'm doing had nothing to do with Elise, whose presence I had forgotten about in my creative endeavors. I held out my short work and dropped it into the paper bag that served as a trash bag below. That crayon ruined it all for me. It was absolute trash, no matter how raw, real, or honest the message on paper was. One small thing was enough to ruin it for me.

I walked out of the bathroom and looked over at Elise, a blank stare on my face and a look of concern on hers.

"Where are your papers? You were just writing something. What did you do?" She questioned. She looked genuinely worried that I might've done something serious.

"Don't worry, nothing's wrong," I said, holding up my hands, signaling a white flag moment. "I threw them away. The crayon kinda ruined it for me," I stated simply, folding my arms, looking at nothing in particular. That was pretty normal for me. I'd write out whatever comes to mind and then realize something is wrong with it; it would be shy of perfect, and then I'll either delete it or throw it out. I never stopped to think of what it might look like to other people to see me do that.

Elise's posture declined a bit, her shoulders hunched ever so slightly, her brows furrowing slightly. I saw her red hair adjust ever so much that it should have been imperceptible. She seemed to have wanted to say something, but hesitated before trying once more.

"If you don't mind, can I read what you wrote? I just have a feeling you'll regret throwing away something you worked on. I get it if you don't want any reminders, but I find a lot of creative work comes from people fresh out of the psych ward," she stated gently, quietly, but not shyly like before. Maybe she was just quiet by nature. Not inherently shy. Maybe it worked better for her to be an observer.

I stared at her. Why would she want to read what I wrote? People have asked before, but that was mainly for fanfiction. This was about my own life. So personal. So detailed. I didn't know if I could trust her with those details.

"Sure. Go for it," I said, trying to remain casual. *WHAT THE FUCK WAS THAT?!* I screamed at myself internally. Why did I just allow a total stranger to read some of the most intimate details of my life? I must have been losing my mind. I felt cold sweat form on the back of my neck, and my heart started to pound fast and hard in my chest.

She moved to get off her bed, and I sat back on my own, looking apathetic. Trying to mimic Killian's affect. Once she emerged from the bathroom, she had the five pages in her arms, clutched close, one in her hand, actively reading it.

She moved without looking up from her place and sat on the bed next to me, placing the other four pages at the edge next to her, completely ignoring the fact that she was sitting on my bed next to me.

I sat there, somewhere between dumbfounded and flabbergasted. Why would she sit next to me? And then not address it? Why is she so interested in that garbage I wrote? It was nowhere near decent or developed enough for a wide audience. I doubted she'd even like what I wrote. I thought of it like a directionless list, but it flowed like a story. Something she could grasp and follow. Something she seemed to be... enjoying? I sat up straighter and looked directly at her, dropping my facade.

There was a small upturn at her lips around the second page, followed by tears forming in her eyes by the fourth, and then she just looked at me once she read the final page.

"I'm sorry. I really shouldn't have asked," she said. My chest felt tight. Was it really that bad? Did she seriously regret reading my writing that much? Was I that bad of a writer? "It's just... It's so..." she trailed off, snapping her fingers like she was looking for the right word.

"Bad?" I said, prepared for the brunt of the hit. Willing her full honesty.

She looked at me, brows furrowed, and her head tilted. "No. The opposite actually. It's good. Better than good, and I'd love to read more. But it's just that it's so personal. I can see why you wouldn't want to share it with other people," she finally finished.

I exhaled shakily. I couldn't believe what I just heard. She liked what I wrote? Even with my truly awful handwriting and it being written in large font in crayon? That meant something to me. Sure, writing fanfiction, I knew I was good at. You don't get thousands of followers just for your writing if you weren't at least decent. I hadn't really written much since I graduated high school, other than a short ten-page piece for a creative writing class for the one semester of college that I actually completed. My teacher back then even told me to keep writing, but I could never make time, or I'd just throw it out.

"Wait, what? You actually thought it was good? I genuinely thought I put that thing where it belonged. I've written so much trash and that was mediocre trash at best," I said, truly loathing my own work. It was too much of a reflection of myself. I was built for a world that didn't exist. I was different.

"Yeah. You don't?" She asked simply, a small smile spreading across her face. I start to feel the flush spread across my entire being, not just my face.

76

I'm nearly as red as her hair. This was genuinely something I popped out in maybe half an hour or so. What would her reaction be if I actually tried to write something good?

"Wha-what did you like about it? Any specific passage?" I asked, trying to understand her line of thinking, trying to understand what I could have possibly written well enough to draw her in.

She pointed to a passage I wrote in the middle of page two, describing how I didn't know when breastfeeding, if your child suddenly unlatches, the milk keeps flowing, and quickly, too. How I was so tired and sleep deprived that I couldn't react and just cried because I thought I was drowning my baby. I remembered my mother had to take Luna from me, told me to go lie down, and she used some milk I had pumped for her instead. I was so upset with myself then, but once I woke up, around twelve hours later, I felt a lot better and thanked her for taking over. Alex was at work, so it wasn't like he wasn't pulling his weight; he was. I was honestly probably coming down from a manic episode that followed birth anyway. Hormones are wild.

"Are you a mother?" I asked her.

"No, but I've always wanted to be. This is something I didn't know, so thanks for the information about breastfeeding. And, I'm sorry for you lo-"

"Mmm-mm! Please don't. I really, really don't like talking about that. I've never really given myself the space to deal with it. And I'm definitely not okay with it being in front of another person whom I don't know, no offense," I said, genuinely hoping she doesn't take any. I just don't know her that well.

She nodded solemnly and looked to the wall. "Can I tell you something? Might make you feel less like you're talking to a stranger," she inquired, not looking at me.

"Yeah, please," I said simply.

She looked at me, looked me up and down, and turned her gaze back to the dark powder blue wall. "My husband just split. Turns out, his swimmers were defective. A bunch of them had double tails or engorged heads or stuff like that. I had a few miscarriages because of that. Once I knew, I blamed him for putting me through that. It's part of the reason I'm here," she said.

I just looked at her. How could she just tell me that with the level of ease?

Like it didn't just happen to her? I felt pity for her, but then reminded myself what I would do if I found out somebody felt pity towards me because of what happened. I hated being the object of someone's pity.

"It doesn't mean I was in the right. Just because I'm in here and I'm depressed doesn't give me a free pass to act however I want. That's also a good part of why I was upset with you for blowing up at Killian, but reading this and hearing the way you've described your past and current anger issues... have you talked with a psychiatrist about them? I know you don't have to tell me. But I'm curious," she said. I sensed no dishonesty or hidden motive from her. Maybe it was safe to open up further. Just for once. This was terrifying, but it also felt good in a way.

"I haven't. It didn't exactly come up," I said to her, being honest with somebody for once.

"Well, I think you should. Maybe show them this," she stated, holding up my previously discarded papers. "It's a strong piece of literature, and it's also very insightful. Your anger, your outbursts, I don't think they're entirely in your control once a certain point is hit. I know people say they black out when they get too angry, but I don't think that's you. It's like you step out of your body and you're operating on pure logic to tear someone down," she said, repeating what was repeated on paper.

"And you got all that from five pages?" I mused, hoping for relief from all this serious talk.

She looked at me with a 'what do you think?' kind of look, her brows raised. "You're very descriptive with your writing, so you should know what kind of imagery you portray. It's clear and strong. Overwhelming, from the sound of it. I'm sorry you have to deal with that. Why so angry, though? I couldn't pinpoint why," she asked, trying, in her own way, to bring levity to the topic.

"I honestly don't know. Sometimes it feels like my default. If someone says something bad about me or someone or something I care about, I lash out. I've gotten better about it. Under normal circumstances, I can walk away and do breathing exercises to deal with it. But not always. I'd say like seventy percent of the time, I can walk away," I thought out loud. I really never considered where my anger stemmed from. I knew I'd almost always felt that way. I couldn't stand it. It'd gotten to a point where I feel like my anger was dangerous, and I tried to avoid it at all costs.

"Well, you may wanna dig deep. When you start therapy, they're gonna drag it out of you," she warned lightly. I could tell Elise was finally starting to not be so shy around me, despite her having every reason to be.

"Thanks for the heads up," I said, as I moved to stand from the bed.

Elise stood as well, but moved just to sit back on her bed and pick up her book, giving me a final nod before returning to it. I walked out of our shared bedroom door, prepared for what comes next. Invigorated by mine and Elise's talk. I was going to apologize to Killian.

8

Truths

Stepping out of my room was the easy part. I looked around the ward and saw everyone pretty much as I had left them, either talking with each other or working on something like a coloring page or word search. Killian was still talking with Olivia, but he seemed more into the conversation. More lively and animated. I thought I saw an actual smile behind his mop of blonde hair, but I couldn't tell for sure. I didn't want to interrupt that. I knew he needed it—the smile, to feel happy. I really regretted lashing out at him like I did.

I was faced with a new dilemma: did I interrupt a good conversation to make my apology, or wait and let it hang in the air, letting people think I was incapable of owning my shit? I didn't want to interrupt a moment of happiness for him, but what I wanted to say was incredibly important. *I need to get it out now, before any more time passed,* I thought, my resolve strengthened.

I stepped forward towards the grey and green couch the two of them were sitting on. Killian was facing away from me, but Olivia saw me approach, and I could see her face fall a bit. She stopped talking and simply looked at me sadly. At least it wasn't with contempt.

"Hey, Killian. Can I talk to you? I wanted to apologize for yesterday," I got out, my fists balled around the pants leg of my scrubs, nervous as all hell.

He turned around and had a total look of neutrality. "Yeah, I'm willing to hear it," he said, gesturing to the empty seat next to him.

I took his offer and sat down. Olivia looked between us and decided then would be a good time to make her exit. She stood up and walked away to join Alice and Renee in coloring. I looked at him for any signs of anger or sadness, and I was surprised when I saw neither.

"You didn't deserve any of what I said yesterday. It's not an excuse, but I was already hurting, physically, mentally, all that. Sometimes, when things line up like that, I just lose it. I know I need to work on it more. So, I'm sorry for lashing out at you yesterday. And thank you for being willing to hear me out. And for getting me help without judgment. That headache was a killer," I rushed through my apology. I was worried he'd withdraw his calm demeanor and start ripping into me for how I treated him the previous day, which wouldn't have been uncalled for, but I was met with patience and continued calm.

"I could tell. And thank you for your apology. I accept. I owe you one as well. Elise came out and talked to me once you were out. She said you regretted what you said and wanted to get my side of the story. It looked like it took everything in her to keep from running from the conversation. Guess she's still working on her shy side."

My eyebrows raised in surprise. He owed me an apology? I remembered Elise saying she spoke with Killian, but she was vague on the details. I wondered if it was because deep down, she really was just a shy person. Her directness with me might have come from the fact that she was upset with my actions. I wasn't entirely sure; I just speculated.

"She asked me exactly what set you off. I told her, and she kinda just looked annoyed with me. Told me it was no wonder you blew up. She gave me a whole speech about the struggles of neurodiversity and getting daily tasks done. I figured by then I was in the wrong, and I owed you an apology for coming at you with a pretty messed-up view of people and their struggles. So, sorry," he said, running his hand through his dyed blonde locks, offering me a rare view of his face, which was a bit red, his brows furrowed a bit downward, not making eye contact with me.

"I accept your apology," I said simply.

"So, no more batshit flip-outs if I say something that pisses you off?"

I laughed. Probably the first real laugh I'd had since arriving on the ward.

"No promises. I can say I'll do my best. And maybe you could just be less of an ass. That would help me not flip out." I stated, very matter-of-fact, but with a huge grin on my face, showing I meant no harm.

He nodded, and we fell into an easy conversation about the time I'd flipped my shit over my sister, Abigail, taking my homecoming dress in high school and wearing it for a Halloween costume. She wanted to go as Carrie from the Stephen King novel. How pissed I was. How I threw my phone in her direction and shattered the screen. It didn't hit her, but it did come close. I regretted that the moment it happened, too. I was grounded for three months over that, and all she got was a week for altering my dress without my permission. I was pissed over getting grounded for that long, and that turned into a screaming match with my mom. I really was a volatile person. I sighed at the thought.

Killian remarked how things could have been much worse. How the phone could've actually hit my sister. "What's your guys' relationship like now?" He asked, seeming genuinely curious.

"Good. She's a mom to two little ones, my niece and nephew. She's in the middle of a divorce, which, unfortunately, we all saw coming. I'm not gonna go into details, because that's not my story to tell, but she plans to celebrate once it's finalized and it'll be well worth it."

He nodded once more. "Sucks that some people can't get their shit together, you know?" He said, leaning his head back against the couch, acting more like his chill self. I couldn't tell if this was the real him or a persona he put on for others, but it really was disarming. "Breakups, divorces, they all suck. For everyone involved, not just the couple," he said, and I could sense there was more to the story.

"You divorced?" I asked.

"No, my parents are. It happened when I was, I don't know, like four? I don't remember all the details, but there was a lot of yelling. Lots of talking to doctors and court-appointed officials. But that's not a story for today," he cut himself off. "I don't like to linger on the heavy stuff. I'm just a guy who's chill and likes a drink. I go to work, clock out, go home, have a beer, and go to bed. I don't bother anybody and nobody bothers me. You know?" He said, far too casually. It felt forced. Like he actually did want to talk about it, but couldn't make himself. I wasn't going to force it out of him.

"Yeah. I get it. I try my best not to bother other people, too. I know it's a problem. I struggled to even ask for the tylenol yesterday. And then the way they have everything set up in here... not a fan. You have to ask for pretty much everything. I'm a very independent person. I don't ask for help. People come to me for help, not the other way around," I ranted, shifting in my seat uncomfortably, but it had nothing to do with the uncomfortable furniture beneath my bottom.

"Veronica was right about one thing. You really do get it." His mention of Veronica reminded me that she got out yesterday. I nearly forgot, looking around for her pink hair only to find it nowhere to be seen.

"Well, she really was insightful. And entertaining. She really knew how to make the time pass. Did she seem less manic when she left or was that just the drugs they gave me?"

"She was less manic. Everyone saw it. I think your outburst connected with her in a weird way that kinda made her snap out of it. Not sure, but it's my only theory." He shrugged, head still leaning against the back of the couch.

"Well, guess we're gonna have to find a new way to entertain ourselves with her gone," I replied, shifting in my seat once more to fully face Killian. "My mother-in-law is gonna bring me some books. What about you? Got anyone coming to visit today?"

"Nope. My family are all busy with stuff. Nobody is gonna visit me today. But I should get to see my dad tomorrow after he gets out of church," he stated, a glimmer of hope in his eyes.

The conversation flowed naturally for several long minutes before Olivia rejoined the group and the three of us started talking about what we should do while we were waiting, running out of things to talk about.

"Monopoly?" Olivia suggested.

"Bad idea. I have flipped Monopoly boards before. I'm not typically competitive, but that game... fuck that game," I stated firmly.

"Okay, the batshit bitch can't handle Monopoly. Got it," Killian joked, a smile forming on his face.

"Fuck you, too," I said, pointing at him and laughing, showing him I mean nothing by it.

"Okay, well, what about Uno again? We had fun playing it the other day." Olivia pointed out.

"No, I'm all Uno'd out," Killian said flatly.

I thought back to my time in high school. When I was in drama class and participating in activities. I remembered a game I thought was fun.

"Two truths and a lie?" I suggested.

They both looked at me, puzzled.

"What's that?" Olivia questioned.

"It's what the title implies. You say three things about yourself, two true, and one a lie. Then, the other people in the group have to guess which one was the lie. I learned it in drama class. We were working on believable acting and showing people's tells for when they were lying. You guys wanna try it? I can go first and give an example."

They looked at each other, nodded, and then looked back to me.

"Go for it. This should be interesting at the least," Killian remarked.

I thought for a moment. What weird real-life experiences could I share with these guys that might make a simple lie sound believable?

"Okay, I've got them. One, I've broken my left leg twice. Two, I've jumped off a high dive once and did a bellyflop. Three, I correctly guessed the plot of an episode of my mom's favorite show before she finished watching it, and she was pissed at me for spoiling it. Now, you guys guess which is the lie. Feel free to tell me why you think the way you do about the suspected lie."

Killian and Olivia looked thoughtful. Olivia crossed her arms in thought and Killian stroked his beard, really thinking.

"Okay, I know which one it is. But let me tell you which two I think are the truths. It's entirely believable that you did a bellyflop off a high dive. I bet you never jumped off one again, did you?" He asked.

"That would be correct. I've never been on another high dive since. My belly was bruised for days after that."

"And I already know you're smart and can see connections in things other people miss, so I wouldn't be all that surprised to hear you ruin show plots frequently," he assumed.

"Right again. So you know it was number one that was a lie?" I smiled. Killian was good at this.

"Yeah. That was obvious. If you'd broken your left leg twice, you'd have a limp or something. You don't. But you do walk weird, you know?" He said.

"I walk weird? How?" I asked, genuinely confused. What did he mean by that?

"You look like you kinda walk more on the sides of your feet than the bottoms. You find the middle of your shoes wearing out faster than the rest of them, right?" He pointed out.

I shivered. The fact that he was so astute was a lot to take in. Did everyone there have the ability to see right through me?

"Yeah, I guess. That's kinda unnerving, you know. Both of you can read me like a book, can't you?" I asked.

Olivia looked up, as she was previously playing with the ends of her hair.

"I'm sorry if that bothers you, but it's like you can't keep your emotions off your face. You're very easy to read," she said, shrugging.

I looked towards nothing in particular directly in front of me. I didn't like being read that easily. I could feel my fists clench in the fabric of my scrub top. A small, slow heat started to rise. I shook my head and dismissed it away. Their observations about me weren't coming from a place of malice. It came from something far more harmless. From wanting to understand me better.

"Okay, moving on. Killian, since you figured out which was the lie first, it's your turn. Two truths and a lie."

He sat up, concentrating for a moment. I could see the thoughts flicker across his eyes as his brows raised and lowered in concentration, playing with different ideas.

"I've got it. One, I kissed a dog on a dare once. Two, I never learned to tie my shoes. Three, I've jumped off a cliff into the ocean once."

I decided to wait and see if Olivia could decipher the lie.

"Two. I saw you tie two folded up pieces of paper together when we both first got here," Olivia said.

He nodded and congratulated her. I asked the question I really wanted answered. I needed to know for sure.

"Why did you jump off a cliff? That sounds incredibly dangerous."

Killian looked at me, and then looked away. "I was going through some stuff, saw an ad for cliff diving and signed up. It helped to clear my head," he replied quickly. I was worried he did it to hurt himself, but it sounded like it was done to clear his head and he was under the instruction of trained professionals. I hated the idea of him wanting to hurt himself, despite only knowing him for two days. He was a person, and I didn't want him to suffer.

"It's my turn!" Olivia exclaimed excitedly. "Hmm. How about this? One, I've never drank alcohol before. Two, I'm a devout Catholic. Three, I listen to rap daily," she stated, her back straightening and a look of triumph on her face.

I knew what it was instantly. "You're not Catholic, are you?" I asked.

"Darn. I thought I had that one in the bag. You're right. I'm not Catholic. I am a Christian, but not Catholic. My faith means a lot to me, but it's not the only thing about me, you know? A lot of times, people assume individual parts of me are the whole of my being. But I want people to know there's a lot more to me than just Eminem and my faith. Like, I can draw. I'm involved in my community. I volunteer when I'm not on campus. I help run my sister's Girl Scout troop," she listed.

"So, you're a multifaceted person with complex emotions and thoughts? Who would've guessed?" I joked.

She laughed. "Yeah, I guess I can also get a little wrapped up in my own head at times, too."

We were all laughing and smiling while sharing difficult things. Was this what it means to have friends there? I questioned whether it was inappropriate to request their contact info. I felt like they both had some interesting stories to tell that maybe they couldn't tell in there. I wanted to get to know them both better.

"So, would it be alright to look you guys up on social media when we all get out of here?" I asked impulsively, wanting to get the awkwardness of the question over and done with.

Killian lolled his head in my direction. "Sure, you can look me up. It's Killian Ross."

Olivia nodded her head and said I could find her under the name Olivia Hugh.

"I'm glad you guys agreed. If you're out before me, my name online is Brina Rogers," I told them. I hadn't noticed Lucien joining us in the rocking chair to the right of the couch.

"I can see all the kids are getting along again. I'm glad to see it. It's always crappy to see youngins' fighting with each other," he said as he took a seat. I could see he was sucking on something in his mouth. A lozenge, maybe? I didn't know they had lozenges there.

"Youngins? I'm thirty-two. Hardly youthful," I said rather sardonically. I hated it when people referred to me as anything remotely childlike. Probably because I had to take up an authoritative role very young. I always felt because of the role I had to fill, that it excluded me from being young, as if it was somehow a bad thing. Something to be embarrassed or ashamed of.

"You're younger than me, therefore, you're a youngin'." Lucien reaffirmed. He motioned in my direction with his shoulder and looked at me. "You're obviously older than her, but you remind me of my daughter. Kid is a real spitfire, but also a sweetheart. She's a senior in high school this year. I couldn't think of a more amazing person than the one I've created," he said, clarifying he was coming from a place of familiarity. I felt the heat that had started to build subside rapidly. "Yeah, I don't have custody of her. My own legal issues, but her mom, as much as I hurt her, still let me keep in contact with my daughter as long as I kept sober. I was until recently. She found out. Stopped letting me call. Probably for the best, but I was so pissed at her for it. I tried to break into their home. Not my smartest move," he explained. I had a feeling there was more to the story, but pressing felt like a bad idea. As nice as Lucien tried to come off, how fatherly and protective he was, there was something about him I couldn't entirely place. Something dangerous about him, but it was dormant. Something I recognized in myself.

The game we were playing had long been abandoned and replaced by more easy-flowing conversation between the four of us. It was still early, I thought, when I heard the door buzzer go off. I heard the high-pitched whine I'd heard the other day before a woman's voice over the speaker in the ceiling said that lunch was served in the behavioral health unit. I made a beeline for the dining area and took a seat at one of the tables, joined quickly by the three people I had just been speaking with.

Maybe being in there wouldn't be that bad. The food wasn't terrible, the people were more chill and understanding than I had originally thought, and the showers got really hot. Not too bad. Maybe I can really have a fresh start. Enjoy myself, even. That all felt strangely right. Like I was exactly where I was meant to be right then.

9

A Different Kind of Full

Lunch was once again served on the same paper tray liners and in those all-too-familiar styrofoam containers. I opened mine, bracing for the squeak of the lid. Inside, there was a salad with pieces of chicken and a side cup of ranch, as well as a fruit cup. This looked absolutely delicious; I had always been a fan of salads. I was the weird kid growing up who requested raw broccoli as a snack. My mom didn't think much of it back then, just glad I wasn't asking for ramen noodles.

When I was five, I went through a phase where I wouldn't eat anything but ramen noodles. She tried offering me different food, but I refused to eat it. When she stopped buying it, I stopped eating altogether. People tried to tell her I'd eat if I got hungry enough, but I wouldn't. Eventually, she found she had to bribe me in order to get me to eat something other than those sodium-laced noodles. It was cheap, only a dollar, as I had no concept of the value of currency back then. But it worked. She needed to bribe me for about a week, so she only lost a few bucks. I started eating whatever was put in front of me, whether I liked it or not. But around that time is when I discovered I loved eating fruits and vegetables more-so than my peers.

I'm glad that one has carried over from childhood. I looked around the table to see what everybody else was having. Killian had a cheeseburger, which he looked like he was thoroughly enjoying. Lucien had the same meal and was devouring it as if he hadn't eaten in days. Olivia had a salad like my own and was eating it slowly, seemingly lost in thought. She was looking straight ahead, not focused on anything in particular. I thought it was odd.

"Olivia, are you feeling alright?" I asked her.

My words snapped her out of whatever trance or state she was in. She blinked a few times and looked over to me.

"Sorry, what did you say?" She asked, a little out of it. She tapped her fork rhythmically on the side of the table, clearly following some beat in her head.

"I was just checking on you. You seemed a little lost for a second. You good?" I reiterated. By that time, Lucien and Killian looked up from their meals at me and Olivia, curious about our interaction.

"Yeah, I'm alright. I was just thinking about an idea I had for a song," she said, not talking about her sudden lack of focus just then, her eyes scanning the room. She returned to her meal, muttering under her breath incomprehensibly, but with a clear rhythm. Probably working out lyrics.

I got up from my seat, abandoning my meal. I went over to the larger table, the two smaller ones that were pushed together to create a craft area. I pulled a piece of lined paper from the pile and got a pink crayon, remembering Olivia's favorite color from group the other day. I strutted back over to the table I was previously sitting at, and reclaimed my seat once again, handing the crayon and paper to Olivia.

She looked up at me, still purposefully mouthing things. She nodded and took the crayon and paper, writing down the lyrics she was clearly hearing in her head. I returned to my meal, chowing down on the so-called 'rabbit food' that I loved so much. It wasn't long before I cleared that and noticed Olivia hadn't touched her food. She was still busy muttering and writing on the page I had provided her.

I looked down at her work, which she quickly covered. She looked a bit taken aback, like I'd just done something offensive. My brows furrowed in confusion, a slight frown appeared on my face. What did I do wrong? I just wanted to see what she'd written. Her gaze softened a bit at my visible confusion.

"Sorry, I don't like sharing my lyrics with others. They're personal," she said quietly, before setting down her crayon in favor of the fork next to her tray. She flipped her paper over to the blank side and then started eating her own food slowly, once again. *Got it, lyrics are private for her. If she shares, I won't pass any judgment,* I decided internally.

"My bad. I know artists can be private with their work. I'm sorry, I should've asked. That's how I am with my writing," I said.

Olivia's gaze fell upon me once more, mouth full of salad, and she just nodded. "'S'alright," She got out, mouth still full of lettuce.

I looked around once more. The guys had finished their burgers and were working on some steak fries I saw on the inside of their containers. This hospital food really was pretty damn good.

"It was pretty sexist of them to give the ladies salads and us burgers," Killian pointed out.

"Mmm- not at all," Olivia interjected. "I ordered a salad, and Brina, I hope you aren't mad, but I just ordered your food for you since you were out yesterday. I hope that's alright."

"Totally fine. Thanks for doing that for me. I like salads." I said to Olivia, who visibly eased. "So yeah, not really sexist if it's what we ordered," I replied to Killian.

Killian shrugged and finished his fries, leaving the table in an unusual manner, using his arms to balance on the chair arms, leveraging his legs to jump out. It was so odd, but it looked fun. He paced back to the living area where he started watching whatever it was we left on the screen. Nobody was paying attention to it by the time lunch was served. We were all too caught up in conversation. I thought it was Mrs. Doubtfire. Not sure. It was definitely something with Robin Williams in it.

I finished my fruit cup relatively fast. I got up from my seat in a relatively normal fashion compared to Killian. I glanced once again at the sole readily available clock that now read 11:30. We had managed to kill a good amount of time. It was an hour before my mother-in-law and the other visitors would be there. This was a time I knew would be harder to pass, as I could feel the conversation drying up at the table while we were eating. We'd simply run out of things to talk about.

Perfect time to get some writing done, I figured. I grabbed about half a dozen pieces of notebook paper and the red crayon from earlier and went back to my room, seeing Elise still there, reading her book. I figured she skipped lunch. Why was she so adamant about my change and growth if she couldn't do the same thing? Why not go and eat with us? She got breakfast. Maybe she just wasn't a lunch person. I know some people don't do breakfast. Maybe this was the case for her.

"Hey," I started. "Did you get any lunch?"

She lifted her head from the book to look at me blankly. "I'm not hungry," she said before returning to her book. Simple enough answer.

I sat on my bed and got to writing. A fictitious story about a woman who was trapped in an environment she put herself in for prize money. She was facing a lot of medical debt due to a debilitating disease her only son was battling. I wrote about how desperate she was, how much she needed the money for her son's medicine, and how insurance decided his pre-existing condition wasn't one they'd be covering. I really had a knack for giving my characters complicated situations to work through.

I didn't feel time passing as I wrote, page after page, front and back, something I couldn't have done if I were using a marker. The words flowed from my hands easily, as writing was always one thing I could do without much effort. I questioned whether or not my voice was one worth sharing. I had written a lot ever since elementary school. I stopped for years after having my daughter. Maybe that was part of why things felt so hard during that time. I didn't use my normal outlet for stress.

Minutes flowed quickly as I drove the plot further, making the woman choose something unbelievably difficult in order to find a way to survive in the environment she put herself into. She had to choose whether or not to light a fire in order to stay warm, since she had no additional clothing, or risk no heat to avoid being found. A truly challenging decision that I was making her weigh until I heard a rap of knuckles on mine and Elise's bedroom door.

"Brina, you have a visitor. You too, Elise," a friendly-looking tech told the pair of us. I was excited and it showed on my face. I loved when Mama, what I called my mother-in-law, visited when I was back home. She always had a good story to share.

I practically jumped off the bed, thrilled at the idea of seeing Mama. As I left the room, I noticed Elise wasn't moving as quickly as me. *Is she not excited for her visitor?* I wondered.

As I left the room, I scanned the main common area for her, for Mama. I made out her short frame almost instantly. She was a little shorter than me with shoulder-length curly chestnut hair, just like her son's in color. She has a sweet smile waiting for me. I nearly ran into her arms.

She squeezed me tight and just held me for a minute, before I initiated the end of the hug. "Hey, Brina," she said as I left her embrace. I saw her look me over, a sad smile on her face. "You've lost weight," she pointed out. At least she didn't point out the dark circles on my face.

"Yeah, fun part of being manic. You forget to eat. Greatest diet ever," I shrugged, trying to downplay the symptoms of my latest episode. Her hands moved to her hips, disapproving of my joke, giving me the 'mom' look. I backed down rather quickly at that.

"Doesn't sound all that fun to me," she stated, sternly. "How are you doing, Sweetheart? Are you at least eating now?"

"I am. Starting to get my appetite back. I had a salad and a fruit cup for lunch. The food here is pretty good. Way better than the food I had when I was in the hospital after having Luna. That stuff was so bland, but this stuff actually has flavor," I informed her, raving about the deliciousness that was a hospital salad.

"Well, I am glad to hear that. I brought the book you asked for, and Alex said that should be enough for you to read while you're in here. He didn't give me the other books you asked for. I'm sorry about that. But to be fair, you're getting out Monday, right? It's only a few more days. I know you're a fast reader, but this book has over 800 pages. It should be enough to keep you occupied for a while," she said as she handed me the book she had tucked under her arm. "The staff already checked it to make sure I wasn't bringing in anything other than the book itself. I'm surprised they didn't do a check on the content, but I guess since you're an adult and voluntary, so you can read whatever you want."

I was grateful for that. I knew this particular book was a bunch of fairy smut.

That was a very specific genre both Mama and I read enthusiastically, part of our bond. Joking about the tropes and the at times awkwardly written sex scenes. Picking apart the plot and looking for holes together.

"Thank you, Mama. I really appreciate your willingness to bring me this. I've been losing it a little bit here. I don't think I get along with confinement," I stated.

"I'd imagine not. Alex said there's not much of a schedule in here. I bet that's not helping. But at least you've got group therapy, right? Is that helping?" She asked.

I sighed. She had no idea. "Group doesn't happen on weekends, and the one I did attend was just all fluffy crap about how interconnected our emotions are. I expected digging down deep and getting to the roots of our problems. But no."

She looked at me, eyes wide, surprised by my words. "No group on weekends and no set schedule other than meals. That sounds awful. No wonder you asked for a book. Does it at least help to talk with the other patients? Did you apologize for whatever it is that you did? I don't need the details if you don't want to go into them, but please tell me you owned up."

I nodded my head, indicating that I had apologized to Killian. I was so nervous too, so worried he'd meet me with anger, that he wouldn't accept my apology, but he really surprised me when he not only accepted it but apologized to me for upsetting me in the first place. That incident was about twenty-four hours ago. Crazy how time both flies and drags in the ward.

"Good. That's really good to hear. I know you've been working hard on your blowups. Did anybody in there say anything about it? Have you mentioned the blowups to the doctor yet?" She inquired further.

"I got called out by my roommate. But she let it go once she saw that I was remorseful. She was the one who helped me after they gave me meds for a really bad headache. I think it was a migraine or something like it. They don't let me have any caffeine in here either. I guarantee that's why I had the headache in the first place. I was drinking a ton of soda and coffee before I landed myself here," I told her. She was aware of my caffeine intake, as she's commented on it a few times, so she knew how important it was that I actually had some.

"They had you off caffeine cold turkey? I'm so sorry, Sweetie. That must've really sucked. What did they give you for it?" She looked so concerned.

"At first, tylenol. When that didn't help, they gave me what they called a 'migraine cocktail'. I didn't ask for details. I just wanted my head to stop trying to kill me," I explained.

"Well, I'm glad they eventually got you something. Alex called me later last night. He said he was waiting for you to call, but you didn't. I think it hurt his feelings, but if they gave you a migraine cocktail, you were probably asleep the rest of the day. I'll talk to him and let him know you weren't ignoring him and keeping him out. He seemed to think your not calling was a deliberate action against him. I don't know where I went wrong with that particular thing, but I wish I could go back and fix it."

I could tell that was a particularly difficult thing for her. Where she recognized her shortcomings with her parenting of her two children, now that they were both adults. She made mistakes with Alex and his younger sibling, Dean. I was there for some of those mistakes, but I wasn't going to bring it up. There was no point. What was done had been done and she'd apologized to her kids for her mistakes over and over again. They'd forgiven her.

"I know, Mama. But you know how you keep reassuring me I'm a good mom because I worry about being a bad one? Same goes for you. You overall did a good job. Alex is a wonderful man now because of you. Sure, he's got his quirks, but who doesn't? And Dean is also great. I love having you guys as in-laws," I said, trying to lift the mood.

She smiled at me and gave me another hug before I led her to the quiet social room. We sat down and she immediately pointed out how uncomfortable the seats were. I apologized, looking a bit sheepish. I knew she wouldn't like the furniture, but what can you do?

"You don't need to apologize for furniture you didn't pick. Stop that," she scolded me. "I wanted to talk with you again in person. I know Luna's party is supposed to be tomorrow, but we really can reschedule. I don't want you to miss it, Brina. A birthday is a big thing to miss."

I crossed my arms at her. "Don't even think about rescheduling her party. You were so involved in putting it together. You got the venue for us this year. I don't wanna miss her party either, but I don't want you to lose the money you put towards the venue and all her friends having to reschedule doesn't seem fair. If people ask where I am, just be as honest as you have to be. Tell them I'm in the hospital, but I'm getting better. Not everybody needs the full story, but I know me not being there would raise some questions. Just... take lots of pictures and videos so I can watch them later," I offered, hoping she would stop asking about canceling Luna's birthday. I was so tempted to say yes, to reschedule it so I could be there, but that felt so selfish, I couldn't bring myself to do it.

She seemed satisfied with my answer, though still had a certain look in her eyes that I couldn't identify, something sneaky. "Okay, we won't reschedule. I promise to take lots of pictures and videos for you. They'll be in the family chat for you to check out when you get your phone back," she finished.

Minutes flew by as we discussed topics from the outside, talking about family stuff, things Alex had mentioned about Luna last night, about the book she brought me. She didn't give me a description but promised me that I'd love it. She had a bad habit of giving spoilers, so a description from her might as well have been reading the whole book.

Just as things started to feel normal, a nurse came to the quiet social area where we were seated, smiling and talking about the mundane, informing us that visiting hours were over. Visiting hours. They need to call them what they really are: visiting half-hours. They didn't allow us a full hour.

Mama got up off her seat with a groan. Those seats really didn't sit well with her. She moved to give me a final hug and promised to call Alex and clear things up for me.

"Okay, I love you, Mama. Safe trip home, okay?" I requested of her.

"Of course. I love you, too, Brina. No more picking arguments with anyone here. Staff or patient," she replied, smirking at me.

I watched her leave through the door I arrived in just two days previous. It felt like a lifetime ago. How was I going to get through the next two days with no visitors? *Oh right, I have a book now,* I thought as I clutched it closer to my chest, moving towards my room to get started reading.

10

Why the Furniture?

I went back into my room, door open as per the unit rules. I turned on the reading light switch near the wardrobe, then plopped down hard on my bed, practically giddy at the thought of reading the book Mama brought me. Elise wasn't back in the room yet, so I had the whole place to myself to just read. *How nice,* I thought.

I opened the book and started to read before realizing I didn't have a bookmark. I didn't want to be one of those heathens who bent the corner of the page to mark their place. I looked around the room to see if there was anything I could use as a bookmark. Nothing. The room was bare other than the bedding. I was gonna need to leave and get a little creative.

I got off my bed and started to leave as Elise came back in. Her eyes were red and puffy. Her eyes swam with tears left to shed. I was so preoccupied with my own visit with Mama that I didn't even see who her visitor was. I wanted to ask about it, but didn't know if it was okay or not. I settled on a safe question.

"How are you feeling?"

She looked at me, sadness clear on her face. "I'll live. That was my husband. He came by to tell me he's going forward with the divorce. He's going to have papers served to me once I'm released. I don't even know why he came here. I don't know why I even put him on my visitation list. It was such a bad idea," she replied, her lip quivered, telling me her tears were about to return.

Despite having experienced loss several times in my life, I wasn't great at handling it. I never knew what to say to people. Nothing I could say would fix things for them or make them less hurt.

"I'm sorry that you're going through that. I really wish I knew what to say," I told her earnestly.

She sniffed and wordlessly moved to lie on her bed, not saying anything, her auburn hair falling around her, hiding her face. I could tell she needed some alone time.

I grabbed my book and told her briefly, "If you need anything, please tell me. I'll help where I can," before leaving, not needing a response. I knew right then what she wanted was most likely space.

I went straight to the largest of the few tables, grabbed a mandala coloring sheet, and decided I would use it as my bookmark. I chose to color it and turn it into a nice bookmark. I got a red marker and started coloring carefully within the lines. I used a mix of reds, purples, and oranges to make it the way I wanted. I ended up only coloring about half, as my patience was running out. I really wanted to get to read the book.

Once I was finished coloring, I moved once again to the quiet social area with my book, plopped on a sage green plastic rocking chair, and started reading. Or, rather, I tried to read. I couldn't focus. My attention span was gone. It took all my effort to make it through a single chapter. *What the hell?* I thought. *I wanna read! Why isn't my brain letting me read?*

I could feel my frustration rising. Not at any particular person this time, but at my own inability to do what I wanted. I loved reading. I could normally read extremely fast. I used to finish books so quickly, my mom put a limit on going to the library to twice a week and let me use her personal card to get additional books to keep me occupied. My not being able to sit still and read was highly unusual and beyond infuriating.

I let out a groan, placing my freshly colored bookmark where I left off, and closing my story. I let my head fall back hard. Why couldn't I read? Where did my attention span go?

And then it hit me. I was off of my ADHD medication. No wonder I couldn't focus. I had been on it for the last year or so. I suspected I was different all of my life, but it wasn't until the last year that my primary care physician assessed me for ADHD and bipolar disorder and put me on meds for both. They were life-changing for me. Up until the side effects from the antipsychotic made it impossible to continue taking it. I developed a damn movement disorder that eventually went away after I discontinued the meds. My doctor wouldn't write me a new prescription for different meds for the bipolar stuff, so I was determined to figure out how to function without them.

If only my mom had seen the signs when I was younger for the ADHD and bipolar...

Nope, don't go there. She didn't. That's a fact. I can't change it. I can only try and move forward. Don't live in the past, Brina, I told myself.

Before long, I was joined by Renee. She sat beside me, and asked if I was alright.

"I can't focus long enough to read," I told her.

"That's gotta be hard, Sweetie. Why do you think that is?" She offered me a kind smile.

"I think it's because they took me off my ADHD medication. I'm still waiting to see the psychiatrist today. I need to get it back. Or something else to make my brain just work right. I can't function like this," I told her, letting my real thoughts out.

I could feel some of the frustration ebbing away, but not the majority of it. It was nice to talk with someone about that particular stressor.

"Thank you, Renee. I appreciate you listening. I normally try not to let it all out like that, but it feels like something was taken from me, you know?" I added.

Her face, still smiling, resigned further. A matronly look. I wondered if she was a mother.

"Any time, Sweetheart. I was just gonna ask you if you wanted to join Alice and I. We were about to start up another game of Uno, if you need something to occupy your mind," she offered. I wanted to say yes, but I felt it wasn't my mind that needed to be occupied, but my body. My excess need to move.

I saw a small frown on her lips, but she nodded in understanding. I felt bad. I didn't want to be rude to her or decline an offer of friendship, or at least someone to talk to. She was nice. A good person, I thought. I needed to say something to her that didn't leave her feeling like I was rejecting her after opening up. "Do you know how to play the card game War?" I asked her.

She looked puzzled and shook her head. I smiled at her and told her after I figured out how to sit still long enough to focus, I'll teach her. Her smile returned after that.

"Okay, I look forward to it," she said.

I moved to get up off the couch, practically leaping with unspent energy. I decided to do some laps around the unit. As I was walking, I fidgeted with my scrub top. I often messed with my shirt when I paced at home.

Around my third lap is when I started noticing that I was speaking out loud. My ideas for the story I was writing about the woman and her child. Talking about different twists I could add or plotholes that needed addressing. I noticed Lucien watching me from his seat on the couch in the main social area. I waved at him briefly and he waved back, before returning to the show on the TV. The furniture was out of place and I moved to that area to fix it. I moved one of the round sage green ottomans towards the couch, then noticed the couch itself was made up of separate, moveable sections, each seat a section that could be shaped. Some were placed too far forward and the others too far back. I decided to fix them as well, while I was at it.

I moved the other ottoman to the rocking chair where Lucien was at and then went to center the coffee table in the middle of the setup.

"Why are you rearranging the furniture?" He asked.

I stopped and really thought about it. Why *was* I rearranging the furniture? That's something my mother would do. I turned to Lucien and prepared to give him my honest answer.

"No idea. I think I'm bored," I told him truthfully. "Is it bothering you?"

He snorted at me. I didn't really see what was so funny, but perhaps my perspective was lost on that one.

"Nah, you're fine. Just try not to block the TV too much, and we're good," he informed me.

I went back to fixing the furniture, making sure everything was just so. I noticed a nurse watching me, and suddenly wondered if I was even allowed to be doing that. She would've told me to stop if it wasn't allowed, so I continued.

Once I was done, the couch was perfectly centered, as was the coffee table. The few loveseats and rocking chair Lucien didn't occupy formed a semicircle all around the TV. Everything was perfectly symmetrical. I felt rather proud of myself, a warmth spreading in my chest.

But then, I had nothing else to do. *Now what?* I thought. I had no clue what else I could do. I knew I wouldn't be able to sit still long enough to work on anything on paper. And there weren't many options for physical outlets. So I decided to pace some more, allowing myself to ramble freely as the ideas came to me for my own story.

"What if I just let her win? No, that's not very satisfying. I need to find a way for her to win in a roundabout way. She's going to be victorious, but how? What can I figure out for her right now? Hmm. What if...?" I trailed off to nobody, my hand balanced on my chin, deep in thought.

"Sabrina?" I heard from across the room.

I looked towards the sound of my full first name. There was an unfamiliar man wearing a white coat. A doctor. Probably the psychiatrist on rotation. I walked towards him saying that that was me.

He led me to the consultation room on the ward. The one I was in the previous day with another doctor. I was told that I would be seeing a psychiatrist every day while I was in there and that the one on the weekends is a different person than the one doing the weekday shifts. Made sense to me. *Doctors need days off, too,* I thought.

I sat down across from him in that white, sterile room. He had my notes and chart on a clipboard in front of him. He read through it quickly, frowning a bit.

"I see you had an altercation with another patient," the doctor informed me.

"If you really want to leave here Monday, I'd suggest you try harder to get along. How are you feeling after that?" He asked me, his professionalism clear and unwavering.

"I know. I did apologize to him afterwards. I guess I feel embarrassed. I try not to let my anger get the best of me, but sometimes, it's like another person takes over. Well, not exactly. It's still me, but I feel like I can't stop once someone has pissed me off. I lash out. But I always feel terrible after," I informed him, my face flushing red.

He made a note with his pen and returned his gaze to me.

"I see. Well, in addition to that incident, I see you didn't attend the second group of that day. Can you tell me why?" He asked. That bothered me. Did he not look at my chart at all? Or was it just not there? I wasn't sure.

"I had a really bad headache, so a nurse gave me what she called a migraine cocktail," I replied simply, letting him fill in the blanks.

He nodded his head, returning once again to making notes in my chart. "I see. I apologize, it was noted here. I just didn't see it. No worries about the group then," he said, not looking at me.

"When can I get new medication for my ADHD?" I blurted out, wanting to get to the heart of the issue.

"Well, I don't think you getting stimulants right now is a good idea. There are non-stimulant options, of course, but you'll have to wait until your med check after you get out to have anything like that prescribed," he replied, a bit shocked at my abruptness.

I sighed. Of course that would be my luck. He probably could've given me the meds if he wanted to, I figured. Maybe he just wanted to observe what I was like without the meds. I wasn't sure why he couldn't just give something to me, even if it wasn't a stimulant. I just wanted my brain to work right.

"I understand you must be frustrated. But so long as there's nothing else that comes up regarding you not complying with the rules, your release should be on Monday, as planned," he informed me, his professionalism still in check.

I nodded my head and he moved to get up, a sign of my dismissal. *That was quick,* I thought. As I left the room, I decided to walk more laps, noticing that it gave me an outlet and let my thoughts flow freely. I passed the nurses station once more and saw that it was still only about 2 o'clock. Time felt like it was moving so slowly. What did people do to pass the time during the day in there?

Read. They read. And I couldn't do that. Or could I? I got that idea in my head and went back to grab my book from where I had left it in the quiet social room. Luckily, it didn't seem like anyone disturbed it. I was going to try and read the same way I did when I was younger. Without medication.

I opened the book and removed the mandala bookmark I made, making my way back to my room. The reading light was still on on my side of the room. Elise was snoring once again, probably exhausted from such a hard talk with her husband... soon to be ex-husband.

I sat down on my bed gently and started to read. It was challenging, even though I knew I would enjoy the book if I could just keep going. I made it through another chapter before I finally allowed myself a break. Trying to focus on that was so fucking hard. Why couldn't I focus on something I genuinely liked? That didn't feel fair. At all. I was so frustrated and angry that I could feel the anger starting to boil over, so I got up to go the bathroom and forced myself to calm down, not wanting to wake Elise.

I sat on the cool, smooth tile floor. It was grounding. As I focused on the feeling, my breathing slowed and the heat of my anger faded entirely after a few minutes. I got back up and walked out to the nurses' station. The feeling of the tile left me a bit chilly, so I figured then would be a good time to ask for a jacket, as I said I would do once I felt cold. Even if it was just a promise to myself. Progress.

As I reached the counter, "Excuse me," I said to the nurse in front of me, a brunette woman. "Would it be possible to get a jacket? I'm feeling a little chilly."

The nurse nodded and moved from her seat out into the main area and towards the closet where all the clothes for the patients were kept. She grabbed a darker blue jacket, darker than the rest of the patients' jackets, matching the shade of blue on the walls nearly identically, and handed it to me, nicely folded. I uttered a word of thanks and moved away to put it on.

There. One problem solved. I thought, relieved to have gotten one thing done that I'd been putting off. I was glad I asked for help in that moment. Maybe I could learn to do that again once I was released. Ask my family and friends for help. I knew they would if they could.

I looked back at the clock once more. It was only 2:30. I had managed to kill only half an hour. I groaned again. This was going to be a long stay if I couldn't make myself read to pass the time. I decided to pace the floor once more, knowing nothing would change other than my place in the room.

11

Balancing the Imagination

What did I really think I was going to solve by just walking in circles around the unit? Absolutely nothing. There was nothing I could do except keep moving and coming up with new ideas for my story. Left, right, left, right. I started keeping track of my steps, even pretending I was walking a tightrope, carefully placing one foot directly in front of the other. I held my arms out for balance, which wasn't really needed. I used to actually walk on small, skinny surfaces a lot as a kid, so my balance was pretty decent.

"What if... I had her walk a tightrope while trying to carry her son's weight over an expanse of... what would be a good thing to put under her? Acid? Lava? Legos her son left out?" I wondered out loud, still trying to come up with story ideas.

"Wait, why would there be acid or lava in a rainforest? Oh! I got it! Piranhas! A piranha-infested river. No, that's dumb. Overdone. Maybe I will make it Legos and turn it into some psychological challenge. Maybe she's tripping on something that was forced into her system. Yeah, that sounds more interesting."

I didn't realize it immediately, but I was being watched by nearly everyone on the ward. They were watching me rant while pretending to walk on a tightrope. Even here, in a psych ward, I must have looked completely nuts. I found humor in that thought. *I'm the craziest bitch in here,* I joked internally, smiling like a madwoman while continuing my unusual walk.

"Brina? You good?" Lucien called out. I looked over at him, mid-step, grinning from ear to ear.

"Yeah, all good here. I'm finally getting ideas for my story," I told him. Walking like that actually did help get my brain flowing for some reason.

Killian used his arms to launch himself off the side of the couch and walked up to me, slowing his pace to keep up. He left Olivia and Lucien talking in the living area.

"So, you're getting ideas, huh? Need someone to bounce them off? My sister gets like this too. Not the weird walk, but writer's block. And no, I didn't mean to rhyme," he offered.

I paused and looked at him. That was a really generous offer. I hadn't had anyone to do that with in ages. I beamed even brighter.

"I'd love that! Thank you so much, Killian," I exclaimed. I was thrilled to have somebody to talk about my writing with, especially with someone who just seemed to get how I operate without questioning it.

"No problem. So, walk me through your story and where you're stuck." He started to mimic my walk, wobbling and flailing his arms. "Jesus, you make this look easy!"

I laughed and began explaining the synopsis of my story. "So, there's a woman, right? She's trying to earn a lot of money by completing some weird tasks to afford an operation for her son that his insurance is calling optional but doctors are calling necessary. She's appealed the decision three times, and nothing has changed. Anyway, she got an anonymous text from an unknown number offering her twice the amount needed for the surgery. She accepted, flew out of her country to claim it, only to find she's being put through a twisted game show where she has to complete trials to win the money."

He was still trying not to fall over several feet behind me, so I made a very deliberate backward turn, still with my feet pointing one in front of the other. He stared at me as I approached him.

"Huh. Interesting. So, like that one show on that streaming platform? The really popular one?" he asked.

I stopped. "Damn. I thought I was being so original. I'm still going to write it, though. The main theme is a mother's love for her son." I'd just have to get really creative with the challenges she faced. I couldn't risk them being too overdone.

"Okay, so you see where I might be running into some issues?" I asked him.

"Yeah, definitely. Please tell me you're not doing something with quicksand. That's so corny. I'm not even sure quicksand is real," he stated as he tried to regain his balance.

"Oh, quicksand is real. I've fallen in it before chasing after my dog. You don't sink slowly, either. It sucks you up quick. That's why it's called quicksand. I lost a shoe, but I got out thanks to a guy nearby who heard me calling for help," I recounted, not missing a step. "I did get my dog back, too, by the way."

Killian nodded and nearly fell as I walked away. I heard him let out a "whoa" a few times before he caught himself. "Seriously, how do you do that for so long?" he asked about my tightrope walking.

"Easy. You know those weird concrete barriers in front of some parking spots? I used to balance on those and the edge of the sidewalk as a kid. I jumped from spot to spot, too. I wanted to join the circus at one point, but my mom wouldn't go for it, no surprise there."

Killian chuckled. "I can juggle. I learned when I was 16 or 17. So, it really wasn't that long ago."

I stopped. "Not that long ago?" I thought Killian was closer to my age. His beard really threw me off.

"Killian, just how old are you? I thought you were closer to your thirties like me."

"Ha!" He guffawed loudly. "I'm only 22. But I get that a lot. It's the beard. It started growing at 14 and never stopped. Grown men were jealous when I was just a teenager. I get mis-aged all the time."

I was relieved by the fact that people thought he was older frequently. I just wished I wasn't one of them. I hated being part of a statistic of people assuming things about others. I really needed to work on that.

"We got sidetracked. So, I'm at a part where she's about to tightrope walk over a pit of something. I just can't figure out what I want it to be. I don't wanna do acid or lava. I want it to be more visual than that. Like shards of glass... or Legos. I swear, all parents know what it's like to step on a stray Lego. Not a good time." I got us back on topic.

"Hmm. You don't want to do anything too obvious. I heard you say piranhas earlier. What about a vat of piranha solution? It dissolves meat off the bone in under 15 seconds and is a very violent reaction. It's not a slow melt like acid, you'd be alive long enough to watch the flesh melt off your bones. How does that sound to you?"

I took a moment to consider how he just described that and questioned how dark his mind was. It might match my own. I know I had a dark sense of humor. It was not always appreciated by the general public, but I had a feeling it would be by him.

"I think that could work. A twist on the acid thing. Maybe I could make her carry a weight the size of her son for added challenge. Or not. That might be a bit much. But I feel like I need to up the stakes. Maybe the slowest person to cross gets tossed in the fluid if they don't fall in naturally." I knew that was dark, but I wanted to see if his imagination was on par with mine.

"Oh, absolutely. For sure, dude," he replied. I beamed at him, so glad I had somebody I could bounce these ideas off of.

We fell into an easy rhythm once again. Killian was getting better at balancing, but he couldn't match my speed. He threw out suggestions for challenges, and we took turns taking them apart. It was very productive. We managed to spend nearly 2 hours talking before I felt the urge to write it all down. I had my focus back, even if it wasn't for reading.

I thanked Killian for his assistance and walked regularly and quickly to get several pieces of paper. I headed to my room at the end of the hall. Elise was awake, reading once more, but her face was still puffy and as red as her hair. I wanted to ask how she was, but I wondered if this was the time to do so. Her brows were furrowed, and I could see her eyes still glistening. It didn't seem like the time to pry.

I moved to sit on my bed, got the red crayon out of my jacket pocket, and began to pour everything from my discussions with Killian onto the pages. I had at least 20 pages and filled them out fast, not caring how sloppily I wrote. It only needed to be legible to me, not to anybody else. Though, I would share if anyone asked. I wasn't like Olivia. I didn't mind sharing my work, but I felt most people didn't care to read it.

Eventually, a loud speaker announced, "Dinner is served in the behavioral health unit." I leapt from my spot, abandoning my writing and crayon. I knew what was coming. Olivia had ordered me a burger for dinner with steamed broccoli. From what I'd heard from the people who had them, the burgers were pretty good.

I sat at the same table as before for lunch, soon joined by Olivia, Killian, and Lucien. I glanced at the clock at the nurses' station. It was just past 5 o'clock. We ate dinner early, I guess. This would be my first dinner there, despite it being my second full day. I was unconscious during dinner the previous night and made it in too late for dinner the night I arrived.

A tech called my nickname and placed my styrofoam container in front of me with a side of orange juice. I was getting used to having orange juice with every meal. It was nice. Inside the container was a burger, steak fries, and steamed broccoli, along with ketchup and mustard packets for the fries. It all looked so appetizing. I dug in immediately, starting with the fries. They were the part of the meal I was least looking forward to, but they were still really good.

"Olivia, what did you get up to today? I haven't really seen much of you after visiting hours," Lucien asked her, eating his own burger.

Olivia looked up from her Caesar salad, fork in hand, and looked sheepish, her cheeks turning a bit pink. "I didn't really do much. After my dad came, I was feeling a little down, so I went to take a nap. I did see Brina and her tightrope act first, though," she joked. It really must have been amusing.

"Did you see Killian join me?" I asked, curious.

"Killian joined you? Huh. No, I didn't see that. I bet that was something to witness," she giggled.

I snickered to myself. I can only imagine how funny, or insane, what I was doing earlier looked. Especially with the rambling. And then when Killian joined, I bet the entire ward stopped questioning why we were both there.

By the time I had nearly finished my meal, we had all been making good-natured jokes about my and Killian's adventure. It really did feel like fun and was productive. Maybe we as humans just need to make time to be silly. It was cathartic.

"You know what we should all do? Play charades," Alice suggested from the next table over. I could hear murmurs of agreement from about half of the ward. I wanted to play. It sounded like fun. It had been forever since I last played, probably not since my sophomore year in high school.

The five of us who wanted to play charades, Killian, Alice, Renee, Olivia, and I, moved to the main living area. I had previously rearranged the space, and it really was set up for this pretty well, everything rounded and centered, like an amphitheater. I grabbed a few pieces of paper to write ideas on. I hated when people tried to do abstract concepts, so I said out loud, "Can we please just use nouns? People, places, or things only. I beg you guys," I pleaded. Trying to figure out abstract concepts was a pain in the ass for me.

"I think that's doable. What are we gonna do about a timer, though? None of us has our phones or an hourglass," Renee pointed out. I didn't think about that.

"Hold up, I have an idea," Killian said. He moved off the couch in his unusual way, striding up to the nurses' station. He asked for something I couldn't make out. The nurse smiled and moved to get up. She walked around the station and towards us, a key in her hand. She walked past the group, unlocked the cabinet beneath the TV, and produced a mouse and keyboard. After relocking the cabinet, she went back to the nurses' station. Killian walked up to the keyboard and mouse and typed something on the TV. He searched for a countdown timer and set it up for 1 minute.

"There. That should solve the problem. So, how are we gonna divide up teams? There's an odd number of us," he reasoned.

"What if we all just played alone? All in it for ourselves. That's how my family used to play it when I was a kid," Olivia offered. It was a fair suggestion.

"And we take turns going no matter what. It doesn't matter who wins, we all go in order. Oldest to youngest sound okay to you guys?" Alice suggested, her gray hair hinting she might be the oldest player. There was a collective sound of agreement. We sorted out who was oldest and youngest and I learned everybody's ages. Alice was 51, Renee was 49, Killian was 22, and Olivia was

20. I was firmly in the middle at the ripe age of 32.

I passed out the papers and a few green markers so we didn't know who wrote what. I started writing as many nouns as I could think of, still invigorated by my brainstorming session with Killian. I made a list of at least 20 words. I started tearing the words out into individual pieces, placing them into a styrofoam cup someone had recovered from dinner.

Once everyone had written their suggestions and placed them in the cup, we were ready to play. Alice got up and grabbed a word, putting it in her scrub pocket. Killian hit start on the monitor and yelled, "Go!"

Alice started moving her arms in a broad sweeping motion and then moved them like a windmill.

"Pool!" Renee shouted.

Alice stopped and nodded. It only took Renee a second or two to figure it out. I wondered if all of them would be this easy. Alice moved to sit on the couch with the rest of us as Renee moved to take her place.

"That was really good acting, Alice. That's the only reason she was able to figure it out so quickly," I pointed out, seeing Alice look a little down, probably because her action was figured out so quickly.

She perked up and muttered a word of thanks. Killian had started the timer again and Renee's face spilt into a huge smile. I found it a bit creepy.

"Smile?" I guessed.

She shook her head, still looking as though her face would split. She started moving her arms, bent at the elbows in a jaunty way, and dancing.

"Performance?" Killian suggested.

"No way, man. Look, she's doing something specific. It's not performance," I pointed out.

32 seconds remained. Renee changed her approach. She stopped smiling and started using her hands to mime pulling something apart. She took one end of the invisible thing and mimed blowing into it. As I thought about that, it dawned on me.

"Clown!" I exclaimed, as the timer hit 19 seconds.

She nodded her head and sat down. It was my turn. I was reeling from the rush of getting it right. I stood up, grinning. I reached into the cup, shuffled my fingers around, and pulled out a single note. It was one of mine. Flame. I recognized the irony of pulling out not just my own word, but that particular one. If I'd miscalculated the pressure on the trigger of the blowtorch, a flame would have scorched my face off. I shuddered a little at the thought.

I moved towards the center of the setup and stuffed the note in my pocket. I thought for a moment about how I would present this. It was technically a noun, and I decided I'd accept "fire" if somebody got it.

I heard Killian yell, "Go!" and started waving my arms rapidly. I crouched down and waved my body up, shimmying from side to side.

"Seizure?" Alice guessed.

I suppressed a laugh. Was my acting that bad? I was trying to show what a flame looked like. I could hear the digital timer ticking behind me. Maybe 10 seconds had passed. I needed to change my approach. I held out my hand and pretended to light a match, my right hand striking against my left.

"Match?" Killian tried.

I shook my head. The ticking continued. I had maybe another 30 seconds to get my message across. I changed my approach once again.

I held out my right arm and pretended to flick on a Zippo lighter.

"Lighter? Fire!" Olivia guessed, pointing at me.

I pointed back at her. "The word was 'flame', but I'll take fire," I said, conceding a small amount. I turned and walked over to Killian's place at the computer, allowing him to take his turn.

I was genuinely enjoying myself. I was so bored before. Who would have guessed that the psych ward could be a place of both intense boredom and loads of fun? Not me.

12

The Elephant in the Room is Purple

The ward was filled with the sound of laughter. It was now Killian's turn, and he had his cheeks puffed out and his arms flapping up and down like a large bird. While I had no idea what he was trying to portray, I knew it was hilarious. He had maybe 25 seconds left, but no one was guessing at this point. Everyone was in stitches, laughing at Killian's attempt at... something.

There was a loud buzz, and the door at the end of the hall clicked open. We had already had dinner, so I wondered why the door was open. I turned my head to look, my face still smiling from laughing at Killian's antics. I could see a bald man in powder blue scrubs entering the unit, his head down, not making eye contact with anyone. I wondered briefly if that's how I looked when I first got into the unit. The game was still going. Killian was still carrying on, unaware of the new person entering the unit.

The timer dinged, and I stopped it. Killian stopped doing his weird dance and told us his word was baboon. It was now Olivia's turn, but everyone had turned to see the new arrival, the game forgotten. I wondered what the newcomer was in for, but quickly dismissed the thought, not wanting to bombard him with something so personal upon first meeting.

"You guys, stop staring at him. He'll come join the group when he's ready. He's not a new exhibit," Olivia pointed out, slightly exasperated. She was right. We needed to give the new guy space. *He'll come out of his shell at his own pace,* I decided. I turned once more to give him a final glance, hoping to catch his eye, an invitation for conversation. He took a quick look at me, then left, entering a room with a technician.

The atmosphere had taken a turn—one of grim anticipation for a new potential friend. Someone new to talk with, someone to teach the strange, unspoken rules of that place. But I needed to remember that this was a man who was there for help, not necessarily to make new friends. I needed to give him time to settle in and gauge when would be a good time to talk with him. Patience wasn't my strong suit, but restraint was crucial at the moment. I didn't want to scare him like Veronica did with Olivia. He looked young, maybe his early 20s. I remembered what I was like then, looking to what I called 'adultier adults' for guidance. He might've been like that, too.

I turned back to the semi-circle of furniture. Olivia had abandoned her turn and the group. I couldn't see her anywhere, so I assumed she had gone back to her room. Killian was still sitting in his spot, as were Alice and Renee. The pair had begun chatting between themselves about yarn textures and different brands.

"He'll come out eventually. Everyone does. Olivia went back to her room to grab a book. I figure charades is over," Killian stated, as if reading my thoughts. I moved to sit next to Killian, prepared to either sit in silence or have a lively discussion. I wasn't in the mood to read just then, but I still craved entertainment. I didn't want to watch a show or movie; that required more attention than I was willing to devote energy to.

"Hmm. I'm bored." I sat on the couch by first putting my feet on the edge, guiding myself down, and folding my legs lotus style. Why not try to sit comfortably if the seats weren't great? I figured Killian wouldn't ask questions about it. I hadn't said anything about the way he got up, after all.

"Same here, dude. But it's not like there's a lot we can do about it," Killian replied. I puffed out my cheeks, letting my lips blow out a sigh. He looked at me and mirrored my action. He then lolled his head over to look at me, and I smiled. *How far will he take this?* I wondered.

I lifted my arm and looked at him expectantly. He raised both an eyebrow and his arm, silently accepting my challenge. After seeing no nurse or staff member looking in my direction, I slowly moved my lifted arm to be outstretched in front of me, pointed toward Killian. I adjusted my wrist so my fist was upright. He perfectly mirrored my own actions, his arm outstretched, a huge grin plastered on his face. This childish fun seemed to awaken something in him. I used my other hand and motioned it in circles around the side of the outstretched one and slowly lifted my middle finger. Killian didn't miss a beat. He motioned with his own opposing hand and lifted his own finger at me. We both burst out laughing, arms slapping to our legs. Our sudden loudness alerted the staff to look in our direction, making sure we weren't causing a disturbance.

I sighed, wiping away a single tear that had formed from laughing so hard. Killian once again mimicked my motion, wiping away his own tear. That renewed my giggles, and I asked him why he was copying me.

He shrugged his shoulders. "It was something to do."

That was a fair answer. It was absolutely better than doing nothing and letting our brains rot away while we waited for our release. Absolute nonsense is what I needed right then. There was no better place for it.

"If you were a purple elephant, do you think you'd ever think about flying?" I asked Killian. My face didn't betray the seriousness I was trying to portray.

He just stared at me, mouth agape.

"What? Why...? Why would an elephant be purple in the first place? Let's start there," he retorted, astounded at the randomness of my question.

"Diet. Don't distract from the actual topic. Do you think you'd think about flying? Yes or no and why?" I reiterated, not letting him diverge from the chaos I was determined to create. I was going to pick his answer apart. Question everything he said. I needed to find a way to pass the time.

"Umm, maybe as much as I think about it now. I think I'd be more worried about why I was purple, though."

"Interesting. Why are you so fixated on the color, Killian?" I asked, a sly smile spreading across my face.

"Hey, you're the one who said the damned elephant was purple, not me."

"Yes, but you're the one who is fixated on the fact that it's purple. Care to explain why that is?"

"Because, generally, I'm not sure if you're aware of this or not, elephants

116

aren't purple. They're grey. Or grayish brown," he said, running his hand through his hair, looking a bit flustered. I grinned wider.

"Well, let's not get too worked up over that one detail. Maybe this particular elephant just eats a bunch of purple berries and turns purple as a result. Good enough?" I said, trying to ease the discussion away from the color of the metaphorical elephant. "Do you think wolves ever wish they could be vegetarians?"

"What the fuck? What is with you and these weird ass questions?" Killian asked me.

I knew the game I was trying to get him to play was weird, but I figured he'd be on board. He hadn't questioned me so far since I'd been there. Not once. Not even when I blew up at him. Somehow, his questioning felt personal. I felt the smile abandon my face, replaced by a frown.

"Sorry, I know that was weird. I won't do it again." I balled my fists into my scrub top, prepared for him to start digging into me, for him to demand to know what was wrong with me and why I'd come up with such a ridiculous question. But that wasn't what happened. I was met with silence, followed by a new statement.

"You don't have to be sorry. You didn't do anything wrong. I was just... I guess weirded out would be the best way to put that. I'm sorry if that's insensitive. I just wanted to understand why you were asking what you were asking." He said gently, looking at me. I didn't meet his gaze. Mine was fixed on the floor in front of me, still feeling embarrased.

Why did I come up with such weird questions? Why did I crave chaos the way that I did? I didn't know. I was just built differently. Weird. I'd always been the weirdo in every group I've been a part of. Often told I was too much. My ideas were too outlandish. I asked the wrong questions and focused on the wrong things. *Wrong. Wrong. Wrong.*

I took a deliberate, calming breath. *I'm not wrong. I'm not built badly or wrong. I'm different, not wrong,* I reminded myself.

"I like asking nonsense questions sometimes. I feel like when we get too fixated on serious situations, we forget to make time to be silly. I find we spend too much time focused on being serious, and it makes us sadder and sadder over time. Asking my weird questions makes me happy. Picking people's answers apart is fun, too," I explained as my fists started to unball from my scrub top, my gaze still locked on the floor. I was slowly starting to feel better, but I wasn't ready for eye contact just then. That would have been too much.

Killian didn't say anything. He simply nodded his head, which I saw out of the corner of my eye.

"I get it. No worries, dude. Ask away. I just wanted to know why you were doing it," he stated, his tone comforting.

I wondered briefly if Killian was trying to manage my emotions for me out of fear of another blowup, but I dismissed the thought quickly. He wasn't the type of person to do that. He likely was just trying to offer me comfort. I felt patronized. I wanted an out.

"Hey, I think I want to spend some time writing. I'll talk with you later," I stated, not looking at him as I got up to leave. He didn't say anything. I walked to my room, noticed Elise wasn't there, and plopped on my bed hard. The papers with my story, half-written from earlier, were at the head of my bed, resting on my incredibly thin pillow. Why the pillows were so thin, I didn't know. I resolved to ask for a few extras before bedtime. I pulled out my trusty, familiar red crayon and started writing. Or, at least, I wanted to. I put the crayon to the page, but nothing came from it.

"Come on. Do something. Write," I willed the crayon verbally. Why wouldn't it move? I had ideas. I just needed to get them onto paper.

I groaned. More writer's block. Exactly what I didn't need right then. I knew logically that Killian wasn't trying to hurt my feelings, but I could be so sensitive at times. He was trying to understand the why of things. Why was I asking weird questions? That's all he wanted to know, but I took it wrong. All because of the way he said it.

Why did he have to go and phrase it the way he did? ' What is it with you and these weird ass questions?' He sounded so angry when he said it, too. Like I had been getting on his nerves. Just like he had when he didn't understand the struggles neurodiverse people had with day-to-day tasks.

Then again, I probably read his tone wrong. I do that a lot. He was probably just so confused. I went from one weird question to the next and didn't give him any time to process things. It was only natural that he'd question why I'd ask him things that were so odd.

Elise had wandered in from walking laps around the ward. She looked rather apathetic, or possibly just neutral. I couldn't quite tell. Maybe she was just bored. I figured it wouldn't hurt to ask.

"Have a nice walk?" I asked her, hopeful that she at least had a decent experience. Not that it was particularly scenic. Several slightly darker than powder blue walls and a handful of windows lined the outer parts of the ward. Nothing stimulating. Not even any art. I wished they at least had a mural or something colorful we could look at. If we were expected to stare at the same walls for hours on end, they might as well make them worth looking at.

She looked at me with the same expression on her face and shrugged her shoulders. "It was alright, I guess. There's not all that much to do here. I can only do so much reading. I figured getting some steps in wouldn't hurt."

She took a seat on her bed, and I was surprised when she didn't immediately lie down or grab her book. Maybe she wanted to talk. She was facing me, after all. We made awkward eye contact before I broke it, uncomfortably staring at each other.

"Have you ever thought about getting a divorce before?" She suddenly asked, after a few moments of awkward silence.

I looked at her. Her question struck a chord with me. The first few years of my and Alex's marriage were rocky, but I never seriously considered divorce. I may have thought it in passing, joking about it when Alex would do something to embarrass me or make me mad. But never with any weight in it.

"No, never," I told her honestly. I recalled the start of our marriage. How there were so many miscommunications. How we argued so much over money problems and how we wanted to parent our daughter. How I wanted a second child when he didn't. I was surprised the day he said he'd try for the second with me. Even more so when, just a few months later, there were two pink lines on a home pregnancy test.

She looked down. I couldn't make out her expression, but something told me it wasn't one of joy. I recalled that Elise had told me she had several miscarriages. I had as well. Well, I wouldn't call three several, but it was still more than I was okay with. After the last one, Alex and I agreed to stop trying, not wanting to put me through any more physical loss. The other two I had were with exes before Alex. I don't know what I would have done if I had had those pregnancies go full term. I couldn't have parented well with the fathers of the other two. I hated that they all happened, but I assumed it was for a dark, awful reason beyond my understanding.

"I hope you never have to consider it. I have to look into getting an attorney as soon as I'm out of here. I don't even know if I still have a bank account. We had a shared one. He could've cleaned us out, for all I know. But I'd like to think that isn't the man I married. Then again, I never thought our marriage would end. So, really, who knows what he's capable of? I just try to get through by putting my faith in Christ. Not that I'm preaching. I'm just saying," Elise told me. That was the most I'd heard her say since I'd met her. What a shame it was something so profoundly sad.

"I hope not, too. And no worries. You can talk about your faith. I'm not gonna shame you for being a Christian. I just don't want to convert. Fair?" I asked, not wanting to seem insensitive, but I also wanted her to feel safe enough to talk about something that clearly meant a lot to her.

"Yeah. That's plenty fair," I heard her mumble through her curtain of auburn hair. "Is it awful as bored as I am, I'm not looking forward to getting out? Real life just feels like too much right now. I know the Lord wouldn't give me more than I can handle. That's why He put me here. But I just don't feel ready. You know?"

I thought about what she said. I knew what she meant. The idea of me trying to get out of here and jump back into my old life—jump back into parenting—that was a lot to consider. I hadn't before. I needed to talk to Alex. We needed to make a plan for my release. I had never been so grateful for my husband as I had been in that moment.

"I know what you mean. Going back to the way things were before doesn't feel like much of an option. I know life is going to change when I get out, but I don't know how much. I don't think I'll be allowed a blowtorch any time soon." I smiled, trying to bring some levity to the hard conversation.

"Why wouldn't you be allowed to have a blowtorch? Why would you even want a blowtorch in the first place?" She asked, lifting her head to meet my eyes. That's right. She wasn't here when I explained my story.

I laughed. A real belly laugh that verged on sounding manic. I probably seemed completely batshit. The blowtorch was the whole reason I was in there, and she had no clue. How nuts was that?

Once I could breathe again and took in her confused expression, I started to explain the event that led to my being there. I told her how I was doing dabs in my bathroom, the ranting and raving, the talking to pretend people, and then the moment I pointed the torch at myself while thinking it was funny. I watched her face grow from horror to stifled laughter. She had sucked in her lips, her hands on her knees, and her face was turning red. She started coughing. I looked at her, wondering what was wrong. Had my story shocked her that much?

"Are you okay? You look ready to blow a gasket," I asked. She looked like a tomato.

"Mm-hmm. I'm fi-" She started before bursting out laughing. "I'm sorry! I can't! I know it was serious, but that is so funny! It could have been so bad! You could've been disfigured, dead, and/or set your home on fire, but I can't help but find something about that hilarious!" She got out between laughs and gasps for air. Nobody had laughed at my story before. Or even found it funny. Not even me. To each their own, I supposed.

Once she was able to compose herself, I moved to get up off my bed.

"I'm glad my story was able to bring you some amusement," I said, slightly bemused myself. If my story could get that kind of reaction, maybe it wasn't as bad as it initially sounded. But she pointed out what I hadn't dared to think about. I could have been disfigured. Burned. I could have died. I could've caught my home on fire. My daughter would've been in danger. *Yeah, it really was that bad,* I decided then and there. I had previously questioned whether it was as bad as it was made out to be, but the thought of putting my daughter in danger was what solidified it for me.

She wiped a tear from her eye and sighed. "Thank you. I needed that. I know you weren't trying to make me laugh, but it's just so different from how you seem right now. Like, right now, you make such logical decisions, but when you're manic... It's like you do a 180. It's such a stark contrast to the person I see in front of me," she explained.

"That actually clears a lot up. I was so confused for a second. If you'll excuse me, I think there's a phone call I need to make. Plans to set up for my release," I replied. She nodded, and I walked out the door to the main living area once more. Time to call my husband and talk about our future... which didn't include him divorcing me. *He's stuck with my crazy ass.*

13

Squeaky Lids

Nobody was on the phone when I got there. Lucky me. I hurried over to it and quickly scanned around to see if anyone nearby was waiting. I felt relieved when I saw no one else. I picked up the phone and dialed out, looking over at the clock once again. About two and a half hours had passed; it was 5 o'clock. Dinner was supposed to be soon, so this might have to be a quick call.

I heard the line ring once, twice, and then heard Alex pick up. "Hello?" he asked.

"Hey, Honey, it's me. I wanted to call and apologize for not calling last night. They gave me meds for my headache that knocked me out for the rest of the night," I explained.

"Yeah, that's what Mom said. I'm sorry I didn't give her the extra books for you, but I figured you'd be fine with the one she gave you. It was huge. But you'd know that. How is it?" He sounded to be in better spirits, not so down in the dumps.

"It's really good, but that isn't the only thing I wanna talk about. I need to talk with you about my release. We need to make a plan for it," I started.

I could hear the words tumbling out of him, faster than usual. "You're still getting out Monday, right? I know you need help, but if I don't work next week, I'm risking my job. I don't wanna rush them, or you, but... you know what our situation is like." His words dripped with worry.

"Yes, Hun, I'm still getting out Monday. That's not what I mean at all. I'm talking about getting a plan set for the transition from hospital life to home life again. I can't just jump back into things the way they used to be. That isn't sustainable and will land me right back in here," I pointed out. We didn't have a plan in place. We had hours to talk during my intake, but we were so focused on the immediate crisis that we didn't use the time wisely. I mentally kicked myself, remembering we were literally waiting for me to be placed in the psych ward. We weren't prioritizing what came after my release.

I heard a sigh of relief on the other end of the phone. "That's honestly a relief. I wanted to talk with you about that, too. Your mom is flying up."

I paused. My mom? She hated flying. What the hell? Did I hop into an alternate reality or something? "Umm, okay? Why? And how'd you convince her to get on a plane?" I asked, truly bewildered.

"You're her daughter. She wants to be here for you. Physically. She's agreed to help out at home for the first week. To help you adjust. She's gonna help with schedules for Lulu, meals, and errands," he listed off.

"So, she's filling my role." I felt a pang of sadness in my chest. She wasn't filling my entire role, but I hated the fact that I needed to step back from doing everything.

"No, Hun. Nobody could fill your role in our lives. You're still my wife. She can't fill that role. Think of it like her being a temp. She's gone after a week. I thought you'd be happy to see her. You said you missed her a few days ago." He tried to comfort me, but it fell short. I felt like I was being placated.

"I do miss her. I do want to see her. I just wish it wouldn't be under these circumstances. I'm ultimately glad that she's coming, you know? But still. I just wish things were different. That I was different," I admitted.

I heard a small sigh of exasperation on the other end of the phone. I've said this to him before, wishing that I was different, better, not mentally ill. His next words were spoken with a deliberate, firm tone.

"Yeah, well, guess what? I love you. I don't wish you were different. I love you the way you are. I just wish it didn't cause you the strain that it does." He didn't miss a beat. I stopped speaking for a second just to process what he'd said. He was so matter-of-fact about it. So blunt.

Why would he want me if I'm like this? I thought. I really didn't see the appeal in that moment. Because of the way I am, where it's ultimately landed me, how it had Alex worried about our livelihoods. Why would he choose to be with someone who made his life that much harder, even if it wasn't intentional? If I were him, knowing what I knew about myself, I wouldn't have wanted to have any sort of relationship with myself. In fact, I'd rather be a mile away from myself at all times, if possible. Maybe further. But it wasn't. I was stuck with myself. The way that I was then.

Well, I guess that means I'll have to make some changes. I was not going to sit there feeling bad about myself. That was the opposite of what I was in the hospital for. It was time for me to start feeling better. To start doing better. I just needed to figure out what step one was. And then I realized I was already doing it. Making the decision to change was the first step. I just needed to figure out the next one.

"You're allowed to have your opinion, and I'm allowed to have mine, but you're factually right on one thing: It does cause me strain. So, we need to strategize ways to alleviate it. You with me?" I asked, showing him I was willing to grow.

I heard the buzz of the unit door. In walked two food technicians and the large food gurney, as I'd taken to calling it. I thought it was actually called a meal cart, but I decided food gurney sounded cooler. My mouth watered at the idea of dinner, but I really needed to get through this conversation with Alex. Maybe he would have been open to me calling later?

"I'm with you, my love. We can do that. I think we can start by saying you don't get access to the torch anymore." He sounded ready for a full-length discussion, but my stomach was practically screaming at me to go get my food.

"Hey, Alex? Can I call you back in like half an hour or so? Dinner just got here," I pleaded gently.

"Yeah, of course, Hun. Go eat. But I'm gonna have to wait to call until after Luna's bedtime. Fair?" He asked. It was a fair request. He needed time to make dinner, feed her, bathe her, do homework, and then Luna's wind-down routine.

"Okay. I love you. Talk to you later. Bye," I said sincerely before hanging up and nearly running to the dining area. I zoomed to my seat next to Killian and across from Olivia and Lucien. I was met with a head nod from Killian and a small look of concern that was barely perceptible under his mop of blonde hair. He was probably still worried about things from earlier.

I nodded at him in return, trying to convey that all was okay now. That I was fine and had everything under wraps. No permanent damage was done.

The techs started calling out names and placing styrofoam containers in front of us skillfully. The tech that handed me mine called me by my nickname, my preferred name, Brina. I wonder if that was a note someone made in my chart somewhere. That I preferred going by my nickname. If not, the staff around here were incredibly accommodating. They're both pretty accommodating, but one is definitely more so.

In addition, I was also given a menu to choose my breakfast, lunch, and dinner for the next day. I still had my red crayon in my pocket. I decided I'd fill it out as I ate.

Inside my squeaky lidded meal was a beautiful-looking burger, complete with a ketchup and mustard packet and steak fries. I dove into it. The burger was beyond good. It was amazing. I'm certain a bit a drool escaped me as I ate. I quickly swiped at it with a napkin before anyone could notice. I started circling my breakfast and lunch selections as Olivia spoke.

"Is it just me, or did anybody else notice the new guy isn't out here?" She asked quietly. I looked around. He wasn't out here. If he didn't eat dinner, there was always snack time later, but that wasn't enough.

"I don't know if we're allowed in each other's rooms, especially if we're the opposite gender. Lucien or Killian, would one of you two be willing to try and talk to him? Get him to eat something?" I suggested. I really didn't like the idea of this guy missing his first meal on the ward. Like I did.

"On it," Killian said as he gulped down his last fry, hopping out of the chair in his unusual way. He walked casually to the door at the end of the right-hand side, the door directly across from my room. I didn't hear what Killian said, but the sound of our new friend's voice was unmistakable.

"GET THE FUCK OUT OF MY ROOM!" If anyone was unsure about what he said, they must've been deaf.

Killian quickly retreated, his arms up in defense. He rejoined us and wordlessly began eating his own burger, his hands trembling ever so slightly. He looked shaken up. That was the second person to yell at him in 2 days. Me being the first. I still felt bad about that. Why was he such a target for people to yell at? I wondered if it was like that for him out in the real world, too. Not that the unit wasn't real, but at times, it did feel separate from the life I lived on the outside. Like it was its own little pocket dimension.

"Not friendly." Those were the only two words he got out between bites of food.

"I don't know, Killian. Maybe you just pissed him off. You've got one of those faces." I attempted to bring some levity to the situation.

He smirked in reply. "Hmm, I don't know. Maybe I'll try again later. When I'm not in his room. Dude really was ready to rip my head off. Well, he actually had his pillow in his hand, waving it around at me. Like the pillow was gonna do something. I don't know what the end goal was." Killian shrugged while scarfing down the last bites of his burger. He was really good at letting this kind of stuff roll off his back.

At that point, we had all finished eating. Olivia had zoned out again and was tapping rhythmically against the side of her container. Lucien hadn't said much, but he was looking over at the new guy's door. He looked ready for something, but I couldn't tell what. It didn't seem like he was in the mood for a conversation.

There was no point in my sitting there anymore. I had finished my meal, as had everybody else, but knowing I had to wait to call Alex again meant, once again, that I had nothing to do. I had a feeling that if I tried to read right then, I wouldn't have been able to get through more than a few pages. My brain was going a million miles a minute. My mom was flying in. Alex had the forethought to ask her to come, or at least, that's what I had assumed. I'm going to get things handled, but I didn't like how out of control I was when it came to the outside world. Things with Alex, my mom, and my daughter. *Oh god, her birthday party,* I thought. It hit me hard. I was going to miss it. I had been coordinating things with Mama for it. The theme, the presents, the food, the games. I was going to miss all of it.

127

That was it. The moment all the tears felt like they were going to burst through the dam that was built. I was prepared to let them. Nobody at this table would judge. I sat there, letting the sadness and defeat show on my face, but no tears came. Again with this crap. Why couldn't I cry? *This is getting annoying,* I thought.

Killian looked at me, his brows raised in concern. "What's got you down in the dumps? It wasn't like you were the one who just got yelled at."

I shrugged my shoulders, not making eye contact with him. This felt like all too much. Too many things were happening at once, but the air in the ward was entirely too still and stale. Too much to process. I could feel my heart start to beat faster, and my chest felt tight. My stomach started to ache a bit. Anxious. What I was feeling was anxiety. Something I was all too familiar with. I'd had panic attacks before, but this didn't feel that bad. I had so much I needed to talk through with Alex and my mother. It felt overwhelming.

My mother. I could call her. She had no more small children in her home to care for, unlike Alex and me. My youngest sister was away at college, getting ready to graduate. I knew she'd be free to talk right then.

I stood up, excusing myself politely, and walked over to the phone, picked it up once again and dialed my mother's phone number. It rang four times before she picked up.

"Hello?" I heard her voice, clear and bright.

"Hey, Mom. It's Brina. Alex told me about your flight. You're getting on a plane? I thought I was the one in the nut house." I smiled, knowing she'd pick up on the humor.

"Damn it, Alex," She cursed my husband. "That was supposed to be a surprise. I was going to show up at your discharge and wait to see your reaction. Guess it might not have been the best idea given the circumstances, though. Surprising you, that is. I'm still coming up there, but I'm never trusting your husband with a secret again." She sounded a bit miffed, but I knew she'd get over it quickly.

"Yeah, no surprises, please. Hearing you're coming up... I'm happy about it, but I don't think I'm in a place to host or anything. I hope you don't mind, Mom."

"No, Honey. I'm your mom. You don't ever need to do anything fancy for me. Especially now. I'm coming up there to be there for you and your household. Anything you three need right now," she reiterated. I wanted to hug her right then.

"Thank you, Mom. I really appreciate you. You have no idea how much." She really didn't. I didn't know how I was going to get through the first week without someone home to help me. Alex couldn't take that kind of time off from work. I would have had to just jump back into things the way they were before. I would have wound myself back up and landed myself in the hospital again.

"I can take a guess as to how much, but I'm not gonna argue. How's life in there, Sabrina? Things falling into routine for you or not really?" I loved my mother, but I wish she would have stop calling me Sabrina. *It's just Brina.*

"Things are going alright. There isn't really a routine to settle into. I wish there was, honestly. I'm so bored. I wish I had my phone. Or my laptop, so I could write faster," I whined. I really was getting bored in the ward rather easily.

"I know, Baby. I wish there was something I could do to make it better for you. Can you read? Do they have books?" She suggested.

"I have a book, but Mom, they took me off my ADHD meds. I can't focus long enough to read."

"Do whatever you did as a kid to read. You can read without meds. You've done it before," she directed. That was going to piss me off. She did that a lot. She pointed out everything I've accomplished without ADHD meds as a reason for me not needing them. What she didn't understand was that the meds made it much easier to do things. I had to struggle through everything manually without their help. She didn't understand why executing the simplest of tasks took me so much mental effort.

"Mom, it's not that straightforward. I've been on the meds so long, I don't know how I functioned before. I don't know how I coped."

"Well, I'm not gonna rehash that little argument again. I still don't think you need the meds for your ADHD, but it's your life. Maybe the doctor taking you off of them will help reteach you how to get by without them again. But enough with all that. If the cat's out of the bag, then we can make plans for when I get there. What do you want your dinner to be the first night you get out?" She changed the subject so fast, I nearly got whiplash.

"What? Mom." I sighed. "Pizza. I just want pizza. I don't want to live without the meds again, Mom. They make things so much easier for me. I don't know how to explain that to you. You wouldn't tell me to go without the bipolar meds, would you? Because I got by for years without them, too, didn't I?"

"Sabrina, I get your point. I just don't like what they do to your brain chemistry. But it is your life. You can make whatever medical choices you want for yourself. I'm allowed to have a different opinion. But know, you can't go off your bipolar meds again. I'll ground you," she threatened.

"Mom, I'm 32. I'm married. I have a kid. I live in a whole different state from you. You can't ground me," I laughed.

"Watch me," she retorted. I could hear the slight lilt in her voice, a clear, albeit playful, challenge.

"Fine. I'll keep taking the bipolar meds, as if I ever planned to stop. Seriously, though, I never planned to go off them in the first place. The side effects were just way too bad. My primary pulled me off of them. Not like it was my choice," I pointed out. It really wasn't my fault that I went off my meds. My primary care physician pulled me off them cold turkey. I figured it was fine because I was operating under the instructions of a medical professional. I was wrong.

"Good. I'm glad to hear it. Things around here aren't bad, but it's pretty quiet. I painted my nails coral this afternoon. I know it's a small thing, but I really like painting my nails," she said. I loved hearing about the small, mundane things my mom could do without three kids all over her. It's nice to be able to talk about small things like this with her.

"Nice. I'm glad you picked coral. It suits your skin tone, if I remember right. You should take a picture and send it to my phone. I'll look at it when I get out of here." I focused on trying to listen to whatever details she was willing to share about her day. Anything to keep me from thinking about missing Luna's birthday.

"Yeah. Also, I wanted to talk to you about Luna's birthday party." Never mind. I guessed I was gonna have to talk about it. "I ordered her that doll set she wanted. As well as some hair chalk and a few sets of markers, crayons, and mandala coloring books. Do you think she'll like all that?"

I swallowed the lump in my throat before I spoke. "Yeah, Mom, she'll love all of that. I love you, I gotta go. Someone else is in line for the phone," I lied.

"Oh, okay. I gotcha. I'll talk to you later. Love you, too, Sabrina." She sounded a bit upset by the abrupt end to the conversation, but I couldn't take any more talk or thoughts of missing my daughter's party. I hung up the receiver and made a beeline for my room. I needed privacy.

14

Flying Bananas

I made it back to my room without anyone stopping me. I wanted so badly to shut the door, but I knew that wasn't allowed. Elise wasn't in the room at the moment, probably still eating dinner, I assumed. My chest felt tight and painful, my eyes stung with tears that refused to fall. I sat on the floor at the foot of my bed and held my knees tightly to my chest.

I knew my mother was only trying to help, but I really wished she would keep her opinions to herself. And her mentioning the party I was going to be missing? At the very least, that was rude. Did she seriously think that was the best time to bring up her dislike of a medication that had been life-altering for me? Something that significantly improved my life. Why couldn't she accept that it helped me? Then again, she did say it was my life and I could take the meds if I wanted. Not that that stopped her from saying how she was against them in the first place.

I could feel my breath grow ragged and short. My vision started to tunnel. *Why did she have to go and say all that? Why couldn't she just be the loving mother who accepted whatever I needed to feel normal? Why couldn't I just be normal? Why did I have to be like this? So sensitive. So quick to get emotional,* I thought. I hated that part of myself.

I sat there, in my own self-loathing, before remembering I decided I was going to try and do better. Maybe I could try that right then. I took a deliberate deep breath and said out loud, "I'm allowed to be sensitive. I'm allowed to be emotional. I'm allowed to feel things." It was the best I had at the moment, but it was better than nothing. I had remembered the group meeting room and all its affirmations posted all over the walls, and ran with that. And it did what I wanted it to; it calmed me down. My heart was no longer racing, and my body didn't feel as tight as before.

I still couldn't cry, but I did feel better then. I felt lighter. Like a weight was lifted from me. I stood up from my spot on the floor and moved to lie on my bed. I wasn't trying to sleep. I wanted to be able to sit with how I felt, and I figured I'd at least be comfortable while I did that.

My vision slowly returned to normal and so did my breathing. Anxiety was one hell of a thing. Definitely not something I'd recommend. Zero stars. My chest felt less restricted, and I could feel my heartbeat level out as well. Sitting there, just noticing how I felt all of that, was so different than just going through it and not thinking about it.

Alex would normally try to comfort me in moments like that, where I didn't feel good about myself. He wanted me to feel better after, but somehow, his trying to reassure me made me feel worse. Why was that? Why couldn't I accept comfort from others? I didn't know. Maybe it had something to do with my diagnosed 'trauma in childhood.'

I knew even then I'd comfort my daughter if she ever felt like this. The way that I was feeling. This level of anxiety. Of contempt for myself. I wished she would never experience such low self-esteem. Alex and I had been trying so hard to raise her with a strong sense of self-confidence, so I held hope that she would never know the way I felt about myself. She would never feel that way about herself.

After a few minutes of quiet contemplation, Elise returned to the room. She looked at me lying on the bed, and her brows furrowed in confusion.

"I didn't take you for the wallowing type. What's going on?" She asked.

I looked over at her and just stared for a moment. Why would she be judging me for this? She spent a significant amount of her time hiding away from people and sleeping, so it really was hypocritical of her to call me out like that.

"You're one to talk." I pointed out. "You spend most of your time in this room. Shouldn't I be the one asking you what's wrong?"

"Yeah, well, I wasn't the one of us that held a blowtorch to their own face. Talk. What's bothering you?" She asked as she crossed her arms. She wasn't letting this go. I had two options: either open up or shut her down. I decided earlier that I was going to change and grow. Now would be a prime opportunity to try and open up. I hated spilling my guts to people. But now, at this high point, I realized I had to. Anything else was going back on the progress I was determined to make.

"A hard talk with my mom. She's flying up, which I'm thrilled about, but my relationship with her, well, it's complicated. Of course, I love her, but she has some opinions I don't agree with. That and my daughter's birthday party is going to happen tomorrow, and I'm stuck in this fucking place. She just had to bring that up," I finished rather sardonically, a dark smirk on my face.

She nodded in reply. "Your mom sounds like a lot of mothers. She'd probably get along with mine. You wouldn't know it, but I was raised by a hippy. A real flower child. She didn't believe in God, like I do. I was raised to love Mother Earth, which I do, but my faith brings me so much comfort. It helps me accept things I can't control. She's never understood it, but she accepts me as I am. She never talks about it, though. It's like the whole Christianity thing is an uncomfortable topic for her."

My mom would've called hers a nut. Probably would have bullied her in high school. But Elise didn't need to know that. My mom is a goth Wiccan. I call her a goth hippy. It annoyed the hell out of her. There was no way our mothers would have gotten along, despite Elise's attempt to relate.

I decided to try and roll with it instead of just dismissing it like I normally would. "Did your mom at least believe in vaccines?"

"At first, no, but as my brother and I got older, she got us our vaccines. She was in really deep for a while, but exposure to the internet and more widespread science helped. We were on a delayed schedule for them, but by the time we were adults, we were caught up," she elaborated. She moved to sit on her own bed, both our reading lights on from earlier. She grabbed her book, but her gaze remained on me. I didn't want the conversation to end there. I felt like I was really starting to figure things out.

"Are you okay with me talking about my family and stuff? I don't wanna overwhelm you," I asked.

"Yeah. Go for it. I kinda love family drama when it isn't mine." She chuckled a bit.

I let out a small laugh and cleared my throat, preparing to go into some of my less-than-stellar family history. "So, I was raised by a single teenage mom. She was barely 18 when she had me, 17 when she got pregnant. My father didn't come into my life until I was 14, but we don't talk now. He has a lot of growing up to do. Anyway, my mom did her best with me, and eventually, she had a new boyfriend and along came my sister, Abigail. That relationship didn't last, and about 8 years later, my mom had another boyfriend that didn't work out and had my youngest sister, Zoe. She's in college now. I think she's nearly done with her bachelor's in early education."

"Okay, so, a little bit of some broken home stuff. Gotcha." She nodded her head along, putting her book down beside her.

"Yeah, well that's just the surface. There's a hell of a lot more, if you're willing to hear it."

She shook her head yes once more, and I continued with my family drama. "Mom was a yeller. We got yelled at over a lot. She didn't learn to regulate her emotions until after Abigail and I were grown, but while Zoe was still in elementary school. But she was still one of the most lenient moms I was aware of. We were allowed to have sleepovers with the doors open with the opposite sex. We could stay out late if we just told her roughly what time we were gonna be back. We never had to sneak alcohol because she'd offer us some every now and then. Like special occasions, and if we wanted some otherwise once we were 18, all we had to do was ask, and she'd buy it for us. I didn't know any other parent who would do that for their kid," I added, not wanting to paint my mother as some unredeemable monster.

"She was also a bit of a neat freak. If things were out of place, yelling would occur. The problem was when I started yelling back. Things got really bad between us. When I turned 15, it was like a switch flipped. I went kinda wild. I stayed up late working on personal projects, skipping school to do so a few times. I picked fights with my mom and Abigail and yelled at Zoe a lot. I felt like I was on top of the world, and all they were trying to do was stifle me.

135

We think that's when the onset of my bipolar disorder started. I was writing more fanfiction than ever and gained quite the following, only to drop the stories altogether when I crashed from the high into a low. I still fought with my mother in the low, but that was about me being lazy and not participating in class, in addition to not wanting to do anything at home either. We didn't know then what was going on. Hell, I didn't figure out I was bipolar until after I'd gotten married and had my daughter. That's when I got my diagnosis. Maybe a year or two ago now. But that's not the subject right now."

I was looking at Elise during all this and taking in her reactions to what I said. She looked bewildered when I mentioned the things about the sleepovers and the alcohol. Right then, she looked sympathetic. What did I say that warranted sympathy? That wasn't what I needed or wanted.

"Please don't look at me like that. I haven't even touched on the hard stuff yet," I requested of her. "Anyway, my mom is really against me being on meds for my ADHD. She thinks it's messing with the chemical makeup of my brain. She's not wrong, but the way it's messing, or rather, messed with my brain, is highly beneficial to me. When I have my ADHD meds, I can pay attention so much easier than before. That was another diagnosis I didn't get until recently. My mom didn't think I had it because I wasn't literally bouncing off the walls or something like that. It's my mind that's hyperactive, not my body. I've tried to explain that to her several times, but she always ends it with something like, 'Well, you must've gotten it from your dad or something.' It's so frustrating. Like, she doesn't deep dive into research about it. She doesn't even start trying to learn about it at all. She just listens to the rhetoric about it that comes from skeptics."

Elise just stared at me. I couldn't make out her expression. It wasn't neutral. Her brows were slightly furrowed, and she wasn't looking directly at me, but at the air next to me.

"Anyway, things got better for me when I met Alex, my husband. We met in our sophomore year in high school. He was still short then. Shorter than me, even. He really did shoot up out of nowhere. He's always been such a rock. Someone stable, kind, and understanding. He supports me unconditionally, but sometimes, I wish he would question me more. We might have sidestepped this whole situation had he asked about my manic symptoms before I was admitted. That's one thing I wish he would do more often. Question things when they seem out of place. Not just accept them. That's something I'll actually have to talk with him about tonight when I get the chance to talk with him again," I continued.

"Well damn, I wish my husband were that supportive. He questioned everything I did. Right down to the brand of bread I bought. He was upset I got the store brand to save a few cents because his favorite brand was a bit more expensive. I guess I don't have to deal with that anymore." She smiled at that last bit. I think I helped her have her own small breakthrough. Maybe I could help her even more.

"Oh yeah, that sounds like it'll be a welcome change. I'd hate to be married to someone who nitpicks over everything I do. That would drive me nuts." I laughed a bit.

"It did. That's why I'm here." She pointed out.

The air grew still. My gaze locked on her, and my mouth agape, I panicked. I tried initially to get something out. Anything. No sound came at first, but I eventually was able to form something close to a coherent sentence.

"Oh God, I'm sorry! I didn't mean to be insensitive." I got out, pushing out my arms and hands, showing I meant no harm.

"No, you're fine. I got what you meant. But yeah. Part of why I'm here is his nitpicking. The thing that broke the camel's back was when he asked me why I picked a certain brand of banana over the other. I just wanted a regular banana, not the organic ones he was used to. I just broke. Started crying. Bawling really. Something just snapped. He had to call 911 to get me out here in an ambulance because he couldn't get me off the kitchen floor. He was really crabby about it, too. He was so annoyed that I couldn't answer him when he kept asking what was wrong. I think I threw a damned banana at him at one point. He yelled at me for that. It was bad. The EMTs were a lot more patient with me than he was. They got me here, the doctor did his assessment, and now, I'm here. I'm not sure for how long. It'll be a while, they told me."

I wanted to laugh when she said the thing about throwing a banana at her husband. I would have tossed the entire bunch at him if he wanted to be that damn particular about brands of bananas.

"So, you made a banana fly, and he complained? What a loser," I joked, hoping she'd find it funny, too.

My joke paid off. She laughed unexpectedly hard. Perhaps a bit too hard for such a half-hearted attempt at one.

"You're right. I married a total loser. Hell, I'm the breadwinner and I keep the house up. I manage everything, and all he did was question me and go work part-time at the dollar store after he got fired from his construction company for insubordination. God, what was I thinking?" She asked between laughs and gasps for air. I laughed too, but before I could get another word out, her laughs turned into sobs.

"God, I married a loser. Why?" She managed to get out. As she continued crying, I didn't know what to do. Did she want physical comfort? Did she want to be left alone? I wanted to help, but I didn't know how.

I moved without thinking and practically leaped from my bed to hers and held her in my arms. She hugged me back, and I could feel her sobs wrack through both our bodies.

I sat there and let her cry into my arms. She held me tight, and I matched the pressure. I wasn't going to let her be alone for this. That place could be really isolating and I didn't want her to feel that way when she had so much to work through.

We sat there for at least 5 minutes before her cries turned into sniffles and she let me go.

"Thank you. If you don't mind, I think I'd like to lie down for a bit. You don't have to leave if you don't want to, but I am gonna kill my reading light, and I'm not really feeling up for much conversation. Sorry," she said softly, reminding me of the shy, quiet person I saw her as just a day ago.

"No worries. I think I wanna go get a snack anyway. I'll talk with you later." I slid off her bed and moved to turn off her reading light at the switch near our door. Before I left to rejoin the majority of the population of the ward, I turned back once more and gave Elise a final, reassuring smile. Then, I headed out into the wild ward. Where anything could happen while I waited to call my husband again, grateful now for his lack of questions.

15

Showing of the Talents

The air in the ward was somehow more dynamic, despite no windows being open. Not that they could be opened. I walked over to the nurses' station once more to look at the clock again. It was 5:45 in the evening. Not a lot of time had passed. I needed to wait until 9 o'clock to call. Luna's bedtime is 8:30, and it usually takes her a bit to fall asleep. So, just over 3 hours. That's how long I had to wait to call Alex once more. What could I do to pass the time until then?

I wasn't hungry, unlike what I had told Elise when I told her I was going to get a snack. I was still full from dinner. I scanned the area to see who was doing what at that moment. Killian was having a discussion with Lucien that looked rather one-sided, as Lucien kept his eyes on the new guy's door. Olivia was writing something out at the largest table. Renee and Alice were walking laps together and talking animatedly.

Good lord, I missed Veronica now. I was so bored, and she was a very good source of entertainment. I hoped she was doing alright. I remembered she was less manic when we last spoke, so I thought she probably was. She would've provided me with a few hours of entertainment. Easily.

I walked over to Olivia and grabbed a mandala coloring page before carefully taking my seat across from her. I got my trusty red crayon out of my pocket and started coloring.

"Heya. What are you working on?" I asked, not looking up from my coloring.

Olivia took a moment to respond. "I'm just working on more lyrics. I'm stuck on one. I wrote "you're standing here, you're trying to lie," and now I can't think of what to write next. I want to rhyme both."

I thought for a moment, my hand stilling above the page I was working on.

"Hmm. Give me a moment. I'm happy to help you come up with something." I started going over possible rhymes in my head that would fit the flow of her song.

"What about ' But I see right through your alibi?'" I suggested.

"Ooh, I wanted to rhyme both, but that's really good. Thank you!" She exclaimed.

I was happy to help her get a few lyrics out. I was just glad she was sharing. Even if it was just a little bit. When she hid her lyrics from me earlier, after I had gotten her the paper and crayon, I felt a bit dejected, but this really helped. I knew then it wasn't personal, but that didn't change how I felt. Positive changes all around.

The mandala was a great way to kill a bit of time, but it wasn't enough. I continued to help Olivia with her rap lyrics and we passed maybe an hour or so. Once I was done with the mandala, a colorful barrage of shapes, I leaned back in my chair and sighed.

"What's on your mind?" Olivia asked, setting her lyrics to the side.

"Not much. I'm just bored. I need to kill 2 more hours until I can call my husband and get things started for my release. Plans and stuff," I explained.

"You know what would kill time?" Killian said, having stopped talking with Lucien and joining us at the table. "A talent show. Only rule is no singing. That's so overdone. And no property destruction."

"What kind of talent shows have you seen that had property destruction?" I asked, a bit bewildered.

"You'd be surprised. Guy in my school once destroyed his ex's yearbook in an attempt at a magic trick." He nodded, recalling that time like it was a fond memory.

"Okay, that sounds like fun," Olivia agreed, grabbing her new song off the table and clutching it to her chest. I secretly hoped she'd perform it. Rapping wasn't singing, exactly.

I moved to get up and realized I didn't exactly have a talent to show if it wasn't singing. I was a musical theater and choir kid growing up. Music was in me. Singing was one way I coped with hard emotions. The fact it was off the table annoyed me, but I understood why. They didn't want to sit through amateur hour.

I decided I'd share the first chapter of my story that I had been writing. Writing was another talent I held. Something I knew I was good at. I moved to get it, but then remembered Elise. She was alone in our room and I was certain she wanted some space after sharing something so difficult with me. Maybe she wouldn't mind me popping in to grab my writing quickly.

I moved swiftly and walked into my room wordlessly, looking over at Elise. She was asleep. Thank goodness. I wouldn't have to worry about bothering her as long as I was quiet. I grabbed my writing off my bed and left the room as quickly and quietly as I could, but I ended up tripping over my own foot. I stumbled and fell to my hands and knees, letting go of my papers and scattering them across the floor.

"Shit!" I exclaimed, before I was able to stop myself. I heard Elise stir and begin to move, sitting up in her bed.

"Did you need something?" She asked groggily, her eyes not really open, talking to my bed, not me.

"No, sorry, I just fell," I told her, feeling bad for falling and waking her.

"You fell? Are you okay?" She inquired, opening her eyes and scanning the room to look for me. She saw me collecting my papers from the ground, trying to put them back in order.

"I'm fine. Sorry for disturbing you. I just wanted to get my writing from here," I reiterated.

"Will you stop apologizing? You fell. It was a total accident. You didn't hurt me. You're all good," She said, sounding a bit annoyed with me.

"Okay. I'll stop. Thanks for understanding. I just wanted to get these to share, and I'll be out of your hair. Didn't mean to rhyme. Can't help it. I've been helping Olivia write rap lyrics for the last hour."

"To share? You didn't even want to share with me. What's changed?" She asked, curiosity overpowering her lingering sleepiness.

"Talent show. No singing or property destruction allowed, though. Killian's rules. Which sucks because it took away what I do for talent show anyway." I decided I was going to mess with her a bit.

"What, you destroy things for fun? Or you sing?" She asked, a bit of humor in her tone.

"I'm a fire performer," I stated, seeing if she'd catch on that I was joking.

"I don't think you should be trusted with flames in the first place, no offense. It's just what you told me about the blowtorch incident. I wouldn't want you to do something that could cause anyone permanent damage," she retorted rather curtly.

I shifted a bit and stood up. "I was joking. I do sing. It's actually one of my coping mechanisms."

"Then why haven't you sung anything? I haven't heard you sing once."

"I didn't want to bother anyone. Some people don't like others singing around them, and I want to respect that," I stated, uncomfortable with being honest about my reasoning.

"You're allowed to sing. I promise. If you don't want to, that's fine, but don't stifle yourself for others."

I paused for a moment. Her words struck a small chord with me. I lived my entire life stifling myself for others. Who would I be if I didn't?

"Maybe you should be a therapist. You give really good advice," I pointed out to her.

She chuckled a bit. "Nah, I couldn't do it. The number of people in there just to complain and not do any work towards improvement would drive me up the wall. I'd probably get fired for calling them out."

I thought for a moment. "Do you want to join us? You don't have to participate in the talent show, but it'd be nice to have you out there with the rest of the group." I wanted to see if I could pull her out of her shell a bit more, like I did with Olivia. She shared her rap lyrics with me. Elise shared her reason for being there with me just over an hour ago. Maybe she'd be willing to join the group.

"I don't know. I'm not really a people person," she said, trying to avoid coming out.

"Please? You can come back in here at any point if you're uncomfortable," I pleaded. I thought some interaction would be good for her.

She sighed. A long, drawn-out sound. "Okay. You've convinced me. I'm not in the talent show. I've got nothing to share like that. But I'll watch."

I nearly jumped with joy. I was finally managing to get her to participate some.

"I'm so happy to hear that! Come on." I led the way out of the door, not looking to see if she followed.

My papers in hand, I moved speedily and purposefully toward the couch. Killian was standing in the center of the living area setup. I guessed he was going to be the MC for the show.

Olivia was to my right on the couch, Elise joined me on the left. Lucien was sitting on a rocking chair, and Alice and Renee were sitting on a smaller sofa to the right of Elise. Everyone but the new guy was there. I hoped he would eventually calm down and join us. Apologize to Killian for yelling at him. *Seriously, why was it always Killian who got yelled at in here?* I wondered.

"Ladies and gentlemen, welcome to the psych ward talent show. Where we put the 'crazy' in crazy talented." Killian started.

There were a few chuckles and groans from the crowd. I guess his joke only landed with some. I was one of them.

"Our first act is here instead of jail. Give it up for the one and only, Lucien."

There were a few half-hearted claps from all of us. Lucien got up, and took Killian's place as he moved to sit on the couch between Olivia and me.

Lucien stood there for a moment and began to speak, but it wasn't with his own voice. It sounded much too high and feminine to be his.

"Howdy y'all! It's Linda here from marketing!" He spoke, and it unnerved me. He normally had a deeper voice, but this was a stark contrast to that. It really did sound like he could be Linda from marketing.

"I've got a few ideas here that would really knock the socks off of these here patients. And that's a challenge with how well they grip the floor, am I right, y'all?"

I nodded my head. His acting and voice were spot on. He was moving his arms and walking about so animatedly feminine, I could've sworn he was a drag queen in another life. Maybe he was.

"Here we have the proposed insanity be gone spray. Just two sprays in the mouth and your mental illness is cured!" He mimed holding a spray bottle and mimicked spraying two pumps into his own mouth. "Hmm, refreshing." He laughed his real laugh, and I jumped. As did the others. It was such a huge difference between his own laugh and the voice he was just using.

"Thank you, Linda! Fantastic, isn't she folks?" Killian said as he moved off the couch, resuming his role as the MC.

We all applauded more than halfheartedly this time. That was a truly impressive display. I hoped to be able to talk with Lucien later and find out when and why he learned to change his voice like that.

Lucien moved to sit back in his seat and called out in that high, feminine voice once more, "Who are you calling she, mister?" We all laughed at that.

"Next up, you know her as the lady who loves white. Please help me welcome Alice to the stage," Killian announced.

Alice stood up and took Killian's spot on the 'stage'. In her hands, she clutched several papers. She turned to face us, with one picture faced out. It was a handmade drawing. A really impressive one at that. It looked like a really stylized self-portrait made with crayon. Alice's short hair in the portrait was covered with daisies and greenery throughout it. The background was a swirl of warm colors. The style reminded me of Starry Night, but with warm tones.

"I call this one 'Warm Florals,'" she stated simply. She flipped the page to show the next picture she had drawn. It was filled with greens and blues everywhere, and it looked like Renee was the subject this time. Her hair was replaced with roses and thorns. I wondered what the thorns represented.

"I call this piece 'Blue Renee.' My specialty is drawing, not naming things." We all laughed once again. I liked the way she named things. I wondered if she made portraits of all of us.

She showed us her next page. It was a pink-toned drawing of Olivia. She had large headphones on and was looking off into the distance with her hair drawn as vines. I thought she captured Olivia perfectly. The next picture showed Killian in green with dandelions for hair. She flipped through some more of all of us. Lucien was also in green with grass for hair, which made sense for how short it was. She even got Elise in her soft pink. She had carnations for hair. It was a very pretty drawing. Last was me. She drew me in red, and I looked very contemplative. No grass, vines, or flowers were drawn for my hair. She drew red lichens. It was so unusual, but I loved it. I wasn't delicate like a flower, I was resilient like fungi. I think that was my favorite detail.

"That's all I have. Thanks, you guys," she said as she moved to sit down next to Renee once again. We all applauded once again, genuinely impressed with her work.

"I'll be taking over for this next round. I hope you all like stand-up and dark humor," Killian announced, taking his place in 'center stage' again.

"I would joke about the hospital food, but I think we can all agree here that it's pretty damn good, right?" He paused for our reactions, where we were all nodding and agreeing to what he had said. "But the rule about no caffeine; what's up with that? It's enough to make someone homicidal, isn't that right, Brina?"

I turned a bit pink but chuckled nonetheless. As did the rest of the patients in attendance. It was funny.

"I had such a bad headache from the lack of caffeine, I think it would've eased it up a bit to just go slam my head in the wall. You guys know what I mean? It's tempting, given how much time they give us to ourselves, you know?"

Elise and I laughed, but nobody else did.

"Oof, tough crowd. You two get it, don't you, ladies? Anyway, if that's how I'll be received, I think it's time for our next contestant. Please put your hands together for Renee."

We applauded, and Renee rose and took to the 'stage.' She turned to face away from us, moving to squat low like she was going to jump on something. Then, she placed her hands in front of her feet and slowly shifted her knees to the outer parts of her arms, leaned forward, and lifted her leg, then the other. All her weight was on her forearms. It was a sight to see. I had no idea she knew yoga.

The crowd was silent, and I could hear her say that it was something called the crow pose. As she slowly lowered herself back down, we clapped once more. That was a truly impressive feat.

Killian stood again and took over his spot at the center again. "That was something, everyone! Let's give Renee another hand. I don't know of many people who could do that." Renee had moved back to her seat next to Alice and was bright red, whether from balancing like that or from embarrassment, I couldn't tell. She wasn't shying away, so that was a good thing.

"Up next is our resident bipolar maniac. Please put your hands together for Brina!" I wasn't expecting to get called next, but I rose from my seat and clutched my papers closer to my chest, nervous to share.

Killian sat down once again, and I took his place, facing everyone. I took a breath, held my papers in front of my face and began to read the story I had been working on. Just the first few pages, anyway. It was a story of a woman named Sally living just above the poverty line, and doing what she needed to do to provide for her son. Eventually, it was found out that her son needed an operation that the insurance company called unnecessary, but the doctors insisted it was needed. After three appeals to the insurance company, all rejected, Sally felt dejected. And then she got an offer from an anonymous source offering her twice the money it would cost for the surgery. She accepted.

The crowd around me had fallen silent, side conversations had ceased, and all eyes were on me. After I was done, they kept staring for a few moments before bursting into loud applause.

"Please tell me there's more. Ladies and gentlemen, I can't believe she just left us on a cliffhanger like that. I'm not sure more applause is warranted, but feel free. I'd like to welcome our final act to the stage. Someone who had previously been too shy to share, but has really opened up. Please help me welcome our resident rap enthusiast, Olivia!"

I moved to sit and gave Olivia a passing look of reassurance as she looked nervous upon standing. Killian sat down once again and Olivia took his place in the center. She looked down at her papers and started tapping against her thigh, creating a beat. We began to mimic it with our feet as a group, showing our support and allowing her to go without having to hold the beat herself.

She took a deep breath and started to rap, shaky at first, but with each line, her confidence grew.

"My mind's a room with a lock on the door,

No one would listen to what I was here for,

I kept it inside, all the feelings I fought,

A prisoner of all the dark thoughts I brought.

The days all blend into a blur of the same,

Just playing this mental and boring old game.

Tried to escape, to make a new scene,

But got stuck in a place in between.

We never go back, killing our time,

I've moved on from that beautiful crime.

Now the words come out, they feel heavy and real,

'Cause I'm finally ready to show you how I feel."

We all paused and let the lyrics fall on us. The meaning heavy on our hearts. It was a great song. And then applause, louder than anything before, burst from the group, especially me and Killian. That was truly something to behold.

"Ladies and gentlemen, I'd like to think that was our winner. Congratulations, Olivia, and thank you all for your participation," Killian finished.

I looked over to the clock once again, and another hour had passed. I had one more to kill while I waited to call Alex, but I definitely had several people to talk to now. Everyone there was insanely talented in their own right.

Just as I started to speak with Elise, wanting to talk with her about her favorite part of the show, I saw the new guy come out of his room for the first time out of the corner of my eye. He was bright red and walking right up to Killian. This was going to be interesting.

16

Frayed Edges

I watched as the new guy approached. He didn't seem angry anymore, but embarrassed. Sort of like how I felt after I yelled at Killian. He moved with a quick pace. Very deliberate strides.

"Hey, man, I wanted to let you know, I didn't mean what I said. Well, I did. The point is, I'm sorry for yelling at you. My bad." His fists were balled into his scrub pants. That must've been something hard for him to do. To own up and apologize. It took guts.

"No worries, dude," Killian replied in his chill way. "Did you get anything to eat downstairs?"

I listened as the pair of them continued on in their conversation. The new guy, whose name I learned was Nate by listening, said he hadn't eaten since lunch. Killian waved him over and led him to the nurses' station, and I guessed requested a snack for Nate.

"And he didn't even need anyone to talk to him," Elise said slyly. Picking on me.

"Oh, please, I would've apologized eventually. You simply accelerated the process," I said with a smile.

I looked back over to the nurses' station, where Nate had then received a Sprite and a banana to eat. I chuckled a bit, remembering Elise's own story involving a banana and making it go flying. That caught his eye.

"What's so funny? Can't a guy eat a banana in peace?" He asked, a bit defensively.

"Nothing you did. Just something I remembered from earlier," I replied.

"You better not be lying to me. I can tell when people lie." His face showed no signs of humor. His tone was unwavering. He met my gaze without breaking it, a silent challenge.

"I'm not. I promise," I told him, holding his gaze, but feeling my confidence waver a bit. This guy was intense. Different from Lucien. With Lucien, it's like he had his anger in a cage, locked away and tamed. This guy, Nate, seemed far more volatile and like he might have a hairpin trigger. I didn't want to mess with him.

"Fine. Just keep that in mind, and we're golden. I hate being lied to." He took a large, pointed bite of his banana and washed it down with a gulp of his soda, never breaking eye contact with me.

I finally looked away and back at Elise, a shiver running down my spine.

"Well, at least he's friendlier than before. That's something," I said, trying to find the bright side, my voice cracking a bit.

"Yeah, if that's him friendly, I don't wanna see him pissed. I'd steer clear of him if I were you. I know I plan to unless he talks to me directly," she said as she played with the slightly frayed edges of her scrub jacket. Had it always been frayed, or was she picking at it so much that it had become that way? I hadn't noticed.

Just as I was about to speak, Nate came back over and took a seat next to me and Elise. His eyes on me, intense and silent.

I swallowed a bit, trying to hide my growing anxiety about his proximity.

"I heard your story from my room. You know how to project. Loudly. It's not bad. Can I read more of it?" He asked, calmly, in a low, rumbling tone that would've made just about anyone nervous.

I didn't think I was in a position to say no, and quickly handed the papers to him, wordlessly. His eyes scanned the page as Elise and I sat there in silence. Olivia was either oblivious, focused on her lyric writing, or she didn't think he was as intense as I did. She didn't react to him at all. I figured she would've since she was so terrified of Veronica. And all she did was show her manic symptoms.

When he was finished reading my pages, he put them down on the small coffee table in front of us. His gaze returned to mine, slowly and unblinking. "That's a pretty strong story. I'll give you that. It really sounds like you're writing someone strong, though, to pretend you aren't weak. Or did I get that wrong?" He asked, a challenge in his voice.

Anxiety gave way to anger. *Who the hell did this guy think he was to demand my writing and insult me after reading it?* I was gonna mess with this guy. If he was gonna play games, I was gonna be the game master. I was gonna act so oblivious to his challenge that it would push him to show his true colors.

"Oh wow, you caught that? I didn't think most people would. And it's not your general weakness, either. I've got a strong body and a sharp wit, but I lack emotional strength. You know what I mean?" I asked him, giving him just enough of complicity that it should've thrown him through a loop.

"Um, I mean, yeah, I get that," he replied, a bit defeated. "But for real, what was with the banana thing? I need to know."

"That's not my story to tell," I told him truthfully.

"Bullshit." His tone shifted to one of outright anger. He wasn't loud, though. His volume never changed. "You were laughing at me, I know it. Tell me the truth."

The anxiety had returned. I was starting to tremble a bit, my own fists balling into my scrub jacket. I felt my earlier feigned confidence, formed from indignation, falter. I couldn't meet his gaze. It truly wasn't my story to tell.

"I threw a banana at my soon-to-be ex-husband. That's why she laughed," Elise stammered out quietly. She must've felt his intensity, too.

Nate's intensity and anger started to subside. He looked a bit sheepish and no longer tried to hold eye contact with me, rubbing his hand over his head.

"I'm sorry. I get so in my head at times. You know?" He asked, trying to give off an air of levity that simply didn't suit him. Especially after what had just transpired. How he went from ready to rip my head off to being shy and apologizing seconds later. I didn't get it.

I had missed the irony there. Some time had passed since he had started reading my writing. I looked over at the clock once again and saw it was just past 9 o'clock. It was time for me to call Alex.

"I'll be back in a few minutes. I've gotta call my husband." I sensed I wouldn't face any retribution for making a phone call and made my move to leave.

As I approached the phone, I noticed my hands still trembling from my earlier interaction with Nate. I didn't know if I was allowed to talk about him with Alex, but I figured if we stayed on the topic of what his day was like and the subject of my release, we'd be fine.

I dialed the number and the phone began to ring. After a few rings, Alex picked up.

"Hey, Honey," he said.

"Hey, Hun," I replied, my voice a bit shaky. "How did Luna go down? Did she give you any trouble?"

"No, she was fine. Out within 10 minutes of lying down. You sound upset. Are you alright?"

Well crap. There goes sticking to safe subjects. Maybe he would accept a general answer. I didn't wanna keep anything from him, but I didn't want to add to his worry about me being in there.

"I'm alright. Or, I will be. Just a confrontation with another patient. I didn't initiate it," I informed him without going into too much detail.

"Confrontation? Are you alright? For real this time. Did they hurt you?" I could hear the worry dripping from his voice.

"No. Nothing like that. It was just verbal. I can't go into too many details. Can we focus on the reason for the call, please? I don't want to spend time hashing out the details of something I'd rather forget."

He sighed. A sound of resignation. "Fine. I guess you can't say much while you're in there. Yeah, let's get the ball rolling. First off, you don't get access to the torch for a while. No dabs. Fair?" He started.

"Yeah. As much as I don't like it, I think that's fair. I'm also gonna ask for some help around the house a bit while I'm adjusting to the new meds. I don't know how they'll affect me when I get home. I remember last time when I had the antipsychotics, I didn't want to leave the bed. They made me so tired."

"I remember. That was a hard month until you got used to them."

My primary care physician was the one who diagnosed me with bipolar 2.

He gave me a low dose of an atypical antipsychotic initially that did eventually help. I didn't have any hypomanic or manic episodes for nearly a year. And then that damned movement disorder happened. I had to go off the meds entirely and I wound up there, in the hospital, five months later.

"Yeah. Not good times. But anyway, do you think that's doable? Helping me with the household chores I normally do until I adjust?"

"Of course, my love. I'm here for you, and if that means washing a few extra dishes or running a few errands, so be it."

"I'm also going to need to get into therapy after all this. The hospital is going to set me up with a therapist who works at the outpatient facility in the hospital. I plan on fully cooperating," I stated, completely being honest. I wanted to get better for him. For our daughter. For me.

"Good. I'm very glad to hear that. What can I do to help with that?"

"When they teach me how to deal with whatever stuff I have to deal with, I'm going to tell you the techniques they tell me, and I want you to help walk me through them as needed. Do you think you can do that for me?"

"Yeah, of course I can do that for you, Brina. That's a really good idea. Thank you."

I was a bit puzzled by his thanks. All I did was decide to tell him about my upcoming new coping mechanisms.

"For what?" I asked, curious.

"For trying. For actually trying to get better. You have no idea how happy that makes me. God, I am going to miss you at Luna's party tomorrow."

Her party. A topic I didn't want to talk about, but I figured I could suck it up for him.

"It's going to be a lot of fun. Just follow your mother's lead. She has all the plans we worked on together for it. You'll be fine."

He took in a shaky breath and said, "I know. I just miss you."

I felt dampness on my cheeks. I was crying. Actually crying. Finally.

"Honey, I love you. I have to go," I said simply, before the tears took over.

"Okay. I love you, too. Have a good night, my love."

I hung up quickly and outright ran to my room, throwing myself onto the bed and letting it all out into the mattress. My breaths were fast and short, my cries muffled by the mattress beneath me. I let out everything that had been built up. My confinement, my lack of routine, my feelings of self-hatred. Everything. I let it all out into that mattress.

There was a small knock at the door. It was a tech. He had come to do vitals.

"What's wrong?" He asked, concerned.

"Everything. Nothing. I don't know. I just needed to let it all out," I told him between sobbing gasps.

"Well, do you think you could let me grab some vitals here? It's time for that and your meds."

I sat up, swiping at my face with my hands, trying to pull myself together long enough to let that man do his job. He put the cuff on my left arm and the thermometer under my tongue. After it deflated and the thermometer finalized its reading, he said that my heart rate was high and my blood pressure was a bit elevated.

"But that's probably because of the crying," he stated, wrapping up his notes on my chart. "I'll have a nurse come in with your medication shortly. Lights out is in half an hour."

He left, and I just sat there, numb. I pushed my head back against the wall and let my breathing even out. I didn't know what to do or what I was supposed to be feeling then.

Another small knock at the door told me the nurse had arrived with my meds. She opened all of them in front of me, placing them in a small cup. She handed me the cups with the pills and a second, larger one with water. I took the pills, then the water, and handed the cups back to her. She gave me a small smile and left wordlessly.

I sat back in my bed, not caring if I seemed rude to the others on the ward. Not really feeling much at all except an overwhelming sense of exhaustion.

It wasn't long before Elise had rejoined me in the room. She went to the restroom, did her business, and came out, wordlessly flopping onto her bed.

I figured she didn't want to talk. That was okay. Neither did I. I laid back on my bed and covered myself with my blanket, ready to let sleep take me.

17

Like Day and Night

I awoke to a familiar scene. My bedroom. My dresser was next to the bed, and light poured in from the window beside Alex's side of the bed. I turned, sighing warmly, my arm moving to cuddle my husband. Only, he wasn't there. I looked around to find him at his dresser on the opposite side of the room, pulling a shirt from it. I assumed he was getting his clothes for the day.

"Come back to bed," I pleaded, smiling warmly at him, demanding more cuddles.

"I can't," he said.

"Yes, you can; we have the whole day together." I lifted his side of the blankets up, trying to entice him back under the covers into the warmth of the bed.

"You don't understand. I can't do this. I can't deal with your outbursts anymore. I can't do the bipolar crap. I'm done."

I could feel panic start to rise. That had come out of nowhere. Everything was fine the day before.

"Alex, I'm sorry. I'll do better. I–I'm trying. I promise! Please, don't leave!" I begged as he continued pulling clothes from his dresser into a suitcase I hadn't seen before. I moved to get out of bed and stop him, but something held me back. It was like there was a force field around Alex. I couldn't get to him. He wasn't speaking to me. He wasn't even looking at me.

"Alex! Look at me! Please!" My cries seemed to fall on deaf ears. He just finished packing, turned and walked out our bedroom door, his suitcase in hand. I had to stop him. I couldn't let him leave me.

"Alex, I love you! Please, I'm sorry. I can't help all of it. I wanna do better. Please, please don't leave me!" I pleaded once more. I followed him as he went through our living room, bypassing our kitchen and heading straight for the front door of our apartment.

"I'm taking Luna, too. She can't stay with someone as unstable as you," he said, looking back at me just once to say that. I could feel my heart shatter. My chest felt impossibly heavy, and the tears came streaming out.

"No, no no no! Don't take her! Not my daughter! Please, I'm trying! Please!" I cried.

He didn't look back again. He simply walked out the door into the blinding white daylight. I tried to follow him, but I couldn't leave. Something was stopping me. I felt something grab my arm.

"Wake up. Wake up!" I heard. *Wake up?* I was awake. Or so I thought.

I was suddenly catapulted into true consciousness, gasping, my face wet with tears. I looked around me. I was still in my shared room inside the behavioral health unit. The light blue room was painted with the faintest early morning light. Elise was at my bedside, her hand on my arm.

"Hey, are you alright? You were talking in your sleep. And then you started crying," she explained to me gently.

I could feel the tears still coming out. That dream had been different from the ones I had grown used to. So full of anger and violence. This one had neither. It was far too comfortable at first, then cold and calculated. I recalled each detail with far too much accuracy for a regular dream. I wondered if the medications I was on could cause vivid dreams like that.

"I'm sor-no, not sorry. Bad dream. I thought my husband, Alex, was going to leave me and take our daughter because of my diagnosis," I explained through shuddering breaths, swiping tears away from my face, remembering how she disliked unnecessary apologies.

"Well, I don't know your husband, but from what I saw when he was visiting, he isn't going anywhere. That man is head over heels for you," she pointed out.

I laughed a bit through the still-flowing tears I had yet to get under control. You'd think after months of not crying, I'd be better at reeling it in. But I couldn't. The feelings, the emotions surrounding the dream, were too strong. I was still crying despite Elise's efforts to calm me.

I just need to let them fall and be done, I thought. I took a few deep breaths, well, as deep as I could manage, and tried to get the tears under control, urging them to hurry up and finish. Eventually, I was able to get it together and my breathing evened out, but a new nuisance showed its head; I now had hiccups.

"Thanks for -*hic*- being here for me. I really -*hic*- appreciate it," I said, annoyed with them.

Elise was smiling now, trying to disguise her amusement with the newly developed hiccups. "No problem. Try holding your breath. It might help."

I took a deep inhale and held it. At first, it wasn't too bad, but then I started to feel my lungs demanding oxygen. I felt my face grow red and begin to perspire.

"Just don't do it so long you pass out, okay?" She requested.

I exhaled and allowed myself to breathe normally. *Were they gone now?* I wondered.

"I think that -*hic*-" I started. "Never fucking mind, apparently. Stubborn ass hiccups," I grumbled. Elise let out a small laugh at my irritation.

"They'll go away eventually. Do you need the bathroom? I want to take a shower," she said, indicating with her head the direction of the bathroom door.

"Yeah, let me go use -*hic*- the restroom and then it's all -*hic*- yours," I replied.

I stood up, the phantom heaviness I felt in the dream gone. I walked into the restroom, did my business, and walked over to the sink to wash my hands, still hiccuping, but they were becoming less frequent. I happened to look at myself in the mirror. I was red and puffy in the face. *Great, now everyone would know I was crying,* I thought, more than a bit irritated with myself.

Nope. Now is not the time to be mad at yourself. You're human and had a human reaction to something scary, I added. I was going to start trying to be kinder to myself. I just didn't want anybody's sympathy when they saw me. I'd explain if they asked, but I didn't want to have to do it over and over again.

I finished washing my hands, I splashed some water over my unkempt hair and decided I wanted to ask for my hairbrush. I walked out of the bathroom and told Elise it was all hers.

I walked out of our shared room and towards the nurses' station, determined to be able to ask for help for once without shame or embarrassment. I looked at the clock for the first time that day. It read 6:30. I was up pretty early for once. Vitals and meds weren't due for a while. I thought they did them every twelve hours, so I had some free time until then.

"Excuse me," I said to a kind-looking tech who sat at the computer, no longer hiccuping. "I wanted to get into my hygiene bucket, and I think my roommate needs hers, too, for a shower. Could you get it out of the closet for me?" I requested.

The tech smiled at me. Always smiling, these staff members. She stood up from behind the counter, came out of the locked door that separated the station from the rest of the ward, and walked with me to my room. She unlocked the closet for both me and Elise, who had been sitting on her bed. I figured she was waiting to ask for her hygiene products for a bit before showering.

The tech got both hygiene containers from the closet and handed them to me and Elise. I uttered a word of thanks and watched her leave the room. I grabbed my hairbrush from the bucket and began working away at the knots that had formed from my tossing and turning during my tumultuous dream.

"I know I said I was going to shower, but I just needed a few minutes before asking for my hygiene bucket, you know? Mental preparation. Thanks for asking for me," Elise said as I was working out the knots in my hair.

"You're welcome. It was no problem. I figured that's what was up. I wanted to get my stuff anyway. It was no extra effort to ask for yours as well." I continued to work through my thick, inky strands of hair. I had really done a number on it. Maybe I was due for a haircut when I got out. Spending time detangling that mess was a bit of a nuisance.

After I was finished, I found the hair tie I kept under my pillow from when Elise braided my hair. I wanted to put it up out of the way. I grabbed my hair with both hands, swirled my hair around with them, and twisted it into a bun that I secured with the hair tie. That way, it would stay off my neck, no longer irritating me.

Elise picked up her bucket and went to the bathroom, closing the door behind her. Once I was done with my hair, I left our shared room in favor of the common area. I saw a few other people awake. Lucien and Killian were both up and talking. Alice was reading her book in a rocking chair. It looked like everyone else was still asleep or getting themselves ready for the day.

It hit me like a ton of bricks. It was Sunday. The day of Luna's birthday party. And I was there. Going to miss it. I felt that heavy feeling in my chest once more and walked over to sit on the couch next to Killian and Lucien. I let the sadness show on my face rather than try to hide it.

"Morning. What's with you?" Lucien asked.

"Bad dream. Missing my daughter's birthday party. What's with you?" I retorted, not hiding the snark in my voice.

"Hey, I didn't do anything to you. Cool it," Lucien stated. "I *was* having a pretty decent morning. This guy and I were talking about the talent show last night. He was asking about the voice."

"I think we all want to know when you learned to do that. Not just me," Killian added.

"Well, if you need to know, I started doing that voice for my daughter when I used to read her bedtime stories. As she got older, I had more practice and eventually, it became something. Once she was 10, she wanted me to stop, so I did for a long time. Until last night. I figured you could all use the laugh," Lucien explained. It was a short, somewhat vague explanation, but that wasn't unlike him. There was still a lot about Lucien that I didn't know and probably never would. I was going to need the distraction today.

As if on cue, I saw Nate emerge from his room, face still full of sleepiness. He walked towards us and plopped on the couch between me and Lucien. The tension on the couch was palpable.

"Morning," he said, none of his hostility from last night present. "Did you guys sleep well?"

I nearly did a double-take. Was this the same Nate from last night? He seemed so normal now. So calm. Maybe he's at his most calm when he first wakes up. Who knew?

"I slept like a rock. You?" Killian asked. He was really good at just letting things like last night go. Just rolling with the punches.

"Same. They gave me something to help. I wasn't sure what it was, but it helped." Nate sat back in his seat, stretching his arms wide over the back of the couch, trying to wake himself more.

"It was most likely trazodone. That's what they've got me on for sleep. I don't think I could sleep without it here," I said, trying to connect with him a little. If he was willing to try and be friendly, so was I.

"I think that was it. I know it started with a 'T'. Thanks. Why does your face look like that? Were you upset over something?" He pointed out how red and puffy my face was from my time crying both last night and this morning.

"Something like that. Bad dream. Hard conversation last night with my husband. And I'm missing my daughter's birthday party today," I told him. I hadn't even considered to tell the guys about the conversation with my husband. It hadn't come up.

"Oof, I'm sorry to hear about your kid's birthday. I don't have kids. Childfree by choice, but I can imagine that's hard. Don't beat yourself up over it," Nate said reassuringly. Seriously, who replaced the Nate from last night? The one who was so openly angry and hostile? Not that I was complaining. I was just getting whiplash.

"When do they do breakfast around here? I'm starving."

"In about 15 minutes or so. We don't have a strict schedule, but breakfast, lunch, and dinner all kinda roughly show up around the same time every day," Killian explained.

I sat there, suddenly aware of my own rumbling tummy. I didn't realize I was hungry until someone else pointed it out. I was frequently like that, even when I wasn't in the ward. I often forgot to eat unless someone else around me said they were hungry and going to get food. I didn't know why that was.

"I'd go for a banana right now," I said.

"I bet you would," Nate replied, his words laced with a double meaning. That was closer to what I had expected from Nate. At least it wasn't hostile. I laughed, a nervous and unsure sound, as did Killian. Lucien didn't. Instead, he looked beet red and started laying into Nate for his inappropriate comment.

"What the hell, man? Gross. You don't just say that to people," Lucien scolded him. "That's harassment."

"Relax, I'm not hitting on her. I'm gay. I take bananas, too," he stated. That made things clearer to me.

"Still, man. Not cool," Lucien followed up weakly. I wouldn't have taken him for someone so straitlaced.

There was a buzz at the door to the unit, and inside stepped two techs with our breakfast. Overhead, I heard "Breakfast is now served in the behavioral health unit." I launched myself forward. I was excited to eat something I had actually ordered. I'd finally been given a menu last night during dinner and made my selections. I was expecting pancakes with sugar-free syrup and cereal with milk. Also, orange juice. Always orange juice. It had grown to be a favorite of mine.

I sat in my normal spot. Olivia wasn't up yet, so her place was taken by Nate. He was sitting across from me and next to Lucien. It's like he wanted to provoke the guy. I wanted to break some of the tension, so I decided to ask Nate a question.

"So Nate, what brings you to the land of the crazies?" I'd be able to gauge what he was truly like by his reaction to my question.

"I kinda had a very public breakdown. I wouldn't be surprised if it was on the news. I was brought here by an ambulance. I don't remember everything, but I remember waking up in the emergency department. I'm not gonna share everything. You'll probably find out more once you're out. I'm on a 72-hour hold. And they don't count weekends when they hold you. So, my time technically starts tomorrow. I should be out by Thursday if they deem me sane enough. When do you guys get out?" He asked.

I was surprised by how calmly he answered the question. Maybe I should stop comparing him to what he was like last night. I knew the first day on the ward could be hard. Maybe it was just that for him.

Our breakfasts were all out in front of us, and Killian and Lucien had dug in.

"Monday for the three of us. I'm not sure about the rest of the people in here." Killian said between bites of cereal.

"I think everyone but Renee and Nate is due to leave on Monday. I know a little bit about her story, but it's not my place to share. Needless to say, she's where she belongs for the time being," Lucien added.

I started in on my cereal, pouring in the milk I was provided. It tasted like the best cereal I'd ever had, despite being sugar-free. Who knew cereal could be so tasty?

"So, everyone but me and... Renee, you said her name was? Damn. That's gonna be quiet as fuck. And boring. Nothing against Renee. I just don't think she's one for conversation.. I hope last night didn't permanently affect my standing in here. I just get like that sometimes. Never lasts long."

It was clear Nate and Renee were about to be alone on the ward unless more people came in. I hoped they would be alright. I didn't like the idea of them not having the community the rest of us had during our stay there.

Nate looked uncomfortable after finishing his meal. His arms fell to his stomach, and he abruptly left his seat, making a beeline for his room. I guessed his breakfast wasn't sitting right with him. Poor guy. Maybe he was lactose intolerant. Maybe he was overwhelmed from the breakdown he had and didn't like the idea of everyone leaving but him and one other person in the ward. Maybe he just needed a space where he felt in control of his environment. All were genuine possibilities.

18

Mirroring Patients

After such an eventful breakfast, I was looking forward to some quiet downtime. I left my seat at the table and returned to my room to sit and read my book, feeling like I could focus on it for a bit and kill some time. Elise, for a change, wasn't in the room. Maybe she was out in the common area socializing with someone. I smiled at the thought of that.

I read for what felt like hours, but was likely only one or two. I easily cleared fifty pages before I was interrupted by a tech telling me it was my turn with the psychiatrist. That was odd. I thought the psychiatrist came a little later in the day than that, but what did I know?

I stood from my spot in the room and followed the tech to the consultation room in the ward. The one I had previously thought was rather dynamic in comparison to the actual group therapy room. Inside sat the same doctor from the previous day. The one who hadn't looked through my file much. Lovely.

"Hello, Brina. I hope your day is going better than yesterday. How are you feeling?" He asked.

"Better now. I've slept well, eaten, talked with other patients here. I think I'm doing good," I listed truthfully. "We even had a talent show last night and I shared some of my writing," I offered, wanting him to know I was trying to improve.

"Well, that is excellent to hear. How do you think you're adjusting to your medications? Any complaints?" He inquired coolly.

"No, none that come to mind. I think I'm feeling more stable now. Not manic anymore." I wanted to make it absolutely clear I was on track for my release date. I didn't want to stay in there any longer than was absolutely necessary. I wanted to go home. I wanted to see Luna, Alex. My family. My friends. I was tired of being confined away from everyone.

"Okay, that's good to hear. Do you have any questions for me?"

"A few, actually. What's with the new guy? I know you can't say anything about his diagnosis or anything, but are we in any danger? He was kinda hostile last night when Killian tried to invite him to join us for dinner. I mean, he's since apologized, but I can't shake that feeling that something is off with him," I got out. "Also, do you think I'm still on track to get out tomorrow?"

He sighed. I guessed I wasn't the first person to ask either of those questions. "You're on track, yes. I still don't make the final decision on your release, but I don't see why we'd keep you any longer. I'm pretty sure you will be released at some point tomorrow. Make sure you attend group and participate tomorrow, and you should be good. As far as information about another patient, I can't tell you anything. I'm sorry. It's my opinion that you're not in any immediate danger, however," he finished with pure clinical professionalism.

I knew he realistically couldn't give me an answer about Nate, but at least it was something. I wasn't in immediate danger. The most that might happen is a verbal lashing, which I'd like to avoid, but I could work with.

"Thank you for the information, Doctor. I don't have any more questions," I stated firmly.

He stood and shook my hand before opening the door for me and calling out to the next patient on his list, Renee. I started to walk back to my room, determined to continue reading my book, when I was stopped by Nate waiting by my door, not inside my room. His face was unreadable. Maybe he got over whatever caused him to flee breakfast.

"Hey. What's up?" I asked, trying to mimic Killian's aloofness, effectively hiding the spike of anxiety I felt.

"Not much. I figured we could talk. You okay with a talk?" He asked, his arms crossed. I thought he looked defensive, but at least he wasn't combative.

I didn't particularly feel like talking with someone who makes inappropriate comments about others upon first meeting them, but what other option did I have? He was in the way of my room.

"Yeah, I could have a conversation. What's on your mind?" I asked.

"I wanted to say sorry for the banana thing. Last night and this morning. I shouldn't have accused you of lying last night. And I definitely shouldn't have said what I did about you taking bananas this morning. That was definitely crossing a line. I know you don't know me and have no reason to believe me, but I'm working on that. My anger issues. There's a fancy diagnosis title or whatever, but it's anger issues," he managed to get out, not looking at me, his arms still crossed and standing between me and my bedroom.

I thought for a moment. What if that was like my blowup at Killian? What if he was actually just someone trying to ask for forgiveness? I decided to give him the benefit of the doubt.

"I accept your apology. Thank you." I assured him with a gentle smile.

I saw the weight fall off his shoulders as he let out a long exhale. Like he had been holding his breath, waiting for my answer. "Thank you. I've been practicing what I wanted to say to you in the mirror for a bit. I don't know why I just told you that, but it's the truth."

I wanted to laugh, but it seemed insensitive at the moment. Instead, I just smiled at him once again and nodded. He was still standing in front of my door, but it no longer felt threatening. Just awkward.

"Do you think I could get into my room? I was hoping to get back to my book. Not that I didn't mind the apology."

"Oh fuck, my bad. Here, I'll move," he said, and immediately moved out of my way. He looked rather sheepish, and I felt bad for ending the conversation so abruptly. I decided my book could wait. Maybe I'd get my writing instead. He seemed interested in it last night until he insulted me.

I grabbed my writing from my bed and headed back out to meet him in the living area, sitting on the grey and green couch. Lucien looked at us from across the room as he sat in a dining room chair with a sprite in his hand, his eyes darting between me and Nate, asking a silent question.

I met Lucien's gaze and nodded my head, indicating to him I was alright.

He nodded back, but didn't look away, taking a sip from his Sprite.

"Oh? I thought you wanted to read?" Nate asked.

"Yeah, but I figured you could use a friend here. Or at the very least, someone to talk to. Before you got here, I did something pretty similar to Killian. Not the sex jokes, but I lost my shit on him. I mean, he did say something mildly crappy, but he did not deserve the reaction I gave him. I lashed out and yelled at him. Said some really awful stuff. But you know what he did when I yelled at him?"

"What?" He asked, listening intently.

"He got a nurse and told them my headache was really bad. He got them to help me. Instead of getting angry or upset with me, he showed me patience and understanding. I'm hoping I can do the same," I said. I truly wished he had gotten what I was trying to say. I just wanted him to know he deserved the same chance I got.

"Well, I don't have a headache, but thanks. I get what you mean. I think it'd be nice to have one person in here that isn't looking at me like I'm going to rip their head off."

"I know that feeling. Not pleasant. Like you're an outcast or some crazy volatile person, right?"

"Yes, that, exactly." Nate pointed to me as he spoke.

I noticed out of the corner of my eye that Elise was talking with Alice and Renee in the quiet social room, all three of them clutching their respective books. Like their own little book club. Elise caught my eye and looked between me and Nate, raising her eyebrow at me. I shrugged while smiling, showing her I was strangely fine.

I told Nate it may take a bit, but people here tended to forgive more often than not. We were all stuck together, so it made sense to try and get along as much as possible.

"Huh. That makes sense. You know, when I'm not in here, and not having a breakdown, I'm a pretty fun guy."

"Oh yeah? Give me an example of your idea of fun," I said, challenging him a bit, but in a much friendlier manner than the night before.

"Well, I play electric guitar, for one. I'm working on putting a band together.

I write my own music. Too bad I'd never be allowed to bring my guitar in. I usually play during my downtime, so this is kinda like hell to me. It's so quiet in here. I can't stand it," he told me. I related. I wanted to feel like I was able to sing in there, but I didn't want the judgment from the other patients. I couldn't care less what the staff thought of my singing ability. They could go into another room if they didn't like it. The other patients' level of comfort was more important to me than that one coping method. I had others. I didn't *need* to sing. I just really wanted to.

"I get what you mean, man. Music is very important to a lot of people, and it's so often a part of our daily lives that when it isn't there, it feels like a void. Right?"

"How do you know exactly what it is I'm thinking?" He asked, bewildered.

I shrugged. I genuinely didn't know. But I found myself relating to Nate more and more as the minutes and conversation flowed. I didn't notice when Killian sat down in a rocking chair nearby and joined us in conversation. Somehow, the topic had gotten to whether or not narwhals could truly be considered the unicorns of the sea or not when a buzzer went off at the front the ward and in came a small crowd of people. It must've been visiting hours. Or visiting half hour, as I called it. I was very aware of my lack of visitors in the group, but it looked like Nate had some, as he stood up quickly, abandoning our conversation to go hug two people who looked vaguely like him. His parents, I guessed. It looked like Nate, Renee, Alice, Olivia and Killian all had visitors. I was left alone. I didn't know how I was supposed to feel, but it wasn't good.

My chest felt heavy and tight, my eyes stung, and my hand flew to my stomach, where I could feel it turn a bit with unease. I missed my family so much. I looked over at the clock. It was just past noon. Time for Luna's birthday party. Tears threatened to spill from my eyes, but I blinked them back. I was happy to be able to cry again, but I didn't want to in front of a bunch of people I hardly knew.

I wondered where our lunch was. Lunch was normally before visiting hours, I'd gathered from my time there. I stood up and walked to my room, clutching the writing I had brought out, but didn't work on.

I sat on my bed and looked over to Elise's side of the room. She was sitting in her bed, silently reading. I guessed she didn't have any visitors either. I looked at the book she was reading. This one was different than the one she had earlier. It looked like a self-help book.

"Whatcha reading? Some fantasy romance novel?" I asked, my voice dripping with sarcasm.

"Oh absolutely. You know, it's just so romantic when men walk you through de-stressing techniques and breathing exercises. Hottest thing alive," she joked, in her dry way. Her tone was entirely serious.

I laughed. "Yeah, sounds about right. Super hot. Seriously though, anything useful in there?"

"I mean, yeah, it's all pretty useful. I just hate that I understand how it works, you know what I mean?"

"Kinda? Can you elaborate?" I requested, a bit confused.

"I find that often times, the more we understand how something works, the less we actually want to do the thing. Takes away some of the mystery of it. Like the magic is just gone. With this, I understand the psychology behind it and what the physical responses mean. Makes me want to do them less," she said as she shut her book, not placing a bookmark and letting out a huff of frustration.

"What was with you and that guy anyway? I thought he was being a dick to you. What's his name again?" She asked me, irritation thinly veiled.

"Nate. And it turns out he's just another guy with issues. He plays electric guitar. I thought that was pretty cool."

"Huh. Him on guitar, I'll take drums, you can sing, Olivia could rap, and Killian could be our roadie. Call ourselves the CrayZ's or something," Elise joked once again.

"Not bad, but I feel like that's a little on the nose, don't you think?" I asked her, giggling. "Maybe the Insanit-tees?" I suggested.

"Ha! Good one. Make it sound so sophisticated. Like we'd ever be a real band. I hope this doesn't offend you, but I have no intentions of contacting any of you ever again after I get out. I want to forget this place ever happened."

I did feel a bit offended, but I didn't let it show. I knew where she was coming from. But it felt like that meant she was avoiding her problems. She wouldn't accept that from me. I wouldn't from her.

"Well, the reality is you can't. You did come to this place. It's not something to forget. You should want to remember it."

Elise looked at me with a flash of something more than irritation but less than anger. Her brow furrowed and her face slightly pink she said, "Why the hell would I want to remember the place I was at my lowest?"

"Because you have a point of reference now. If this is your lowest, things can't get worse, right?"

She paused for a second, as if considering my words carefully.

"I think they could, but I see what you mean. Sorry, I'm just so ready to get out of here."

"I don't blame you. I just want to hug my daughter and husband," I told her truthfully.

As she was about to say something, I heard from the overhead speaker "Lunch is served in the behavioral health unit."

I nearly leaped off my bed, as did Elise. I had grown to love the hospital food. Not that it was difficult. That was probably my favorite part of being in there.

I sat at my normal place. Elise joined me in Killian's normal spot. Across from us were Killian and Nate. It looks like they had got to talking after visiting hours were over.

My styrofoam container had a chicken salad with some tomatoes and a packet of ranch along with an orange juice and a fruit cup. It looked like pineapple slices. I liked pineapple well enough, but it wasn't my favorite. I ate it first to get it out of the way.

I looked around and noticed the clock said it was now just past 12:30. Eight and a half hours until I could go to bed, I thought. And then it would be Monday. My release day. I looked forward to it. How was I going to continue to pass the time in there? It felt like things got slower and slower as the time ticked on.

"You were playing electric guitar, and mid-strum, your string broke? What did you do?" Killian asked Nate. I was glad to see they were making friends with each other.

"I just kept going. I missed a lot of the notes, but what else could I do? I was mid-performance. High school was rough." Nate stretched his arms out in front of him before taking a large bite of his burger.

I looked over at Elise, who was quietly working on her own burger. She hadn't said a word since we left the room. Then again, she might have just been focused on eating. I wondered if what we had talked about was weighing on her.

"Brina, what do you think?" Killian asked me.

"Sorry, think about what?" I replied, lost.

"We were talking about maybe doing another talent show tonight. Nate has this idea to play air guitar for us with YouTube in the background for his song. Apparently, he has his own music uploaded on there, so he's just gonna work with his own prerecorded track."

"Oh, yeah, that sounds really cool. I'm not sure about a whole talent show, since we kinda saw everyone's talents last night. But I'd like to listen to your music, Nate." I said, still distracted by my own thoughts.

"I don't think we should do an entire talent show again, but maybe we could do a music contest. Karaoke, air guitar, rap. All of it is on the table." Elise said, breaking her silence and giving me a small smirk. She was trying to get me to sing. Sneaky. I liked it.

"Ooh, yes! That sounds so fun! I'm down. What do we get if we win?" Nate asked enthusiastically.

"A gold star?" Killian suggested lazily.

"That works. Better than nothing. You in, Brina?" Elise asked, a playful glint in her eye.

I thought about it. I wasn't exactly in practice. There was a physical ache in my chest from wanting to sing. I usually did multiple times a day at home for fun. As much as I wanted to sing, who would actually want to hear it? Then again, they all thought my writing was good the previous night. Maybe they'd like my singing too.

"Yeah, I'm in."

19

Mania is a Hell of a Drug

We agreed as a group to do the music competition in the evening, something for after-dinner entertainment. So, we all had a few hours to find something we'd like to perform. A new, quiet energy had settled over the ward. Nate was humming a riff I assumed he intended to play with his air guitar. Killian was jotting down notes. Maybe they were lyrics for an original piece. That would be interesting. The energy even carried over to Alice, Renee, and Olivia. They were each taking turns with the keyboard and mouse, looking through YouTube for karaoke videos they'd want to sing along to. Everyone was so excited for this. Except me.

I knew I was a good singer. I've done karaoke several times before. Hell, I'd even starred in a musical back in high school before, but this felt far more intimate. The eight other patients could judge me harshly if my voice cracked or I forgot a lyric. But I knew realistically that it was unlikely. The problem was my own internalized perfectionism. I wanted to give them an excellent performance, but I was so out of practice. I didn't know if I could even give a decent one.

I wanted my voice to be something worth hearing. I wanted the song I picked to be appropriate for the ward as well. A lot of the music I'd grown to like in my late 20s and early 30s had explicit ratings. I didn't think that would be allowed in there. I tried to think back to when I was younger. What did I use to listen to? A lot of pop. Lots of musicals. Some alternative rock. A little bit of country. Not as diverse as my current musical palette.

What possible song could I pick to perform? *There are so many good ones in my range*, I thought. I just had to pick one. Should I go with a love song? No, I didn't want to do anything with romance out of respect for Elise and her upcoming divorce. Maybe a really popular pop song. I just didn't want to annoy anyone with something that was overplayed. *What should I pick?*

I figured it would be a good idea to take a break from trying to pick a song and maybe go call my best friend, Monty. We hadn't spoken since I arrived in the ward. I missed her. It was the weekend, so she likely wasn't at work.

I walked over to the phone only to find it occupied by Lucien, who was speaking in a hushed, angry tone to whoever was on the other end of the line. With the phone occupied, I needed to find another way to pass the time.

And then the perfect song popped into my mind. It wasn't profane, like a lot of the music I liked, but it did kind of describe the way my mind worked. "Too Much" by margo. It talks about how someone views their mind. Wishing it would be quiet, how they think they're too much. I could definitely relate, and I thought the other patients would as well.

I had my song choice now, but I still wanted to talk to Monty. She was probably wondering why I hadn't contacted her at all in the last few days. We normally talked daily. I hoped Alex got hold of her and told her what was going on, so that my call wouldn't be a surprise.

As I waited for Lucien to finish his conversation, which had grown louder and more angry-sounding, I walked some more laps. Avoiding going around him, I adjusted my pacing to only one side of the ward, walking back and forth instead of in a circle like I had been. I wondered how long he was going to be on the phone and how far his anger would escalate.

When it became clear he was going to be there for a while, I hurried back to my room, intending to write some more or read. Whichever would keep my mind more occupied. I saw Elise in the room once more, reading her self-help book. I waved to her, acknowledging her presence. She nodded in return, and I sat on my bed, my book in hand, ready to read.

I opened the book to the chapter I was on and got started. I had left off with the protagonist fleeing her captors and just shy of getting caught. The smooth texture of the pages acted as something to ground me. They helped me focus on something other than Lucien's growing anger towards whoever he was on the phone with.

I continued to read until I jumped when I heard a loud yell of frustration and the sound of plastic hitting metal once, echoing into my room. I nearly dropped my book and looked towards the noise, as did Elise. The sound was jarring and attention-grabbing.

"What are you all looking at?!" I heard Lucien yell. I was glad I wasn't out there at that moment. I probably would've looked at him, too.

I glanced over at Elise, a look of bewilderment on my face. She mirrored my own expression. After a moment, things went quiet again, and I shrugged, not knowing what to make of the sudden silence. I was tempted to go check and see if the phone was available now, but decided against going immediately and resolved to finish the chapter I was on before going to make my call. As I turned my attention back to my book, I took a breath, in and out slowly, calming myself from the residual anxiety following Lucien's outburst.

I read on. The protagonist was about to be caught and ran, giving away her location. That's where the chapter ended. I sighed and closed my book.

What was I going to say to Monty? Would she crack jokes about me now being certifiable? Probably. That's just the kind of person she is. I was more concerned about her worrying about me. I didn't want that. I was healing and starting to grow into a better person. Maybe she already knew that.

Monty had known me almost as long as Alex. She was very perceptive, even when I wasn't around her. She often knew me better than I knew myself. She was always the person to call me out on my bullshit when I started saying I was fine when I wasn't. She never put up with it. Always telling me to admit when something is wrong. I pissed her off several times doing that. Hard habit to break.

I stood up from my bed, looking over at Elise once more, who had resumed reading her self-help book, and made my way out to the phone. It was unoccupied, luckily. I pulled my list of phone numbers from my pocket and dialed the number next to Monty's name.

"Hello?" I heard before the phone could complete its first ring. She must've been using it when I called.

"Hey, Monty. It's Brina," I said, gulping down whatever lingering anxiety I had left. "Did Alex fill you in on... everything?"

"Um, what do you mean? I know you're in the hospital for a manic episode, but he didn't really elaborate. He had to go deal with Luna," Monty explained.

"Oof, yeah. I need to tell you the whole story. I swear, it's not as bad as it- actually, yeah. It was kinda bad. You know how I smoke dabs?"

"Yeah, we've done them together. What about them? What, did you set yourself on fire or something?"

I chuckled darkly, a humorless sound. "Nearly. I pointed the blowtorch at myself,"

"You did WHAT?!" Monty yelled into the phone. I quickly held the receiver away from my ear before cautiously replacing it. "Why the hell would you ever point a blowtorch at yourself? Are you crazy?!"

"A little bit, yeah. I thought it was funny at the time. Mania is a hell of a drug. I know better now, obviously," I told her calmly, even though I wanted to laugh at my own joke. I knew then it was not the time.

"Oh my God, Brina. What am I gonna do with you?" She sighed with exasperation into the phone.

"Love me forever and tell me about the outside world to keep me from going even crazier?" I suggested.

"Is it that bad in there? I thought they sent you there to be less crazy, not more."

"Yeah, well, the boredom and lack of a schedule will get to anyone."

"I haven't really been doing much. Lots of gaming lately. I've advanced so far in the game, that I killed the boss in just a few hits. I think somebody overpowered certain aspects of it, but I am fully going to take advantage of it until the updates and deletes that code."

"That sounds like fun. Any chance it comes with a two-player online option?" I asked, hoping to play with my long-distance best friend when I got out of the ward.

I hated how far Monty was from me, but that was my own fault. I moved away after having Luna so we could be closer to Alex's family, but I missed my own. I missed the friends I made growing up, but it was my idea in the first place, so I didn't feel like I could complain. I hated how he cried quietly the first Christmas we had without his mother when we were living with my mother. He missed his family so much. So, I told him it would be okay to move back to his home state, despite it being 800 miles from my own hometown. I didn't go to high school there, as my family moved around a lot. We moved back home after I graduated. Alex packed up and moved down to be with me.

"Yeah, it does actually. I'll text you the details, and you can get the game when you get out. Tell Alex I said hi and I fully plan on stealing his wife from him in a few months... well, as long as you're still coming down for Christmas."

I had planned to fly down with Alex and Luna for Christmas with my mom. I wasn't sad about the years we couldn't spend Christmas with her like Alex was about his own mother, but that didn't mean I didn't miss her. And Monty. And the few other friends I had left behind when I moved.

"It's still a yes. I'm not missing Christmas with you guys down there. I missed it last year, I'm going this year. Nothing is gonna stop me. Not some bipolar bullshit, certainly." I said, my tone shifting to formality, hoping to make Monty laugh.

My attempt at humor was met with a quiet chuckle. I smiled, happy to make her laugh. I loved making people laugh.

"Okay, you've convinced me. But for real, don't push yourself. If you need to stay up there for the holidays, I'm pretty sure everyone down here will be understanding," she said, conveying that my recovery was the priority, not a single visit to my home state.

"Fine. I promise I won't push it. Prepare to be surprised when I do actually get to come down there, though. I fully intend to be down there for Christmas," I reiterated. I heard a long sigh come from the phone. Not one of relief, but one of exasperation.

"There's no stopping you, huh? Alright. I'm really excited to see you, though. I promise not to be shocked when it happens. But hey, listen, I hate to do this, but I gotta go. I've gotta get laundry started and take my father-in-law to his bingo tournament. It's so competitive. He's convinced today is his day to win big. He's convinced of that every time I take him to bingo."

I laughed a bit at that. "That's totally understandable. I'll talk with you when I'm out of here. Love you, bestie."

"Love you, too. Try not to flip on anyone in there. I know you."

Too late, I thought. I heard the line click off, and I hung up the phone, saddened by the abrupt end to the call. I understood she needed to do normal people things, but I wished I could be out there doing normal people things, too.

I scanned the ward to see who was out of their rooms. Killian was talking with Olivia and Nate, Renee and Alice were debating something between themselves whilst smiling intensely. Lucien was nowhere to be seen, so he probably went back to his room. I wouldn't have blamed him for doing so. His phone call sounded rough.

I wanted to talk with someone, but I didn't want to deal with the short cord attached to the phone anymore. I figured I'd talk to Killian or Elise, and we could talk about the upcoming music competition. See what they were planning to do for it. But Elise was reading in our room, and Killian was already involved in a conversation. I didn't want to interrupt.

I had nothing to do and nobody available to talk with, and I didn't think I could focus well enough to return to my book or writing. I figured I could ask for a snack. I was also supposed to be eating more. I had neglected to eat much in the last few weeks, causing me to lose ten pounds rapidly. My mania had gotten so bad that I simply forgot to eat for days in a row. When I did eat, it was a single meal in one day, and then back to forgetting to eat. Between not eating and not sleeping much, it was no wonder I lost control like I did. I put my body and mind through so much neglect that they retaliated. At least, that's how I thought about it.

I walked toward the nurses' station, looking at the clock once again. We had a few hours left to kill before the start of the music competition. I took a breath, steadying myself before doing the difficult task of asking for something.

"Excuse me? I was just wondering if I could get a snack. A banana and a Sprite, if you've got them, but I'll take anything," I said to the blonde nurse behind the station.

She smiled at me, always smiling, these staff members, and stood up to go to a room behind the locked door. After she returned, she had exactly what I requested and handed both to me. I quickly opened the banana and ate it, not realizing how hungry I actually was. I sipped my Sprite as well.

"Is there anything else I can do for you right now?" She asked me.

I thought for a moment. Did I physically need anything else right now? Maybe a shower. I could ask for new scrubs and my hygiene bucket. It was something to do, anyway.

"Could I actually get some new scrubs and my hygiene bucket, please? I wanna take a shower," I replied, asking as politely as I could.

She walked out from the locked door into the ward to unlock the closet of clothing before handing me a new set of scrubs, towels and undergarments. I smiled back at her and told her thanks, and walked with her back to my room to get my hygiene bucket. I saw Elise, still reading her self-help book. She looked bored. I wanted to say something, but I had already resolved to take a shower. I didn't want to ask for all of this and then not use it. The nurse gave me a final smile and walked out the door, back to her station, I supposed.

"Hey, if you need to use the bathroom, I'd say do it now. I'm gonna grab a shower," I said to Elise, wanting to at least give her that courtesy.

She put her book down wordlessly and moved to go to the bathroom, closing the door behind her. I could hear everything, but I chose to ignore it. After she had flushed, I could hear her wash her hands at the sink. She opened the door once again and said, "Bathroom's all yours."

I thanked her and grabbed my things to go take a shower.

I got into the bathroom, shut the door with its magnetic door strip, and began to remove my clothing. I walked over to the weird shower, with no stall, only a shower head near the toilet, and pushed the single button to turn on the water. It came out cold at first, but heated up quickly. The pressure was amazing. It felt like a massage from the water. I scrubbed my hair and body quickly, but lingered under the pressure of the water. It felt like the most therapeutic thing in that place, washing away the awkwardness of not having anyone to talk to.

I let the water turn itself off and quickly got a towel and dried myself off, not wanting to be exposed to the cold air for too long. There were two towels once again, neither big enough to wrap around my body, even though it was a bit smaller than normal. I wondered briefly how much weight I'd need to lose for the towel to fit, but quickly dismissed the thought, knowing it wasn't a healthy one.

I dressed as quickly as I dried off. I took a look in the slightly steamy mirror, making a note about a new pimple that had popped up, and then left the bathroom, my old scrubs folded in my arms along with the towels. I stepped out of the room once again, not looking at Elise, and deposited the used bunches of fabric into the shared laundry hamper. I looked around the ward once again, having spent about thirty minutes in the shower, to see what had changed. Nothing really had changed except that Lucien was out of his room again. He looked as bored as I was. He caught me looking at him and waved me over. *This should be interesting,* I thought.

"Brina, come over here for a second, I wanna ask you something," he said as he waved.

Against my better judgment, I decided to give talking with Lucien a shot. He still made me nervous, especially after his phone call. His history didn't help. I was glad for his honesty; however, it didn't make it any easier for me to get close to him. But he was here to try and do better... and avoid jail. He deserved a chance.

As I approached, I gripped my scrub top subconsciously, twisting it slightly.

"What's up?" I asked, trying to appear casual and falling short.

"Hey, I wanted to ask about your performance. What are you gonna do for the music competition?" He questioned with light curiosity.

I stared at him, a bit dumbfounded. This was the same man who was yelling into the phone an hour ago. He seemed completely calm now.

"Um, I'm not sure entirely." I lied, not wanting to give away my song.

"Well, are you gonna be actually singing or lip syncing? Or pretending to play an instrument, like that other guy?" He asked further. I felt a small pang of anxiety in my chest and began to twist my hands into my scrub top once more.

"I'd actually like to keep it a surprise, if you don't mind. And the other guy has a name. It's Nate." I said, my tone a bit clipped in Nate's defense. Everyone here deserved a chance, and I was going to make sure they got theirs.

"Nate. Right. Got it. I really don't like him," Lucien stated bluntly. "I'm not gonna start any shit with him, but don't expect me to be all buddy-buddy either."

"You don't have to. But could you try to give him a chance? For me? Maybe what we saw initially wasn't the real him. He seems more pleasant to be around now, less hostile. You've seen it too, right?" I pointed out, willing Lucien to comply with my request.

"Brina, I know I said you reminded me of my daughter, but you aren't her. She's the only one who can make those kinds of requests of me. If you don't mind, I want some space now." He stood up and walked back to his room.

I was a bit shocked. He was the one who called me over, not the other way around. I guessed I touched a nerve. At least he didn't yell at me. I was grateful for that.

I thought for a moment. Rejection. That's what that was. He rejected my request. Maybe that's what my character needed in my story. Suddenly, I was filled with inspiration. I needed to write. To get words on paper immediately. I nearly ran back to my room, grabbed my red crayon from earlier, got my story out, and went to work.

20

The Grand Finale

I was a writing machine. Nothing could stop me or slow me down. I spent nearly 4 hours just working on the story and its plot. My characters were becoming more and more alive, more fleshed out. The main character, Yuna, was one hell of a reluctant protagonist. She really didn't want to have to go through the trials she did just to get the money for her son's surgery, but she did it anyway, complaining the whole time.

"Dinner is served in the Behavioral Health Unit."

I stopped writing and realized how dry my eyes were. I'd hardly blinked since starting to write this round. I moved slowly, not hurrying off to dinner like normal, but taking my time, my joints a bit stiff from not moving for hours. I was looking forward to my last dinner there. Both because I knew it was going to be good and because it was going to be my last. I was going home the next day.

I sat in my normal spot with Killian, Olivia, and Nate. My dinner was delivered in its normal squeaky styrofoam. Inside was a burger, steak fries, orange juice, ketchup, and mustard. I quickly scarfed the fries down, then the burger.

"Whoa, slow down there. You're gonna choke," Nate said to me, seeing me eating as quickly as I could, not full from my snack hours earlier. Nobody really said anything else. I finished my burger at a reasonable speed.

After dinner, it was time for the music competition. I was excited then. I had my song ready, and I was confident that unless I purposefully did a bad job, nobody there was going to judge me harshly. That was going to be one fun final night in the ward. I was ready to dazzle everyone with my unknown talent.

I realized the keyboard was still set out. Somebody was bending the rules for us. I wasn't going to complain. I watched as Killian headed for his 'center stage' again, ready to be the MC once more. I took a seat on the couch next to Olivia and Lucien. Renee and Alice were on their couch. Nate sat alone in a rocking chair, the one previously occupied by Lucien, who stared daggers at him. Elise was also sitting in one of the other rocking chairs. I was surprised to see her participating without me asking, but I was thrilled nonetheless.

I could see Renee and Alice talking with Killian. He looked like he was trying to convince them of something, but failed to do so. Maybe they didn't want to participate. I figured it would be the same with Elise. Maybe they just wanted to watch.

"Welcome, ladies and gentlemen, to the first annual psych ward music competition, where all forms of sounds are considered musical. Even this." Killian let out an ear-shattering shriek. My hands flew over my own ears, trying to muffle the awful assault on them.

"And that's why I will not be participating. I'm not a musical guy. I am, however, happy to be your host and provide this lovely commentary. Our first act is none other than our lovely Linda from Marketing, or excuse me, this note might be a typo. Let me see. Ah, yes, excuse me. Lucien. Come on up!"

Lucien got up and took over the keyboard and mouse. He looked up a karaoke version of a country song that was well-known, but I couldn't place its name. Was he really going to sing?

He was. The music started with the sound of an acoustic guitar playing. Once the intro was over, Lucien began singing in the voice of Linda from Marketing, his original character. It was really good. He had the twang down just right, not a falsetto, but a real-sounding voice. One that was well practiced and did more than carry a tune. The song spoke of easy days, fishing, and drinking a beer down on the river. It really sounded like a female country singer was performing. It was incredible to witness.

Once he was done, the room burst into applause. He took a bow and proceeded to resume his seat next to me. I nudged his shoulder with my own, showing him my congratulations on a fantastic performance.

Killian retook his place in 'center stage'. "What a wonderful performance from Linda, everybody. Our next contestant is set to be the world's most introverted rapper. Please help me gently welcome Olivia to the stage."

Olivia stood up and blushed sheepishly. She took his place, went up to the computer, and looked up not a song, but a beat. A rhythm with a certain tempo. She hit play on it and came back to take her place.

"Hi, you guys. This is my same rap from earlier, but with more lyrics. I hope you enjoy," she said ever so quietly. And then she began to rap.

"My mind's a room with a lock on the door,
No one would listen to what I was here for,
I kept it inside, all the feelings I fought,
A prisoner of all the dark thoughts I brought.
The days all blend into a blur of the same,
Just playing this mental and boring old game.
Tried to escape, to make a new scene,
But got stuck in a place in-between.
But this place is a cage with a key made of pain,
Where they all feel the sun but still welcome the rain.
I see the quiet ones, the loud ones, the broken,
And a whole lot of words that were never quite spoken.
Like the one with the tunes he just hums to himself,
Or the one with the feelings she reads from a shelf.
I'm not on my own, I'm just part of the team,
Living out someone's beautiful, terrible dream.
We never go back, killing our time,
I've moved on from that beautiful crime.
Now the words come out, they feel heavy and real,
'Cause I'm finally ready to show you how I feel."

There was silence at first, then boisterous applause. I gave her a standing ovation. That was one hell of a performance. And those lyrics? Amazing. The fact that she wrote all of that herself was insane. Crazy how words on paper, when spoken aloud in a specific rhythm, could evoke such intense feelings.

"Ladies and gentlemen, Olivia! Wasn't she great, folks? Up next, we have our manic mess, Brina. Show us what you've got," Killian announced.

I took a moment, then stood up, walking up to the keyboard. I typed in the song I wanted to perform, took my place in the center of the gathering, and began to sing my song. I put effort into sounding similar to the original artist, margo. The song started with her explaining her internal world. How she felt like she was losing herself, and how she thought her brain wasn't working right. She felt too much, and her mind was loud. She felt like things would never change. She felt like she had no chance of changing. But I knew better. I could do more. I could keep trying and not go backward.

The song ended beautifully. I took in everyone's expressions. They ranged from shocked to surprised to awe. Eventually, they burst into applause for me as well. I did a small, awkward bow and ran back to my seat, suddenly feeling a little too exposed.

I felt my cheeks aflame and felt Lucien bump me with his shoulder. He whispered, "Great job." A simple affirmation that meant the world to meant in that moment.

"Where did you hear that song first, Brina? I feel like it just described all of us here. Anyway, we've got one more act for you all lined up tonight. Please welcome the one and only Nate to the stage."

Nate got up and went to the keyboard, pulling up his original guitar song that he had posted online. He took his place in the center and took a dramatic, deep breath, closing his eyes. And then he held up his air guitar and started to shred some heavy metal. It was super intense. Big gestures, rapid finger movements, and he was bending at the waist. Really getting into it. At one point, at the end of his performance, he dropped to his knees, head high to the ceiling, and thrashed his head around as he mimicked the last few chords of the song, ending on one final hard strum.

We all applauded his performance and his song. I couldn't believe that was him online. That was so cool.

"That brings our little competition to an end. Applause tells us the winner is... Olivia! Gold star for you. Everyone, give her one final round of applause!" Killian announced Olivia's win. It was truly earned. We all clapped politely, and Olivia turned quite red.

"Thanks, you guys," she said meekly. I gave her arm a small squeeze in support. She squeezed my hand back, showing she got the message.

The night settled into a quiet, easy rhythm after the conclusion of the music competition. Olivia wore her gold foil star with pride for the rest of the night. Soon, it was time for meds, and then I went to bed. Ready to start the next day and go home.

* * *

I awoke to the dim light of dawn. The light was even dimmer than normal. I looked outside to see that it was overcast. Oh well. I would've preferred to go home on a sunny day, but it might as well have been with how excited I was.

I quickly got myself out of bed, ready to get the day going. Ready to get going, honestly, but in a strange way, I was going to miss the ward. Or at least, the other temporary residents of it. I made plans to get in contact with Killian and Olivia after we all got out. I looked over and saw Elise still asleep in her bed. I left for the bathroom quietly, did my business, washed my hands, and walked out to the heart of the ward once more. I wandered over to the nurses' station, eager to see what time it was.

I looked at the familiar clock once again. It was just about 7 in the morning, time for their shift change and our breakfast. After group at 8, we would have our vitals taken, and then it was just a waiting game until it was time to go.

"Breakfast is served in the behavioral health unit."

I quickly took my seat, ate my breakfast wordlessly, and then spoke to Killian, who looked about as excited to leave that place as I was.

"You remember the name to look up to find me online, right?" I asked.

"Yeah, Brina Rogers, right? You'll get a request from me. Don't worry. I'll find you," he said, his words would've sounded ominous if it were anybody but him speaking them.

"You realize that could've come across way creepier than you intended, right?" I pointed out.

"Yeah, but it's you. You know what I mean. God, I'm so ready to get out of here. Group and then waiting around to go home. I feel like today is gonna drag if they don't release us soon."

We talked for about an hour until it was time for group. When we got to that too static room again, I saw everyone was in attendance. Ryan was back to get us going, but I couldn't focus on what he was saying. I tried my best to participate, but it was pretty much exactly the same as the first session, just without Veronica and with Nate. It went on pretty uneventfully.

We got out pretty quickly as nobody really felt like sharing much. We were all too antsy about our impending release. Well, everyone but Nate and Renee. They were going to be there longer.

I went back to my room after the session and started putting together all the papers I had been writing on. I was going to take them home and put everything I wrote on my computer. I wanted to see if my story would go any further outside of the ward.

I had just grabbed the book that Mama had brought me when Elise came into the room, her face full of tears.

"What's wrong? Are you okay? Are you still getting out today?" The questions poured out of me. I wanted to help. I didn't want her to be upset.

"Yeah. I'm still getting out. I don't have a ride, though. I found out my husband refuses to come get me, so I'm going to have to take the bus to get back home," she said sadly. I wanted to punch her husband, or rather, soon-to-be ex-husband, in the face. How could he do this to her? He was the reason she was in there, and now he wouldn't even help get her home. Asshole.

"Can your parents or friends come get you or something?" I asked.

She shook her head, red hair smacking her in the face as she did. "My parents are dead. Car crash when I was in my early 20s. I moved up here with my husband for work recently, so I don't have friends here yet. So, it's either a bus or a taxi, and I don't have the money for a taxi."

Dead. Her parents were dead. How did that never come up? I could have sworn she talked about her mom like she was still alive. And the fact that she had only just relocated? That added insult to injury. Poor Elise. I felt deeply for her.

"Oh. I'm sorry to hear that. I wish there was something I could do. Do you think you're gonna be alright?" I asked.

"I'll be alright. Eventually. Just not right now. Can I have the room for a bit?" she requested, tears still streaming from her face.

"Of course. All yours." I said in response.

I grabbed my things, putting them neatly on the edge of my bed. I then cleared out of the room to give her the privacy she requested. As I walked out to the main common area, taking it in for what might be the final time, I felt a small pang in my chest. This was the place where my healing began. It was up to me to continue it on the outside. Could I do it? I wondered.

"Sabrina Rogers? You're out of here." I heard.

I turned and looked to find a nurse with my bag of personal effects.

"I'm going now? I haven't even had a chance to say goodbye to everyone yet." I said. As eager as I was to go home, I wanted to give everyone a proper goodbye.

"Well, you've still got to change, and then we will walk you downstairs. Your husband and mother are waiting," she told me, her tone indicating there was to be no nonsense.

"Okay. Let me just- BYE EVERYONE! I'm out of here! There, I'm good now. Can I go get changed?" I said, after yelling to the ward, that it was time for me to go. It was far from a proper goodbye, but at least it was something. I grabbed my personal effects from the nurse and went back to my room, where I had only just left Elise to cry alone. I felt bad. There I was going home with my husband and mother, and she was going home to nobody.

I moved with purpose, quickly going to the bathroom to change into my black crop top and shorts. I uttered a word of apology to Elise and changed quickly, wanting to let her get back to her alone time.

"You're leaving now? I hope things get better for you," she said through her tears and sniffles.

I came out of the bathroom and gave her a final hug goodbye. I didn't have any words that could've been of comfort to her, but I could at least give her that.

I walked back out to the ward for the last time and followed that same nurse out the door into the hallway I had come in through. I followed her into two different elevators, going downstairs and out through an outpatient exit. I saw my car parked outside. Inside was Alex and my mother, talking. Unaware of my arrival. I wanted to run to them. To wrap my arms around both.

Alex suddenly turned his head and saw me. He pointed me out to my mother, and they both moved to get out of the car. I walked outside into the overcast day and embraced them both. I was finally out.

"Hi, Honey," I heard Alex say into my hair. "I missed you so much."

"Me too. Hi, Hun. Hi, Mom. It's so nice to see you." I said as I pulled away from their combined embrace. I beamed at both of them. Ready to go home.

"Can we please get some pizza tonight?" I requested.

They both burst out laughing as we all climbed into the car and pulled out of the driveway of the hospital. I was going home. Finally.

Epilogue

I sat in the car in the front passenger side seat with Alex driving and my mom in the back seat. I tried to insist she sit up front, but she wanted me to be able to sit next to my husband. We were driving home. I was finally going home. I was looking forward to getting to see Luna later that day. She was in school when Alex and my mother picked me up.

"Sabrina, what's the first thing you want to do when you get home?" My mother asked.

I thought for a moment. I had planned my first dinner at home, but not my first activity. Maybe I could start a writing project. Maybe I'd start putting the story I'd written with my red crayon onto the laptop. I didn't want to be rude, but I wanted to get it written out while it was still fresh in my mind.

"I don't know. Maybe some writing? I spent a lot of time inside there writing a story that I think I want to continue," I replied, gazing out my window, watching the small town go by us as we got closer and closer to home. The hospital was only about 10 minutes from our apartment. We didn't have long to talk in the car.

"That sounds like fun, but do you think you could hold off until tonight? I have a surprise for you when you get home. My mom had the idea," Alex said. That explained the sneaky look I got from her when she visited me in the psych ward.

"Yeah, I can hold off for a bit." I wondered what Alex and Mama had planned for me. I wasn't one for surprises, and they both knew that, but if they decided to surprise me, then it must've been good.

Not long after I replied to Alex, we pulled up to our apartment building, parking on the side of the street like normal. I got out of the car quickly with my papers from the hospital. I wanted to get upstairs and find out what the surprise was. I wasn't great at being patient, but I was working on it.

Once we were all inside, I saw it. A present wrapped up and not addressed to me, but to Luna. I was confused. "This has Luna's name on it. Not mine."

Alex smiled. "Exactly. Look who it's from."

I looked at the from section of the label. It had the word 'Mommy' written on it. The confusion gave way to clarity. They saved a present for me to give to Luna since I wasn't at her party. I could feel my eyes start to sting with happy tears. I clasped my hands together with glee. If this was the big present I picked out for her, which it looked like based on the shape of the package, then Mama and Alex must've wrapped it up for me to give to her.

"It's the toy violin you picked out for her. Mama came up with the idea to let you and Luna have a moment together where you're reunited and come home with a present for her. I thought it was a good idea, so I got the violin wrapped and put it away until you got home. Honestly, it gave me something to do while you were in there," Alex said as he pulled me in for a hug, wiping away my tears.

"Aww, how sweet and mushy," my mom joked from behind us. She didn't really do big displays of affection like Alex and Mama did, but that was alright. I didn't expect her to. She showed her love in other ways. Like her teasing.

We moved from the hallway to the living room, where my deeply cushioned couch awaited. I was excited to sit on it again, knowing it would be significantly softer than the couch in the ward. My bottom would not hurt from sitting on my couch; that was for certain.

While we waited until it was time to pick Luna up from her bus stop, we chatted about my experience in the behavioral health unit. I talked about the lack of schedule, how good the food is, my, Nate's, and Lucien's outbursts, the talent show, and the music competition. They listened intently to every detail, asking a few clarifying questions every few minutes or so. My mom decided we needed to play Cards Against Humanity to have a few laughs and lighten the mood. I happily agreed, and Alex did so reluctantly, not wanting to disappoint either of us, but he ended up having as much fun as the pair of us, if not more.

Enough time had passed afterward that it was nearly time to walk to the bus stop at the end of our street to wait for Luna. As we walked, I had some time to think. I hadn't seen her since putting her to bed on Wednesday night the previous week. Would she be mad at me for disappearing on her? For missing her party? I gripped my shorts tightly, waiting for the bus to come. I could feel my heart pounding in my chest. Alex was standing to my right, and my mother was to my left. He gripped my hand and squeezed it, reassuring me that everything would be alright.

Soon, I heard the sound of the bus brakes squealing before I saw the big yellow vehicle turn onto our street. My heart nearly flew out of my chest. I was anticipating that moment so much. The moment I got to see my daughter again. I wanted to give her the biggest hug in the world and never let go.

The bus made it to the corner we were standing on, and the doors opened. Soon, children started filing out and walking to their homes. I waited for Luna, who was normally last, as she sat in the back of the bus.

I saw a small flash of chestnut brown hair, the same color as Alex's, through the bus window. The next thing I knew, Luna was leaving the bus and running for us. I felt her hug my waist tightly, saying something into my tummy where her head was buried. I held onto her tiny, warm body tightly, but gently, not wanting to squeeze her. God, I had missed her more than anything.

"What did you say, Sweetheart?" I asked, my voice dripping with maternal love.

She pulled away and looked up at me with her big green eyes. "Mommy, you're back! I missed you. Do you wanna go color with me?" She asked innocently.

"I'd love to color with you, but there's something I want to do first. Let's go home. I've got a surprise for you."

Afterword

Congratulations! You've reached the end of the story. Brina has really made an effort to try and grow, hasn't she? I, Brittany, the author of this book, know what it's like to live with Bipolar Disorder. Unfortunately, from personal experience. I hope that this story helps to spread awareness about living with bipolar and what to look out for in either yourself or loved ones with the diagnosis. If you ever find yourself in crisis, please, reach out to your loved ones and your area's crisis hotline. Below is the information to reach the national Suicide and Crisis Hotlines in both the United States and Canada. Thank you for reading.

US- Call or Text 988 for the Suicide & Crisis Hotline

Canada- Call or Text 988 for the Suicide Crisis Hotline

About the Author

Brittany L.J. Roberts is an emerging voice in contemporary fiction whose writing delves into the raw and often difficult reality of living with mental health challenges. In her debut novel, When the Flame Goes Out, she weaves a story that illuminates the true nature of these struggles with empathy and insight. A proud mother to a neurodiverse child, Brittany draws from her personal experiences to create relatable and deeply human characters. In her spare time, she enjoys the peaceful rhythm of crocheting.

You can connect with me on:

🌐 https://bljroberts-author.com

🅕 https://www.facebook.com/BrittanyLJRobertsauthor

www.ingramcontent.com/pod-product-compliance
Lightning Source LLC
Chambersburg PA
CBHW020147120726
47903CB00007B/2443